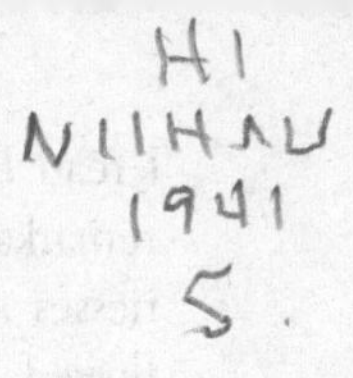

Praise for *East Wind, Rain*

"Paul's graceful, objective tone may be the book's greatest strength. She is at her best describing the sheer physical sensation of being on the island. Sunsets, heat, and dust are rendered in tactile detail. The island becomes a force in its own right. When it's over, we don't want to leave." —*New York Times Book Review*

"A compelling psychological drama." —*San Francisco Chronicle*

"With elegant prose and an eye for the telling detail, Caroline Paul illuminates a small Hawaiian island caught—for seven spellbinding days—between the future and the past. The characters who inhabit *East Wind, Rain* ache with yearning and desire . . . they captured my heart."
—Amanda Eyre Ward, author of *Sleep Toward Heaven* and *How to Be Lost*

"A debut novel that tackles the complex issue of national allegiance . . . *East Wind, Rain*, which is based on an actual event, rarely disappoints." —Associated Press

"If you thought there was little new to say about December 7, 1941, Caroline Paul has proven you wrong. *East Wind, Rain* depicts a Pacific Island world isolated from the conflict between the United States and Japan, and yet smack-dab in the middle of it. This is a complex and beautifully imagined story of evolving meanings and shifting allegiances. An intelligent and impressive debut."
—Tom Barbash, author of *The Last Good Chance* and *On Top of the World*

"Authentic and dramatic. . . . A big war comes to a small place, making its effect even more effective." —*Booklist*

"I read *East Wind, Rain* in a single day. It's a very beautiful and remarkable book, peopled by characters motivated by their weaknesses and their strengths, to tragic consequences. The premise flowed with moment-to-moment precision. I was awed by the depth of Caroline Paul's rendering and the extent of her imagination."

—Po Bronson, *New York Times* bestselling author of *Why Do I Love These People?*

"Paul offers a refreshing and interesting vantage point from which readers may reconsider the episode in history. . . . [A]n excellent job of bringing complex questions to the forefront."

—*Kirkus Reviews*

"*East Wind, Rain* is a lyrical adventure based on the true events of ordinary people caught in extraordinary circumstances. . . . A wonderful parable on our notions of paradise, faith, and, ultimately, love."

—Holly Payne, author of *The Virgin's Knot* and *The Sound of Blue*

"Moves . . . with a lyricism that contributes to [Paul's] characters' development. It's a promising performance."

—*Publishers Weekly*

"This is wonderful, captivating writing about one of Hawaii's most intriguing historical events. Caroline Paul's storytelling clearly evokes the nuances of Island life as her characters grow in realism and complexity."

—Keola Beamer, author of *The Shimmering—ka 'olili*

East Wind, Rain

Caroline Paul

HARPER PERENNIAL

NEW YORK • LONDON • TORONTO • SYDNEY

HARPER PERENNIAL

This book is a work of fiction. References to real people, events, establishments, organizations, or locales are intended only to provide a sense of authenticity, and are used fictitiously. All other characters, and all incidents and dialogue, are drawn from the author's imagination and are not to be construed as real.

A hardcover edition of this book was published in 2006 by William Morrow, an imprint of HarperCollins Publishers.

FIRST HARPER PERENNIAL EDITION PUBLISHED 2007.

Designed by Daniel Lagin

The Library of Congress has catalogued the hardcover edition as follows:

Paul, Caroline.
East wind, rain : a novel / Caroline Paul.—1st ed.
p. cm.
ISBN: 978-0-06-078075-3 (acid-free paper)
ISBN-10: 0-06-078075-4
1. World War, 1939–1945—Hawaii—Fiction. 2. Air pilots, Military—Fiction. 3. Japanese—Hawaii—Fiction. 4. Islands—Fiction. 5. Hawaii—Fiction. I. Title.
PS3616.A935E17 2006
813'.6—dc22 2005043418

ISBN: 978-0-06-078076-0 (pbk.)
ISBN-10: 0-06-078076-2 (pbk.)

07 08 09 10 11 ❖/RRD 10 9 8 7 6 5 4 3 2 1

To my father

Who loved tales of faraway islands

December 9, 1925–February 15, 2004

The natives are yours and you are the new chief and they will work and serve you according to the laws and customs of Hawaii. . . .

—King Kamehameha V, upon the sale of Niihau to Aylmer Robinson's great-grandmother, in 1864

Japan will notify her consuls of war decision in her foreign broadcasts as weather report at end. North Wind Cloudy Russia. West Wind Clear Britain. East Wind Rain United States.

—U.S. War Department's translation of Japanese "Winds Code," intercepted November 19, 1941

Higashi no kaze ame (east wind, rain).

—Tokyo weather forecast, December 4, 1941

Acknowledgments

There are many people who have made this book possible.

Trish Lee, who is from Hawaii, first told me this incredible story.

John Boyle, professor of Asian history at California State University, Chico, combed the manuscript for accuracy and spelling and kindly contacted friends who supplied me with important details.

My fellow Grotto member, writer Lisa Margonelli, volunteered early on to read a draft and I took her up on it. She gave me wonderful advice and even a pom-pom cheer. Michelle Tessler, whom I'm lucky to have as an agent, is the perfect combination of business savvy and compassion. Thank you for your unwavering belief in this story.

Jennifer Brehl took all the stress out of the final edits by being perceptive and kind at once. Thank you for your work. Elaine Pfefferblit read an early version and gave me invaluable advice that set me on the right path, as always. Zoe Rosenfeld was wise and patient and made me a better writer. Alan Holbrook was generous with his time and advice (and savvy about guns and radios).

Allan Beekman, Ruth Tabrah, Gavan Daws, Chris Cook, Rerioterai Tava, and Moses Keale Sr. wrote some of the many books I consulted for my research.

Eric Martin and Melanie Gideon struggled with me through every incarnation. If there were medals for that, you'd both get the one for valor AND the one for wounded in action. Thank you for all your help.

The Grotto continues to be a major force in my life. It was an inspiration to write in an office filled with such great talent. Thank you for the camaraderie during the dark days. And please keep the roof deck neat.

Mom never stopped telling me how proud she was of me and this work, which made all the difference. My brother Jonathan clued me in to the Zero's fatal flaw, as well as made me laugh way too hard during our title brainstorming (thanks also to Ian Murray and Bill Britt for that). My twin sister, Alexandra, has the kind of absurd faith in me that makes me think I can do anything, and as always was the first reader I relied on. My father lived only long enough to see me struggle with the writing of the book, but if there's a bookstore where he is, I know he's first in line.

Mindy Ross found me a vintage warplane to fly, so I could better understand its magic. Thank you, Mindy, for all your faith in my writing, in *East Wind, Rain,* and in me.

East Wind, Rain

1

When the plane finally crashed, onto the dry, rutted grass and into a fence, it did so with a hiss and a sigh. There was no outcry or fuss. No boom, or bang, or screeching rent of steel. It crashed as if it were already part of the midday sounds of that desolate island, the soughing wind across the scrub, the low snuffle of the surf. It sliced perfectly through the glancing, metallic sunlight. It skittered like scree through the red dirt. It came to rest, crooked as a tree.

As if in deference to the quiet island, it crashed with gracious aplomb; a long, low exhalation, right into the ground.

Two miles away Yoshio Harada sat in a small wooden chair and looked out a window. His wife had scissors in one hand; with the other she bent back an ear. Pieces of his hair fell noiselessly to the floor, wending their way down like small, winged insects. From where he sat he could see the back of the bee shed, and to the right the rise of the brown land. Above that a bleached, cloudless sky. It was only morning, but his face was slick with sweat; every now and then he blinked away its sting from his eyes. All the windows and doors had been pushed, canted, or propped open before they'd sat down, but the breeze they sought carried only heat and hardy, finger-sized flies—shiny, black-bodied athletes undaunted by anything but gale-force winds. And there was the dust. Even now he could see it, stars hovering in the slant of light by the sill, falling with his hair. In the two years they had been here, this is what he knew his wife resented the most, the way the land rose up to mock her in tiny red particles of itself, caking the corners of her eyes, coating the kitchen table and the insides of their child's mouth. Let's go back to Kauai, she'd plead. Or somewhere. Soon. But Yoshio had taken to the dry, harsh landscape and its leaden heat.

Suddenly the scissors stopped. Yoshio straightened and lifted one hand to run it through his black hair. He decided against it; she hadn't moved to look at him head-on, as she usually did, appraising her work with that stern, hard stare. He imagined how silly he looked then, with that band of newly exposed skin like a long white chalk mark around his head.

-Irene, *kachan*, am I handsome enough for you yet? He wanted to look at her, but she was still behind him.

-Shhtt, she said suddenly. Did you hear that?

-I only hear the sound of my nap calling me.

-I heard something.

Yoshio, sensing that she was serious, listened. He knew all the sounds of this dry, creaking island. It was a habit of his, from back in the days when he had to be more careful than he needed to be now, to keep an ear open, so even now he would stop his horse suddenly, or straighten while checking a beehive, and listen for no apparent reason at all. The smell of her sweat drifted to his nose. He wanted to reach for her hand. He heard nothing out of the ordinary.

-Perhaps Mr. Robinson is back early. He tried to laugh lightly. He laid his hand on his own shoulder in case she wanted to clasp it. Or church is letting out in Puuwai. All those Christians rushing for the dead pig.

She didn't move for his fingers even as he briefly waggled them. They bounced like lonely anenome on a white seafloor, up, down, around. Still, no touch from her own small hand. Instead the floorboard coughed as she shifted uneasily.

-Wild pig, maybe, he continued. He could feel her fingers stiff against his neck, and he knew that her back had straightened and that her mouth was set hard in a line. They're getting as big as the men here, and not nearly as nice. Mr. Kaleohano said one tried to take his cigarette recently.

When she didn't laugh he said, Sweet, and half turned and reached for her wrist, but she stepped away. He dropped his arm on his lap and clasped his palms together, squeezing tighter than he meant to.

-When we're done, he said, I'll check the fences.

She didn't answer, so he repeated himself and noted she glanced at him distractedly, as if she'd just remembered he was there.

-Yes, okay, she said.

-Are we done, by the way? Do I look like Mr. Clark Gable?

She laid the scissors down on the kitchen table and flapped at the errant hair on his shoulders. He could see each black sliver rise like a moon into the air to meet the invisible, inevitable silt before fluttering silently to the floor. She listened one more time, her cupped hand poised at his neck.

Finally she shrugged.

-Perhaps it was a pig, she said. But she glanced out the window and frowned.

The plane lay still. It was hard to believe that its final seconds had been so wondrous. In another circumstance such a nebula of sparks could have birthed a galaxy. But that was then; once they burned themselves out, there was only utter quiet, as if the place the plane had carved through time and space and dirt was a momentary void in the world. Above, a mynah bird circled clumsily and stared, incredulous to find a plane where her favorite fence post should be. On this driest Hawaiian island, there were no lush trees or balloon-size leaves to cover the wreckage; the vertebrae and fibulae and phalanges of metal lay exposed to the sky, as if angry grave robbers had recently looted. There was the propeller, twisted and grotesque like some huge and evil flower. Farther away, a tire, thrown beyond the *kiawe* tree. The pilot was slumped and unmoving, with one of his arms thrust forward, as if to ward off the earth he had met so abruptly. He leaned sideways in his still intact cockpit, the canopy shattered around him. His body shimmered from the glass shards, as if he had brought a starry night sky with him as he fell to earth. His eyes were closed, he did not look dangerous. The mynah bird wheeled away anyway, unnerved.

Somewhere in the ocean a pod of dolphins slowed their rush away from shore. They'd picked up the cluck of the dying engine well before, had even heard the faint whistle of air where the bullets had rent neat holes in the sheathing. The crash had spooked them, but now there was only silence.

-I feel new, like a present unwrapped. Yoshio wiped the sweat from his brow. Then he opened his arms and gestured for his wife to come close to him.

She bent her head to one side, assessing the haircut. Then she flapped her arms away from her sides as if to cool her armpits.

-This heat, she said, and turned away.

Their young daughter, who had been playing with shells on the floor nearby, began to cry suddenly. Yoshio turned and saw that a piece of his black hair had settled near her foot and scared her.

He dropped to his knees slowly, low, soothing noises in his throat. He picked up a shell and pushed it against his nose; he could count on this to make her laugh. When she finally did laugh, he got to his feet and stretched. He had some chores to do in the honey shed, and then a nap. It was just another hot, dry day on the island of Niihau.

Howard Kaleohano stood by the plane. He had seen it make first contact with his backyard, and finally come to its crooked stop, tangled in his fence. It lay like a huge manta ray in the dirt. On this smallest Hawaiian island, privately held, visitors were not allowed, except by invitation, and with the strictest of instructions and a good disinfecting. His first thought, after the initial shock, was whether Mr. Robinson, the owner of Niihau, would be angry.

It was December 7, 1941.

2

Sixteen miles away, on the lush island of Kauai, Aylmer Robinson had fallen asleep in his library. A half-empty glass of milk rested on the floor by his crossed ankles, a Bible was open on his lap. Every so often his head jerked to one side and his breathing seemed to stop, but he continued to sleep. A servant tiptoed in and put a pillow behind his head. Upstairs someone swept a wooden floor. Somewhere a door clicked shut.

Suddenly there was a loud shout; Robinson rose awkwardly from his chair, fumbling, still half in his dream about riding a horse. His milk glass went sideways and shattered; one hand shot reflexively to his graying hair and sent the pillow skimming across the stone floor. There was another shout and Robinson turned to the open window. Through it he could see the foreman running toward the lanai, yelling a blue streak, waving his arms. Robinson knew immediately by the brilliant red of his cheeks that Mr. Shanagan hadn't gone to church as expected, but to the local saloon. Still, all this hysterical ranting, this was something different. Robinson threw open the window, his pique of righteous fury kept in check only by his strict Calvinist training, and opened his mouth to speak sternly to his man, since it was Sunday after all, a day of humble contemplation and rest in service of the Lord, not drunken tantrums. But Shanagan kept running toward him, oblivious to the fact that he hadn't cleaned up for his employer as he usually did (cramming mints into his mouth and pushing his red hair flat with his hands), and oddly undaunted by the sight of his boss leaning out the bay window with the harshest look he had. Shanagan ran with his arms forward and his chest heaving, a man drowning in an invisible sea.

-Pearl Harbor! he yelled. The Japs have gone and bombed Pearl Harbor!

It was Sunday, a day that Robinson devoted exclusively to the Lord. Usually he didn't pick up a phone, read a book other than the Bible, or get into a car. Listening to the radio was a special sin. But today he knew that the good Lord would forgive him as he knelt next to the Philco and turned it on. A *sneak attack,* he heard through the rush of blood from his face, *the real* McCoy. The words thundered on, unimaginable, impossible. *Nineteen battleships destroyed . . . thousands of our boys dead, that's what they're saying . . . the cries of the wounded . . . Awaiting word . . .*

When Robinson finally pushed away from the radio and rose stiffly to his feet, he called for his horse. His house staff and his ranch hands and all the sugar workers were to be rounded up and informed of what had happened, with orders to wait for his return from town. Shanagan, cold water dripping from his face and a cup of coffee in his hands, stood at the kitchen sink, panting. By the kitchen door the old cook Kaanapapa shifted from one foot to the other, his arms stiff against his sides. They turned to stare at Robinson as he entered.

-And Niihau? said Shanagan. Will you be setting off t'a there?

Aylmer looked at him dazedly.

-I'm not so worried about Niihau, he finally said. That's the safest place to be right now. The devil's on Oahu and coming this way. It's this island I'm worried about.

Kaanapapa and Shanagan nodded. The island of Niihau, owned by the Robinson family for almost a century, was an isolated land spit of dust and scrub. On a clear day it could be seen from the shores of Kauai, but otherwise it was a secret place. Even these two men had never been there, though it was just a half-day boat ride across the channel. They knew only a few things: that Niihau was another working ranch, the arid land just suitable to graze cattle and sheep; that almost all its inhabitants were native Hawaiians; that there were no modern conveniences like electricity or telephones or automobiles; that it seemed a sacred place for their boss, purposefully kept away from the world. It was the "mystery island," a secluded place that Robinson talked about often but rarely brought anyone to visit. Yes, Niihau was not a place to worry about now. No one there would have any idea of what had happened today at Pearl Harbor.

-Lead the families of Makeweli Ranch in prayer, Kaanapapa. Robinson pushed a hat slowly onto his thinning hair. I'm needed in town more than on Niihau.

-Anything I can do, sir? asked Shanagan.

-Clean up, replied Robinson, eyeing his foreman with rebuke. And pray.

He turned, his thin frame slouched in the manner of a man too tall for the doorways around him, and walked toward the large hall. His two employees watched his familiar gait, how each foot hung in the air just a moment longer than necessary, how his narrow chin stuck forward, how the mud on the cuffs of his pants clung unnoticed, how the sprigs of hair in his ears went untrimmed. Most days they thought of how sad it was he had never taken a wife, had never had children. But today they only noticed how he looked so much older than his fifty-two years. He disappeared around the corner and Shanagan coughed and put his cup down with a clatter.

-God help us all, he said.

3

Howard Kaleohano ran toward the smoking plane. He could just make out a man draped over himself, unmoving. There was no time to think that he had never seen anything like this in his life; for all the angry young horses he had shoed and skittish lambs wrestled for their wool under a vigilant sun, nothing had adequately prepared him for a plane dropping out of the heavens. Even the suddenness of the birth of his child was preceded by hours of keening and tumult; though the child had dropped suddenly into his heart, he had not dropped so unexpectedly into the world.

He'd seen planes before, of course. On Kauai, where he had grown up, the airbase had rumbled nearby and as a boy he had done the predictable boy things—pressed his nose against the fence and stared at the magnificent flying machines, the nimble, stumpy army vehicles, the jerky steps of men whose lives he could barely imagine. But he had been on Niihau for almost ten years now. Robinson didn't allow fancy machines here. Things fell from the sky, yes, but they were God's things: dust, rain, birds killed by other birds. Not planes. Maybe somewhere else, thought Howard, but not here, not on Niihau.

As he pulled himself onto the wing to get to the pilot, Howard was already formulating the words he would tell his boss, for everything on the island that was out of the ordinary was passed through him to solve or explain. The time ten lambs died suddenly and mysteriously. The day the church was missing two Bibles. The storm that may or may not have loosened the boat dock. Treading carefully, arms out to the side like an acrobat, Howard made his way to the cockpit. There he hesitated. He glanced at the pilot, still unmoving, and then studied the long, almost female lines of the plane. Despite its torn and twisted body, the plane looked powerful, though Howard did not know just how powerful, or that he stared at a Zero, the best fighter plane ever made. Instead, he thought of Robinson's own long face, the tapered jaw moving slowly from side to side, the wiry eyebrows dropping ever so slightly together like a slow-forming cloud, the occasional nod as he took in the problem that Howard presented and transformed it into something easily remedied, condensing a wild rainstorm into a cistern brimming with form and order.

Howard knew something was wrong. It was not just the wet sparkle of blood that ran from the pilot's forehead. There was the large red sun emblazoned on the plane's side. The thin muzzle of a machine gun glinted in the sunlight. Military insignias were stitched onto the pilot's jacket. Howard could smell smoke, maybe gunpowder. There was no question; this was a fighter plane.

But Howard had little understanding of the great European war that had been raging on a far-off continent for two years. Nor had he heard about how high tensions were between the United States and Japan. Yes, it was in all the newspapers and, on the other islands and on the mainland, heavy in people's minds. It would not have taken much for any of them to figure out what a downed Japanese military plane might mean. But on Niihau, the islanders were cut off from the world. The Robinsons banned newspapers and telephones and radios on the island. They discouraged literacy and the English language—both were considered conduits of evil ideas and thoughts. People rarely left the island, and those who did had to ask permission to return, which was rarely granted. Church was the centerpiece of life on Niihau. Since a posting on Niihau was considered too harsh and isolated, a minister came from Kauai every month or so, handsomely rewarded by Mr. Robinson for his time and his seasickness during the crossing. Nevertheless, every Sunday was full of song and a long sermon intoned from the Hawaiian Bible by Howard, the only man who could read effectively. On all other days of the week work stopped intermittently and the villagers got to their knees; under the Robinsons' insistence the Niihauans prayed five times a day.

There had been a time, years ago, when the island had been less isolated, more open to the outside world. The governor of Hawaii had even visited, and the children had been given new shoes for the event. But gradually the Robinsons decided that the modern world carried too much wickedness for the innocent Niihauans. Niihau became a world unto itself. The shiny shoes were put on kitchen shelves or forgotten entirely.

So it was not a surprise that Howard was at a loss to explain the plane. What should have been telling was now, without context, almost absurd. It was as if an alien spaceship had suddenly landed. There was no way to understand its significance in relation to this island, on this day; only that it was scary and unexpected.

Howard leaned toward the body in the cockpit and peered closely. He saw black hair from under the hat and a small, precise nose, confirming that the being inside was at least human. Otherwise the face was covered with a pair of skewed flight goggles and blood. Howard let his pounding heartbeat begin to slow, and began to take note of the things in front of him. He stared at a machine gun flecked with blood. He squinted at the steel belt buckles. He admired the pilot's flying helmet, its flaps like sagging rabbit ears, its thick leather shining in the sunlight. Finally, he gently pulled the man to an upright position and, as his head flopped to one side, saw that he was still breathing. With small, tentative pats of one large hand he began to shake the pilot awake.

A mynah bird landed on the plane's nose, startling Howard momentarily. He waved to shoo her away but she only cocked her head as if to say, Pal, I'm curious too, so he shrugged and turned back to the pilot. The dark butt of a gun on the belt at the pilot's waist suddenly caught his eye. He pulled it out, slowly, gingerly, fumbling with the holster, almost dropping it. The barrel was as long as a dog's snout, and it had been recently, lovingly, polished. With his free hand Howard rummaged in the pockets of the flight jacket. As he pulled out a wad of carefully folded papers, the pilot sighed. Howard glanced at the papers and saw the treelike marks of what he did not know were Japanese kanji, and some sort of a diagram. He quickly stuffed the sheaf into his back pocket and shook the pilot again, holding the pistol awkwardly, like a sandwich, fingers on the casement and handle. Guns were not allowed on the island—a shotgun was kept at the ranch house only, an almost forgotten relic of the fight against the goats once brought to this island by the venerable Captain Cook; to save the island from death by nibbling, every last one had been carefully, systematically killed—and it had been a long time since he had used a weapon. He began to worry that Robinson would see him with this illegal object, until he remembered that Robinson was not due back until tomorrow.

The pilot finally opened his eyes, and for a long moment stared straight ahead at the mynah bird still perched on the plane's nose, jerking its head to and fro from one shiny object to another.

Aloha, Howard said. The man did not respond instantly, but after a moment he began to raise his hands, which startled both Howard, who stepped back quickly, and the bird, which flew away. The pilot kept his arms in the air and Howard, remembering how confused he had been the time he had fallen from a horse and hit his head, realized the man must have temporarily lost his mind. *Aloha*, he said again, and this time the man turned, and then started in surprise. For a moment they stared at each other. *Hele mai ai*, Howard said. The man said nothing. He had blood on his face and already a fine red dust on his skin.

Was the man deaf? It seemed he could only stare and blink. Perhaps the man didn't understand Hawaiian. Howard raised one of his large hands and now spoke in halting English.

-You okay, mister? he asked. Come on down. Fix head.

4

The pilot had taken off from the aircraft carrier with his heart light, his throat constricted. He'd sat at the controls with a straight posture and one hand tapping his knee, which his instructor had always hated, not so much because it was ineffective or dangerous, but because it reflected a jauntiness unseemly for a Japanese warrior. He was only twenty-one, but he had flown all of his air raids over China like this, except the first few when he had clutched the stick so hard his forearm had hurt for days afterward.

It was a good day to die, he thought. The sky was cloudless, and his squadron navigated the final miles to their target by a Hawaiian radio station that played American jazz music, so that he nodded his head almost unconsciously to words he did not understand. They were sure that they would be spotted and intercepted before Pearl Harbor and the military installations came into view, but they were not. And then here was the airfield, the American planes waiting quietly for their destruction.

He rained machine-gun fire down on men running for outbuildings. A gasoline tank blew, sending orange-black flames into the sky. P-36s, lined up wingtip to wingtip like children holding hands, were easily destroyed. When his squadron leader finally ordered them all to reassemble, the young pilot made one more pass, just for the sheer thrill of it. Below him the ground was littered with the innards of planes and hangars. He saw the blink of scattered machine-gun fire, but otherwise there was little resistance. Smoke blurred the air. He knew that men screamed, heated ammunition popped from its casements, steel collapsed with a moan, but from where he was in his Zero he heard only the roar of the engine against the stillness of his heart. It had gone so perfectly, and as he wheeled toward home—or at least to his carrier somewhere on the high seas—he allowed himself one raised fist, a private moment of unabashed self-adulation that he quickly buried with thoughts of his navy brothers, his country, and the emperor.

But his gas tank had been hit. By the time he realized this, as his engine began to hesitate and cough, Pearl Harbor was behind him and it was too late to turn back and make a final pass, with true warrior *seishin*, right into an American target. He stopped tapping his free hand, thinking vaguely that his instructor would finally be happy, and dipped his right wing, then his left, to get a view of what was below. Somewhere nearby was an uninhabited island called Niihau, designated by his commanders as a crash-landing spot, if necessary. When he saw Kauai off to his right, the deep green of lush forests and high mountains, he knew he was close. And there it was, looking, as promised, like a small, reddish seal lounging on its side. And there, at the northernmost tip, where the head curved toward the body, was the rock Lehua, a beacon of white bird guano. He didn't have much time. Even as he headed for it, his engine died completely, and refused all of his efforts to coax it back to life. But he had the altitude to make it to the island, where he saw enough to realize that most of it was rocky and full of scrub—not ideal for an emergency landing. Off to his right, however, he spotted a small diamond of color. As he turned toward it the island seemed to bloom, with rows and rows of planted trees, herds of cattle, and the white dots of what must have been sheep. The pilot went rigid with surprise. Were there people here? He saw a large yellow field perfect for landing. But a sprawling white house, a mansion really, sat on the eastern flank like a whale bone, a vertebrae of small sheds and outhouses whittled along its periphery. The pilot wheeled to the left and saw to the south more open fields and finally a cluster of houses, though much more modest than the white mansion. The pilot drew in his breath. He quickly glanced at his map; could he have made a mistake? But there was no other possibility. This was the island of Niihau, not uninhabited after all.

The pilot's mind reeled with this new information. People? Americans? Why, of course they were American, this was the Hawaiian island chain. Americans had spread through here like a stain for more than one hundred years. Well, he could not land here. The worst dishonor, worse than a useless plunge into the sea, was the capture of his plane and papers by the enemy. The pilot jerked his head to look at his instrument panel. The altimeter read 1,000; he could still make it to the ocean and dump her there. Deliberately he turned toward the water; he would die with the same calmness with which he had flown most of his three thousand combat hours. But then the silvery sheen of a familiar face coalesced in his mind. He felt a rushing torrent in his stomach, his breathing shortened. His mind flooded with what seemed to be bright colors, though he could not say he actually saw the colors, it was more of a feeling that they were there. Abruptly, he steered back toward the fields. Something in him softened and blurred, and he lined up for a crash landing onto the clearest ground possible.

No, no, no, a voice inside him cried, deep and gravelly, like an officer in the distance shouting over a great wind. The pilot blinked, sat ramrod straight. As if waking from a sleep, he seemed to shake himself, then canted the stick wildly to the left, until the heaving blue ocean again filled his windshield. For the Divine Emperor! he thought, or perhaps shouted. The whitecaps blinked like landing lights in front of him. The roar of his descending plane was wild applause in his ears. He exhaled, willing himself to be calm. He called upon all his years of combat, the *muga* deep inside him. Duty, honor: those were all that mattered now. The altimeter began to drop fast.

But he *had* been told to land on this island. A submarine patrolled offshore to rescue him or any downed flier who made it to this designated spot. He could live. Back went the nose of the plane, once again the scrub stretched before him. Oh, he was weak! He knew why: he had allowed himself to love the fishmonger's daughter (there was her face, glinting, shining), and his yearning for her had softened him, overcoming his years of military duty. Now his mind was a cacophony of differing orders, a shrieking of training against instinct. Until this moment he had been sure he had always wanted the highest honor a Japanese soldier could attain—to die for the emperor. And now he was battling that with some reflex he had not known he had, an unnameable force that shamed him.

The ground was coming up fast. He turned to the ocean. Yes. His free hand gripped the cotton leg of his flight suit, as if he were afraid it would fly to the stick of its own accord. And then he turned again, with something like a cry tearing from his throat, losing more altitude and aligning himself with a rutted brown field. He was committed now, too late to sink his plane into the depths, waterlog it with salt and plankton and let it disappear. His chin jutted with shame. His plane would be vulnerable to the enemy now, his own life a cowardly misfortune if he survived. He told himself that there was hope, that he must yaw toward the water—now, now,

now—but the wheels touched and there was a terrible groan from his plane and then a thunderous yawn, and he felt his body slowly compress and a pain above his eye and then it was dark.

He was moving; he was on the carrier being lifted by the seas. Images spun toward him: the spume of foam when the plane in line in front of him crashed on takeoff into the water; the perfect blue of the morning; how the nose of an American P-36 looked before it dropped away and began to spin. Then all this was swallowed by a sudden billow of black smoke, its angry thrust into the sky: another airfield losing a hangar. How beautiful it was from where he was in the sky, and how terrible. His mind began to fill with the long, dark tendrils; they curled and swam around his plane, buffeting him with tangible fury. Finally there was nothing but its very blackness, as he dropped out of consciousness again.

Then a great wind rocked him. His shoulder was being pummeled by it, pushing him from side to side. Then it subsided, ruffling his coat and pressing his hips. It began again at his shoulder, and First Airman Shigenori Nishikaichi finally came awake. He scrabbled at the goggles and pulled them from his head. Blood arced into the air and as he followed its exuberant spray, the shiny, hard light of midday forced him to close his eyes again. Squeezing his eyelids together tightly, Nishikaichi ran his hand along his hair, understanding with a soldier's calm and cool detachment that head wounds bleed a lot. Next he reached instinctively for his pistol. It was gone. When he opened his eyes again, he saw a mynah bird staring at him from the nose of his plane. The creature flicked his black head to and fro.

-*Aloha*, mister, the bird said, and flew off.

To Nishikaichi, who did not speak Hawaiian and only the rudiments of English, the words sounded garbled, otherworldly. For a fleeting second, he thought that Lord Buddha himself had come to lead him to the other side, and as he watched the bird-God fly away, hammering at the air with ragged, black wings, he raised his hands. He waited for his body to rise silently and follow, thinking then of his mother and father, who would not yet have gotten the letter informing them of his death on its stark, precise military stationery, who had not yet fallen to their knees in a spasm of conflicted feelings, who may only now be wondering if he, their one and only son, had something to do with news trickling in about the great destruction. He only wished that he could assure them by including this part, that Lord Buddha had indeed come, though in an unlikely form, graceless and almost ugly, as a great god should, and taken him to, well, he didn't quite know that yet, but he waited, arms outstretched for the magnificent, unlikely Will to speed him away, and wondering at how this at least they had gotten wrong, that there was no great calm in death, at least not yet. He had been aware of an uncomfortable heat and bright light, and now suddenly that he was not able to move much, far less fly.

There was a heavy pressure on his shoulder and he jerked sideways. Staring at him was an older man with very brown, crooked teeth and black eyes whose corners tilted slightly downward, not unlike his own (in fact, Howard was only twenty-nine). He had a large, square chin, and a mountain of a forehead. His features were as angular as a movie star's but rough with sun and dust. Jet-black hair rose in a curl from the man's forehead and, though the pilot could not know this, was combed carefully whenever he found himself alone.

Nishikaichi would have thought that this was yet another Buddha on a mission—except for the stench. It was an unmistakable man smell, the muddy funk of sweat and something else—horse, it turned out. The stubby fingers were red with dust and there was horsehair all down the front of his white shirt. Startled by

Nishikaichi's sudden consciousness, the strange man took a step back on the wing. For an endless moment the two blinked at each other, wordless, and then Nishikaichi saw his pistol balanced in the man's other hand and any illusion that he was dead quickly disappeared in the ensuing rush of adrenaline.

Nishikaichi considered the distance between him and the man; he was fairly sure he could take him in a fight, but it would mean finding the harness buckle and undoing it, then hoisting himself from the cockpit. He thought his legs would come free fast, but he could not be sure, and though the man seemed clumsy and a little confused, the pilot knew from his own experience that country people were most dangerous like this. Besides, the island was not uninhabited, as he had been told in his briefing. There would be more of them. Nishikaichi lowered his outstretched arms, then raised one hand slowly. The man raised his. He frowned and said something that did not seem to be threatening, but still, it was hard to tell. Nishikaichi did not respond, waiting for the gun to be raised to his face and cocked. Well, it would be right to die, wouldn't it? He had dishonored the Divine Emperor by landing here, and now he deserved whatever this man wanted to inflict on him. Except that to die now meant that his plane was theirs. The man spoke again. He gestured. Nishikaichi unbuckled the harness and pushed himself slowly from the cockpit. He would do as this crooked-toothed man asked, until he could find a way to destroy his plane, and then himself.

5

Howard's house was the same as all the houses in Niihau's only village of Puuwai. It was perched on small stilts to encourage ventilation. There was a front porch and a door that led to a main room with a table and a few chairs. To the right was another room with two single beds; to the left a smaller room for his child. The roof was tin, which occasionally dented in a strong afternoon wind, sending a shudder through the house and a loud *woomph*. To one side was a small shed where animal feed and a few tools were kept. In the back was a thousand-gallon water tank used during the dry season.

The island was big and the population small, so houses on Puuwai were not too close, and were delineated by lava walls on which chickens and children often perched. Usually Howard could see his neighbors if they stood on their porch and waved, but he couldn't tell the expressions they had on their faces when they did so. Now most of his neighbors were crowded into his house. Those who couldn't fit inside milled on his porch and in the front yard, so that the horses that usually found shade there moved reluctantly to the back field. The villagers lucky enough to get a place in the kitchen pushed and squeezed to get a better look at their new guest, a brave few actually within a few feet of him, sometimes touching the chair he sat on, or fingering with tentative flicks the flight hat that lay limply on the table, discolored from blood. The pilot did not turn his head, and ate with the concentration that the islanders had seen in feral cats. His nose was as small as a petal, not broad and flat like the Niihauans', and his skin was pale, not burnt and earthy. Someone said he was Japanese, though he did not look much like the three Japanese on the island: his face, despite the dust and blood, was unmistakably smooth, his hands as delicate as the muzzle of a young lamb. The Niihauans were intuitive people. They sniffed the wind for weather, they felt with their hands for an animal's sickness, they prayed often. Though the pilot's expression was stern and his eyes stayed mostly fixed on his plate, they knew, as surely as they smelled rain, that this man was afraid of them and of their home. They bustled around dropping food on his plate, their way of reassurance.

Howard had no idea why the pilot had landed on Niihau, but his neighbors turned to him for answers anyway. For the sixth time this morning, Howard leaned back in his chair, squinted at the ceiling, and, spreading his arms wide for quiet, began a version that was even wilder and more dramatic than the previous telling only ten minutes before.

-So when the plane hit, there was a ball of flame that almost burned my hair right off . . .

-I thought you said it landed like a bird?

-Like a crazy bird. The explosion was like thunder, and I said to myself, Howard, get that man out before he cooks like a pig. I ran to pull our *malihini* here from what looked like his burning grave. There were bullets flying from the guns on the plane—

-He tried to kill you?

-Well, no, no. The bullets must have shot out from impact. But I thought it would not be hospitable to have our strange friend die on this island, and I ran every which way to keep clear of the guns and get to him in time. He was very happy that he landed near me, and not near one of you, who would have stood staring like dumb cattle at his predicament. Without me that plane of his would have been his *pahu* for sure.

The villagers laughed, which startled the pilot momentarily. He stopped eating and the crowd quieted, sorry they had alarmed him. After a moment they spoke again, but this time in lower voices.

What will *Ka Haku Makua* say when he arrives? We must tell the visitor to leave now. What, ask him to swim? Mr. Robinson will be as mad as when the fever came from Malia's nephew. It's not our fault he fell here like a rock from the sky. He was madder when the church candles disappeared. Look, you all, there's nothing we can do but close that cut on his head. Mr. Robinson comes tomorrow. Tomorrow. *Ka Haku Makua* arrives tomorrow.

Howard sat back and listened to his neighbors talk. He wanted to stay in the excitement of the moment, and not let his mind wander to more troublesome things, but he felt a small knot in his stomach. What was a soldier doing so close to Niihau? Why had he crashed? It was possible a boy so young had simply been completely overwhelmed by the powerful machine. Howard remembered that his own eight-year-old son had been thrown from a high-spirited horse just yesterday. Howard himself had once been bested by an especially small calf that he'd attempted to hog-tie, a fact that he shared with no one, not even his wife, Mabel. The strange boy had simply lost control of his plane. But even so, this pilot was a soldier. Though there were many soldiers on Kauai, this one had come from a faraway place, and soldiers, with their guns and papers, were never a good sign.

Howard had not understood much of what the pilot tried to

tell him or these questions would have been answered by now. After the crash Howard had led the pilot by the elbow to his house to feed him, and when he had seated him, the pilot had become agitated and had begun to speak quickly. Howard thought he heard some English words, but he could not be sure. *Slow,* he'd answered back in English, elongating the word, keeping his lips rounded for seconds after the sound ended. But the pilot only spoke louder, as if Howard was deaf, leaning forward with an expression of great concern. Finally the pilot pulled a pencil from his flight-suit pocket and Howard peeled the label off a condensed-milk can.

To Give Me, the pilot wrote in blocky letters of English on the back side of the label.

Howard was one of the few Niihauans who spoke English, and one of the even fewer who could read the white man's language—he'd gone through sixth grade at the Kauai missionary school—but he did not understand this. The pilot then mimed searching in his flight-jacket pocket, looking for something. He pointed at his holster and back at the paper. Howard, understanding now, shook his head amiably and offered the pilot more food. He had the gun under the bed in the next room, the papers in his pocket. The pilot would not understand that guns weren't allowed on the island, and that Howard was simply saving him from Robinson's disapproval. And by the excited way the man was acting about it, he clearly wasn't in his right mind. That was a nasty enough cut, and surely the crash had rattled his brain. Howard was going to feed and care for his new guest; the particulars would be taken care of by Mr. Robinson, when he arrived on Niihau tomorrow.

The torn-off label on the table was now picked up and passed back and forth. Each person squinted from a wary distance, holding the paper at its edges as if it held some kind of disease; those few whose courage surged stroked the penciled letters carefully with one finger. It was hard not to be swept away in the excitement; after all, little changed on Niihau that was not molded by the wind or the water; when it did the Niihauans preferred to let their boss handle it. The result was a wide-eyed excitement only heightened by their concentrated effort to remain uninvolved, at least until Mr. Robinson arrived.

By now Howard's house was quite full—surely the whole village was here—and Howard considered telling his story yet again. But there was that twist in his stomach and the realization of one more thing that bothered him. A small, nagging memory of an event he had repeatedly read about, but had been unable to put in any meaningful perspective.

Perhaps it was nothing.

In fact, it probably was nothing.

Howard did not know exactly where this event was taking place, except that it was far away. Still, he thought he should mention it, even if it would worry his neighbors. It was, after all, a war. Howard pursed his lips and frowned. A war. A soldier. There might be a connection. He leaned back in his chair and harrumphed in his throat to speak, then stopped. There was, of course, another thing to consider. It might get back to Robinson that he had told people about this war, and that would lead to uncomfortable questions. Sticky questions, about how Howard had come by this knowledge. As it was, Howard often arranged for the Kauaian boatman who ferried Robinson to and from Niihau to buy tobacco, which was forbidden. The boatman stuffed Bull Durham into an old sock and Howard would find it later that afternoon in his fishing gear, limp from the seawater on bad-weather days, stiff from the heat on others. But sometimes the tobacco would come wrapped in an old Kauai newspaper, and Howard would sit down and read. His large, rough fingers slid under each word, his lips moved as if in prayer. If he got the front page, he read sporadically about a faraway war, with its strange-sounding cities and battles. But mostly he got the pages that dealt with fish prices and sugar yields. Even these did not seem relevant to his life on Niihau. A war in a distant country was positively remote. No, thought Howard, it would be more trouble than it was worth to mention this to his neighbors. There was a good reason that Mr. Robinson had never talked about it, and that was that it had no bearing at all on their lives here on Niihau. Besides, Howard could not risk Robinson finding out that he smoked.

-The boy needs a poultice, said a gravelly voice, and Howard looked over at Ella Kanahele. She was shorter than the other Niihauan women, but she was wide and sturdy. She pushed forward, her dark hair falling loose from her bun so that it sprayed around her face like a waterfall. Her eyebrows were in a characteristic frown. Once at Howard's shoulder, she thrust out one hand.

-He's got a good knock on the head, she said, and nodded at her fist, where a paste oozed out, smelling faintly of fish and perhaps pineapple.

-Here, she said, some *laau*.

She swung her arm toward the pilot, who flinched at the sudden movement and then put up his hands to deflect her wrist. She frowned and shushed him.

-Trying to fight an old woman! Put your head over here, young man. I've been known to get grumpy. Just ask my husband.

The villagers laughed again, and some of the tension in the room was broken as men slapped Ben Kanahele's shoulder kiddingly and the women guffawed. Ben was not much taller than his wife, and as wide as a honey crate, a lumbering, quiet man known for the fact that even at fifty-one years of age, he could throw two ewes over his shoulder with little effort. That hearty strength, however, evaporated in front of a wife like Ella, who could get as bad tempered as a boar. But her touch was gentle as she spread the paste on the pilot's forehead and then patted his shoulder with one small hand.

-You may have that fancy uniform on, but you're just a boy. You need taking care of. Now I'm going to say a prayer, because ultimately it's not us that does the healing, but the good Lord himself.

And with this she dropped her head and began to murmur, eyes closed. There was a respectful silence until she was done.

-Amen, Howard said. And too bad he doesn't understand what we say. I'd like to know why he's here, on Niihau of all places.

-Well, said Ella, squinting at the boy. You think he's Japanese. Bring the Japanese to talk to him.

-The Japanese, Howard agreed, and someone ran for the head beekeeper, Ishimatsu Shintani. Shintani had been born in Japan, though he had been on Niihau for as long as anyone could remember.

Old Shintani was pushed to the front of the room by excited hands. Always wizened and a little sour looking, today Shintani looked as if he badly wanted to be somewhere else. His deeply browned skin paled at the sight of the military pilot. His eyes widened. He began to shake his head. The pilot spoke quickly and with enthusiasm as he got close. Shintani, pushed right into the table by his smiling neighbors, stood rigid, with his eyes averted. The pilot continued to talk, leaning forward intently.

-What's he saying? Howard asked, looking from the animated pilot to stiff, unmoving Shintani and back again.

Shintani gripped the table edge and kept his eyes fixed on a spot somewhere to the left of the tabletop as the pilot continued to speak. Once, the pilot reached across the table, as if to take hold of Shintani's wrist, and Shintani suddenly unfroze and stepped back as if he had been stung.

-I don't understand this dialect, Shintani finally stammered in his fluent but oddly accented Hawaiian. Howard nodded and shrugged. The Niihauans passed around the news: Shintani the beekeeper could not tell them why the pilot was here. There were disappointed murmurs. Shintani continued to look as if he wanted to run or collapse.

Shaking his head, Shintani finally backed out of the room.

-Fetch Mr. Harada! said Howard.

Yoshio had just finished cleaning a saddle, which he'd hoisted onto a rack and then leaned against before going on to the bridle, when he heard the horse canter up the driveway. The rider called his name and then came to a halt in front of his house, so Yoshio stepped out of the shed and squinted up the hill to the commotion. Mr. Robinson is back early, he thought first, because the master's arrival always brought a kind of hysteria to the island, the suppressed excitement of a king's visit. Some villagers traveled the fifteen miles to meet him at the boat dock. Others came to the door when he rode through town. But he could not remember a time when someone had actually heralded his arrival with such a ruckus.

"Mr. Harada! *Wikiwiki*, hurry, hurry," the boy yelled. Yoshio saw Irene open the door and frown at the skittish horse and its braying rider, the unnecessary dust they kicked up. Yoshio began to walk toward them. The yelling stopped as the boy seemed to speak to Irene, though from where he was it was impossible to know what was said. He saw Irene step back, and then the flash of her *mu'umu'u* in the sun as she raised her arms like wings. The dust shimmered and cut into his eyes, the sun heated up his neck. Irene's voice, high-pitched and urgent, called his name. Yoshio began to run.

* * *

It was a two-mile ride from the Robinson ranch house property that the Haradas took care of to the village of Puuwai, but they covered the ground quickly in their cart. Irene, who usually complained about the dust, said nothing, only held three-year-old Taeko close. When they pulled up to Howard Kaleohano's house, the villagers overflowed from the inside of the house, to the porch, and down into the dry yard, but parted when Yoshio and his family mounted the steps. The women hissed at the small children to stand aside, the men touched the brims of their hats with their thumbs and nodded. Yoshio felt Irene clutch at his sweaty shirt and for a moment he was glad. But then the kitchen table came into view. He stopped and opened his mouth, but he was suddenly unable to remember the language he had grown up with.

-I am Naval Airman First Class Shigenori Nishikaichi, the stranger at the table greeted him in clear, precise Japanese. Then he said gravely, Your Pearl Harbor has been attacked. We have invaded the United States.

Yoshio heard the words in slow motion, a dust of sound caught momentarily in a breeze that fell through the inner workings of his mind. *A. Tak. Pe. Erl. HA. Boor. In. VA. Aded.* Then the words went from dust to scree, rumbling and screeching on the incline of his brain, gaining sound and momentum. He felt Irene's own suppressed cry, even as she stood completely still, as if the words were instead a solid rock that had fallen in her path and she was frozen first in horror and then with the suddenness of a multitude of choices: turn back, go left, go right. He wanted to step back himself, stumble, more likely, to put immediate distance between him and this murderous pilot, but another part of him knew instinctively that it was not the time to alert his neighbors to anything wrong.

-What do you mean? he stammered in Japanese, trying to keep his face impassive even as it drained of blood.

-Everything's gone, destroyed. The Imperial Navy did its job well. You should be proud of your native country.

Yoshio only blinked at him. The pilot's face, which had been taut with sudden pride, slackened. The Japanese couple was not as pleased as he would've liked.

-Why are you here? hissed Yoshio. Already he could feel Howard's eager impatience, wanting to know what was being said. Taeko had begun to whimper. The room was as quiet as a room full of people could be. There were no loud noises, but it rustled with the sway and murmur of bodies packed tightly together.

-Bullets hit my gas tank. An emergency landing—

But Howard now jumped up with his wide, foolish smile.

-What's he saying, Mr. Harada? Does he know the Old Lord?

The villagers crowded closer to hear Yoshio answer.

-I mean, why'd he land here, of all places? Howard waved his arms around the room. We're not used to guests, and the Old Lord will be angry when he comes tomorrow. You know the rules.

Yoshio nodded and felt Irene's heavy silence behind him.

-Yes, the rules, he said slowly. He frowned and looked down.

He wanted to shout, Destruction! Death! Mayhem! Stand back, all of you. It's evil, right here, in our kitchen. Truss this boy like a chicken, put a knife to his throat and make him beg. Strip him of his flight suit and that stern expression, throw him into the sea. All of you, listen, listen. America and now Niihau have been attacked by the *Japanese*.

But he said nothing. His hands had begun kneading together, and a far-off memory roused itself. *Japanese*, the memory said, its voice slick with disdain.

-Mr. Harada? said Howard.

-It's—he won't say much. Yoshio coughed, dropping his hands

at his sides. He—what does it matter anyway? Mr. Robinson will be here tomorrow, he'll take care of all this. I'm sure the boy will speak more when he's less tired and his wound has healed a little.

There was a ripple of agreement in the room, and even Yoshio felt the palpable relief as the villagers willingly abdicated any real responsibility for the stranger. Howard sat back and nodded fiercely.

-Right you are, Mr. Harada. We'll let the Old Lord handle the *mea mai ka ʻaina ʻe* in the morning. Later, we'll put him in the shed, keep him isolated, like he'd want us to. For now let's eat more and treat our guest as Christians should.

Someone plucked a ukulele and began to sing. Yoshio talked to the pilot for a little while longer, setting a few things straight, gathering a little bit more information, telling the pilot that tomorrow they would go to see the boss of the island when he arrived. Yoshio kept his tone neutral and his eyes away from the strange boy with the ramrod-straight posture; despite this his nausea and panic grew. Finally, he felt his horror about to burst. He excused himself quickly. He and Irene said nothing to each other as they pushed their way out the door. They nodded at their neighbors, smiled tightly. *Errands*, they murmured as convincingly as they could. They fled down the porch stairs, without looking back.

6

It wasn't just the strange airman. Foreigners—*mea mai ka 'aina 'e*—had been coming to Niihau for as long as anyone could remember. Perhaps it was the isolation and the accompanying promise of respite from the outside world. Perhaps it was something directly linked to the dry, flat landscape, which allowed one to see for so far without interruption that some might have thought they glimpsed the future. Something beckoned on that shorn, bare land, the promise of possibility that artists see in a blank canvas stretched before them. There is no other explanation for why Niihau was consistently described as a kind of paradise by the *mea mai ka 'aina 'e* who landed there.

Niihau itself did not seem to care one way or another what was thought of it. It went about its island rhythms as it always had, yielding little rain, kicking up formidable amounts of dust. And so people left even more often than they arrived. For centuries the dry years had forced people to make the treacherous canoe ride to Kauai and settle there instead, often never returning. Kauai was lush and green. Its Mount Wai'ale'ale was the wettest place on earth, receiving five hundred inches of rain a year. Only sixteen miles leeward, Niihau was a flaking, discarded peel of sand and lava. It was smaller than its neighbors, only eighteen miles long, and curled like a lemon rind. The wind was strong, rain was rare. Hawaiian lore stated—and science later confirmed—that Niihau was the first of the island chain to push its way from the ocean floor. Its explosive, frothy, molten birth seemed inconceivable now. It was an island of muted color, understatement, and calm.

Though the rains that soaked Kauai rarely made the trip across the channel, others did. Old Ella Kanehele liked to tell the tale of her great-great-grandfather, and how he had been one of the first to welcome the famous explorer Captain Cook when he'd arrived in 1778. Another family said that they had a gift from one of the crew and frequently pulled a box from under a bed. They would open it reverently and rummage through a few bird feathers, a Bible, and a stick blessed by a *kahuna,* finally pulling out a large iron nail, red with rust and salt. Here, they would say. See?

None of these claims could be verified. But Cook wrote affectionately in his log about Niihau, how he found scattered villages of grass huts and friendly inhabitants. He also found yams, thousands of them, a food item perfect for the long overseas voyages. Welcomed and feted, Cook saw the island as a kind of innocent paradise, despite the harsh landscape. His men saw it as an idyllic respite from the boredom of the high seas. When Cook made sail two days later, it was with the holds of his ship jammed with the hardy root vegetable and plans to return, though he lamented that he was unable to fill his water caskets from the trickle of brackish water Niihauans relied on. He and his crew left behind three goats, two pigs, pumpkin seeds, onion seeds, and venereal disease. All would irreparably alter the flora and fauna of this tiny island.

In 1864 another *mea mai ka 'aina 'e* arrived on Niihau. A restless rancher named Eliza Sinclair—Aylmer Robinson's great-grandmother—had recently sailed with her family from New

Zealand to find land to farm in California. Disliking what she saw there, she took her family and backtracked to Hawaii, landing on Oahu near the place where Pearl Harbor would later be built. Here the matriarch put out the word that she was interested in a large tract of land on one of the islands. But because of the Great Mahele of 1848, which split up the royal lands and allowed private ownership for the first time, unbroken property big enough to ranch had become rare.

On Niihau, however, no islander came forward with enough money to take advantage of the Great Mahele. The harsh climate and subsistence living meant that few of the one thousand Niihauans could afford to pay the annual tax to the king, much less buy their own property; ultimately only one indigenous family would manage to do this. Pleas by Niihauans to lower the cost of land went unheard. Kamehameha V began to tire of the island and, with its taxes unpaid and its inhabitants angry, he wished to unload it; he was glad to show this *haole*—white foreigner—not only available parcels on Oahu and Kauai, but also the whole of Niihau.

It just so happened that 1864 was a wet year for Niihau. The land was green, the springs were abundant. Lake Halalii, usually a huge, dry crater, was brimming with water. Eliza Sinclair's son-in-law visited Niihau and came back with a report that the island was lush and verdant, perfect for ranching. Eliza Sinclair hadn't thought much of Ford Island, which was in the middle of a large, quiet bay eventually named Pearl Harbor, or the property that would in 1941 be downtown Honolulu (and well on its way to being the most expensive real estate around). And the tract on Kauai seemed too small. But Niihau sounded like paradise. She promptly offered $6,000 for the whole island. The king countered with a demand for $10,000, pointing to its lush beauty, its fecund soil. Eliza

Sinclair agreed. Yoshio Harada had always liked this story; it was, he thought, one of the few times that the white people got their shirts taken by a brown people.

Within a few years Niihau reverted to its familiar dry and desiccated self. Eliza Sinclair and her family quickly realized their mistake and bought a new swath of land on Kauai, but they remained infatuated with their island, and began its monumental makeover. They brought building material over the channel. They imported cattle and merino sheep and bees and, eventually, fine Arabian horses. In came the new flora: mango, pear, star apple. Birds were freed on the scrub: peafowl, ducks, turnstone curlew, meadowlark. Turkeys. California valley quail. Partridge. By the time Aylmer and his brother Lester inherited the land, even the water on it had been carefully controlled: it was diverted by hand-laid pipes and stored in cisterns dug with shovels and pickaxes. Everything came by boat, and as a boy Aylmer had liked to watch the herds of animals snort with trepidation as they docked at Kii.

-Like the ark, his father would say proudly with each boatload.

The ranch was never wildly profitable—the Robinson family had their sugar ranch on Kauai for that—but it flourished nevertheless as proof that whatever a man wanted to do with the land, he could, as long as the Lord was willing. The ranch hands were all Hawaiian and the Robinsons wanted to keep it that way; they were an innocent people, good Christians nearly decimated by the vices and diseases of the outside world, but ripe for salvation: Niihau would be a small garden of Eden where the most vulnerable of the Lord's children could live in peace, as well as work on the Robinson ranch. The Niihauans spoke only Hawaiian, thumbed through Hawaiian Bibles, were encouraged to marry their Hawaiian neighbors. They tended the land with the reverence of their Hawaiian ancestors. Under orders from the Robinsons, families gathered to pray every day, and the whole village went to church on Sundays; no one seemed to think there was anything odd about this arbitrary fusion of Hawaiiana with Christianity, or if they did, nothing was said. In addition, the outside world was kept at bay. Communication was limited to news of babies born or family members sick on other islands, and done by word of mouth. There was no electricity, no cars, no newspapers. No telephones. No guns or alcohol or (allegedly) cigarettes. There was no post office, no jail, no police. And if you left the island hoping to make a life elsewhere, you were rarely granted permission to return, for fear that you would bring modern life with you, like a virus. If Niihau was to remain pure, the Robinsons reasoned, it had to be beyond the grasp of contemporary temptations.

At first many Niihauans left, either angry with the new ownership or because the chronic lack of water couldn't accommodate both the old inhabitants and the influx of new ones. Those who remained began to respect their new landlords, and eventually to trust and depend on them.

By 1922 Aylmer began to run the island himself, under his father's watchful eye, and the population of people had stabilized at around 140. Sometimes outsiders were brought in to manage a part of the ranch, as old Shintani was with the beehives, or with hopes of widening the marriage pool, as with Howard Kaleohano. But by the mid-1920s, newspapers had dubbed Niihau "the Forbidden Island" because of its strict rules and increasing isolation. The Robinsons pointed to the dangers of disease and the lack of water for why fewer and fewer outsiders were allowed to come ashore, but *haoles* and *kama'aina* alike whispered that the Niihauans were nothing more than serfs in a bizarre fiefdom. The Robinsons wanted only a pliant workforce, they said. And it was a shame, these ignorant Niihauans happy with the little they got, the situation they were in. They didn't know enough to see what they were missing. The modern world was surging forward; they were content in their small, backward paradise.

But when Aylmer Robinson had wanted someone to take care of his ranch house, after his white foreman fell ill, he'd hired Mr. and Mrs. Harada on a recommendation from a friend. They weren't Christian, but they were quiet, dependable, and hardworking. They had a small child. More important, Yoshio was a good beekeeper. And the fastest way to Robinson's heart was through bees.

-I'm interested in well-run societies, Mr. Harada, Mr. Robinson had said when they'd first met. Bees represent one of the best.

Yoshio had nodded, but he thought that it was an odd interview. His previous employers had never spoken, just squinted at his large shoulders and his callused hands. And if they did speak, it was merely to convey the specifics of the job, or to ask questions about his work background. Certainly Yoshio had never seen such a large house before, never mind been asked inside one to discuss a job. He had expected to meet Mr. Robinson in the paddock or in the doorway of a shed, but he had instead been ushered into the sitting area by the man himself, and offered a mug of cold tea. The room was sparsely furnished, but books were crammed into every nook and cranny. A stack near Yoshio's elbow threatened to fall, so he tried to stay very still, even as Mr. Robinson, at first glance a quiet man, sat down and, on the subject of bees, became almost animated.

-Man could learn a lot from these tiny creatures, he said to Yoshio. If only we could pull ourselves away from the temptations of the devil for a moment, to sit quietly and learn! Why, the workers do everything for the hive—they care for their younger sisters, feed the drones and the queen, clean the combs, collect nectar—well, you know all this, Mr. Harada, but by gosh, if it wasn't blasphemous, I would suspect they were Christians, raised by the teachings of His Only Son, don't you think? I'm never disappointed with bees, not in the way mankind disappoints me. The day I find a man willing to exhaust himself with his arms to cool a room, like bees do for their hive, is the day I see our poor species differently. And my heavens, that dance that they do. The most beautiful thing. It proves there's a God, I say. They dance to tell their sisters where the flowers are, don't they, Mr. Harada. A wondrous thing, that dance.

-Like the *hula*, Yoshio finally spoke up, cautiously. Though he had never seen it, he had heard that this native Hawaiian dance of hand gestures and foot stamping and hip rolling all enacted a story of some ancient god or goddess, of incoming weather, of lost love, or newfound hope.

Robinson blinked, momentarily perplexed, as Yoshio sat politely waiting for him to answer. Despite the fact that Hawaiians were indigenous to the islands, they were far outnumbered by the *haoles* and Asians, and those Yoshio did know spoke English and had forgotten many of their customs. But Yoshio had been told that Robinson loved the native Hawaiian language, which he spoke fluently, and that he was obsessed with the history and botany of these islands. He felt it was an intelligent thing to bring up the islanders' rites, even though he knew little about them, to show he would fit in well on Niihau.

Robinson's face began to darken and his eyes narrowed.

-Not the *hula*, Robinson finally said slowly. That's a *lascivious* dance. Practiced by folks who didn't know better. Have you *seen* the *hula*?

-Uh, no, sir. Yoshio dropped his head and stiffened.

-Well, then, you wouldn't know.

There was a pause, which Yoshio did not dare fill, in case he said the wrong thing again.

-Bees, Mr. Robinson finally said, nodding his head back in Yoshio's direction. People have all sorts of these nonsense ideas about them. How it's some sort of slavery, some sort of *dictatorship* in there for the queen bee. What do you think, Mr. Harada?

-About what? Yoshio shifted to release the pressure of his thighs against the chair. His hands clenched together in his lap. His knuckles striated and the veins jumped and held.

-About bees. About whether it's a dictatorship. The queen, a brutal overlord, the others just slaves.

Robinson folded his own large hands and sat back. Yoshio saw how piercingly blue his eyes were, as if the afternoon sky was trapped there. He cleared his throat.

-Yes, well, the workers *do* do everything for the queen. But, but—well, sure, it seems to benefit them all, what they do for her. The hive gets cleaned, new bees are born, more honey is stored. He bobbed his head. A healthy queen means a healthy hive.

-Exactly. Mr. Robinson nodded in approval and the closest thing to a smile Yoshio had yet seen split his craggy face. He was a puzzling man, Yoshio thought later. He had the bearing and locution of a minister but the skin and clothes of a ranch hand. Yet more money than anyone Yoshio had ever known.

Despite Yoshio's misstep about the *hula*, Robinson must have seen that he was a good family man, and certainly a fine beekeeper. He was hired. Still it took Yoshio months to convince Irene that the job would be a good opportunity for both of them. She dreaded the isolation of that far-off island (it's only a half-day's boat ride, he'd insisted) and the idea that she would be away from her beloved sister. She's just had another child! Irene exclaimed. She'll need my help. But Yoshio was unusually persistent.

-Think of Taeko, *kachan*. It's a child's paradise out there. Farm animals, open spaces. A large house to live in.

-But Taeko needs her little cousins, her family. Irene would not give in.

-She won't be far away. Look, by the time she starts school, we'll be back on Kauai. With money in our pockets.

-You can make money in the fields.

-The fields aren't for a man anymore.

-What is for a man?

-A man needs to have his own life, his own work. This island would be perfect.

-Because it's far from whites?

He shrugged and looked away.

-Perhaps, he'd said.

Yoshio had been born on a Kauai plantation, where his parents worked the fields under arduous conditions. There was a close-knit Japanese community in the Hawaiian Islands that insisted on a solid education and a Japanese acculturation for their American-born children. Asians outnumbered whites ten to one, and people of Japanese descent made up half the population on Kauai, so while life was hard Yoshio grew up feeling, if not American, at least part of his Hawaiian home. He remembered muddy walks to school, with some children wearing geta on their feet; the *hai, hai* as his father laughed at a neighbor's joke; the sweet, insistent smell of mango. Still, to be issei—a Japanese national—or nisei—of Japanese descent, born on American soil—meant that even on Kauai you were looked at sideways by *haole* shopkeepers and housewives. That the *luna* chose you first for a whipping in the fields because you wouldn't fight back. That though you were an American citizen, you'd never really, truly be red, white, and blue. With youthful bravura that he would never show again, Yoshio left for California and what he thought would be a better life.

When Yoshio got off the boat there, it looked as if the Japanese men had successfully assimilated into American culture. They smoked cigarettes and said *Hey, pal* and *You betcha* when they spoke. They patted their shirt pockets and took off their sweaters by crossing their arms and pulling them from the sides over their heads. They walked in long, loping strides. But soon it became clear that California was a terrible place for a Japanese man. There were laws that banned nisei from marrying whites. None could own land. Schools were segregated, as were public theaters and swimming pools and water fountains. Street preachers and local politicians alike yelled and stamped with their fists in the air, blaming the Yellow Peril for all the evils in California. What happened specifically to Yoshio over there, he would not say, not even to Irene when he married her, but he came back after seven years with a watchful eye and a new slouch in his shoulders. He spent the next ten years on Kauai, but some deep humiliation haunted him so that during the day his knuckles hurt from clenching his fists and at night he sometimes woke in a sweat. It was no surprise, then, that when he was offered the Niihau job as caretaker and assistant beekeeper, he ignored the isolation, the harsh climate, the strange fiefdom he was going to. He thought only that this would be the last chance he had to reclaim himself as a man. Truth was, he wanted this job on Niihau because it offered something more than good pay and good work. He didn't tell Irene this, but he had lost something of himself a long time ago and he wondered if he could find it on Niihau.

After seven months of fruitless persuasion—during which Robinson either waited patiently or forgot about the job offer entirely, Yoshio wasn't sure—Irene finally agreed and, clutching her sister tearfully, as if they were traveling 1,600 miles instead of 16, begged her family to write often. Unfortunately, mail was prohibited on the island (so few of the islanders read anyway), but Irene did not learn of this until later. They left by boat for Niihau, and it was with shock that Irene set foot on that hot, peeling landscape with its wind so dense with red dust she thought she might choke. Since then Yoshio continued to promise her that things would change, and that she would begin to like it, as he had, but so far that had not happened. Though the Niihauans were friendly people, they tended to regard anybody not born on the island with the mild caution they gave small but sharp-toothed animals. Irene immediately felt this and put it down to her Japanese heritage; Yoshio insisted that the Niihauans did not compartmentalize their world in this way, that the family simply lived too far from the village for her to segue seamlessly into Niihauan life. In the past year, he liked to point out, the men had included him as one of their own; they showed him *lawaia,* using crude nets or a cowry-shell lure so that he proudly brought home *hee, popolo,* and *moi* for dinner; they listened as he told them about bees. He, for one, began to relax; California would recede in his memory, he thought, and he would no longer clench his fists and stare at his lap at inexplicable moments, paralyzed with fear and shame for no immediate reason he could think of. But Irene became withdrawn and quiet, and even the most open-hearted of Niihauans were puzzled by her. Yoshio hoped that the store that Irene ran would eventually make her feel more at home. The Hawaiian women came by often to pick up what they needed—canned milk, thread, flour—and surely their chatter would lift her spirits. But Irene would not let go of the certainty that the Hawaiians saw them as *mea mai ka 'aina 'e,* and that they would never be fully integrated into the island.

And, now, on the afternoon of December 7, as the pilot calmly explained that Pearl Harbor had been destroyed by the Japanese military, Yoshio knew that his own attempt at a new life had been attacked as surely as the Pacific Fleet.

7

By dusk the Niihauans had drifted away to look at the plane and then drifted back, then drifted away for evening prayer and drifted back again, tidelike, still drawn to the excitement of a forbidden *mea mai ka ʻaina ʻe.* More sweet potatoes and *poi* were pushed in front of the pilot. Someone started a game of *kini kini,* others sang quietly.

Only when they were up the hill did Yoshio stop the cart and look at his wife, who had pushed one thin arm over her face and turned it from him. He glanced furtively from side to side and leaned forward to touch her, then leaned back before he did. For a while they sat canted away from each other—he fiddling with his large, square hands, she jerking with strange wet gulps, like the desperate suckling of a newborn—until Taeko began to squirm. Yoshio finally reached forward to stroke his child's head with his fingertips. He clucked at her soothingly. He felt his wife stiffen at his proximity.

-Why didn't you tell them? she said through her tears. About what the pilot said.

-That news, coming from me? Pearl Harbor bombed? It's too horrible for our neighbors to understand. Mr. Robinson will let them know soon enough.

She straightened and stared at him, and despite the smallness of her bones, her birdlike fragility, her face had hardened into something fearful.

-You think Mr. Robinson will solve everything! she cried. Yoshio squeezed her shoulders to calm her. He *tsk*ed his tongue against his teeth.

-The Niihauans trust him. You know how it is here, he said softly.

-We should have said something.

-*Kachan,* let the Old Lord handle this. It'll be fine.

-You say that, but you don't believe it.

-I do. We've done nothing wrong.

-We're Japanese. That is enough.

Yoshio turned away and brought his hands together unconsciously. Before he knew it he was squeezing them again, the word *Japanese* ricocheting through his skull. He felt the sting of an old blister, the crack of his thumb bone.

-We're American citizens. Born and bred on an American island. Now, time to go home. He lifted the reins and slapped them against the horse's shoulder, but Irene grabbed his arm.

-There will be more of them, she said. He said so himself. Coming on the submarine to take over the island.

-Mr. Robinson will let us know of the dangers ahead. Come on.

-They've attacked Pearl Harbor, now they'll go on to Kauai. Then to us, here on Niihau.

-Quiet! Yoshio glanced around nervously. Enough talk of this.

-We must see the plane, cried Irene. The horse jerked forward, but Irene still clung to his forearms, until finally he pulled back and the cart stopped.

-I need to see it. She was breathing hard and her eyes had taken on a starved look he saw often but could not quite interpret.

-*Kachan,* we must go home. It's bad luck to go near a thing like that. We need to stay away from everything until Mr. Robinson comes.

-Then I'll go alone. She squirmed sideways in her seat and shifted Taeko from her lap.

-Okay, okay. Slow down, sweet, slow down. I'm here. And he swung himself quickly off the cart and raised his arms to take his child.

They walked carefully, Yoshio with Taeko in his arms now, Irene with the hem of her dress bundled in her hands to keep from tripping on it, her mouth set in a grim line. He thought that for once she was glad for the familiar silt against her face and the continuing heat because she looked so drained by fear and strangely light that without the heavy, oppressive air, she would surely float away. As the metal creature grew closer and larger, Yoshio felt dizzy. It was the strong smell of food and intermittent singing from Mr. Kaleohano's house that did it. Such merriment was absurdly out of place, but it was his fault, wasn't it? He should have wheeled toward his neighbors the second the pilot had spoken; he should have yelled at the top of his lungs. Pearl Harbor! he could have screamed. Instead his throat had squeezed shut and his body had seemed nailed to the floor.

He held out his hand when the debris thickened, but Irene did not notice, or simply ignored him, and stepped slowly, eyes wide. Her lips were pursed in something between disgust and wonder. Sometimes, when jellyfish washed ashore after a storm, he moved this gingerly, this warily. But jellyfish did not scare him like this recumbent beast, shattered but still dangerous in a dark, unnameable way. Yoshio followed Irene until she stopped just short of the wingtip and stood with her arms folded. He stopped too, his shoulder in front of her, his hand dangling in case she wanted to hold it.

He was scared, no doubt about it. He tried to remind himself that this was only a lifeless piece of metal and glass, brought here by a boy. He scanned the side and saw nothing too threatening: the red Japanese circle, the large, jutting wing. He had, he realized, half expected a message to be scrawled on the plane. An explanation or a declaration of some kind, something to match the destruction the plane had supposedly wreaked. He was disappointed in the simple red circle and in the gray, silent bulk.

-It's big, Irene said.

The body aft of the wing sagged sideways. Part of the nose gear burrowed into the ground, and the wheel struts had disappeared under the belly, crushed by the emergency landing. Still, Irene was right; despite its damage it was still an impressive size. But to Yoshio it was more the world it came from that struck him as immense, that forgotten place of complicated machinery, so different from the simplicity of Niihau that from Yoshio's vantage point it appeared in a flash as almost divine. Here, in this tangled piece of metal, were the godlike powers to destroy and create at will, and with it all the rage and sorrows of the outside world.

Yoshio looked for the bullet holes that the pilot indicated had drained his gas tank and forced his landing. He could see them if he looked closely, tear-dropped holes near the belly. He turned to Irene to point them out and assure her that no Niihauans would guess they were there and that there had been a conflict. But her face was so white that he decided against it, and neither spoke for a while until Irene realized that Taeko had pulled her hand from her father's. She walked in her stiff, unsteady lockstep toward the plane, her arms forward as if reaching for its blistered metal edges and shattered glass. Irene lunged with a cry of rebuke and fear, pushing past Yoshio's hips and breaking him from his reverie. He watched in what appeared as slow motion as she swooped their child from the ground and pulled her against her breast; and simultaneously saw her leg jerk back as a bright red ribbon of blood leaped from her toe. He heard her gasp and realized with the part of him that quickly grasped and appreciated irony that his wife was the first, but perhaps not the last, on this tiny island to be wounded by the war, and it was, of course, because of him.

8

On the morning of Monday, December 8, Nishikaichi woke with a start. It was still completely dark in the shed, and he scrambled to his feet in a panic. Something moved to his left and he whirled sideways. He thrust one arm forward to ward off any blow, but nothing hit him, though he was sure he heard a growl and a sudden gnash of teeth. He chopped at the air frantically, still feeling nothing, and he knew that he was losing his composure, that he must calm down. Catching his breath, and suddenly ashamed of his panic, he stopped. When his eyes adjusted, what he had taken to be monsters became the long, skinny strips of salted pork draped from rafters and the outlines of large wood crates. The ominous angry snorts were just the heavy snores of his guards beyond the walls and sometimes the wind as it truckled across the scrub. Nishikaichi sat back down on the mat. He put his head in his hands. After a moment of quiet, when it was clear that the natives had not heard his one-sided punch fest, he began to take stock of where he was and the situation he was in.

His first, unexamined, reaction was that he must simply find a sharpened object and end it here, in a large and bloody gesture. He imagined the wide eyes of his guards when they found him, cross-legged on their soft grass mat, leaked of life. He would die in his military uniform—*gyokusai*, suicide instead of surrender. Of course the papers would still be in the wrong hands and his plane would be picked over like carrion by American soldiers. Before *gyokusai*, he would have to take care of that. Then with one thrust of a pointed stick, or a sharp-edged stone, it would be over. He would be on his way to the Yasukuni Shrine, with the rest of the honored war dead.

But what about escape? There was great *haji* in being imprisoned. Even the gentle and hospitable imprisonment of these villagers sent a wave of shame through him. But where could he go that he would not be found? A submarine patrolled offshore, assigned to rescue downed airmen, but it would not see him until the sun was much higher in the morning sky. And the island was dry and searingly hot. He could die of thirst. Or of a bite from a small and pincered insect, who knew or cared nothing of dying for a noble ideal. It would be a waste of his death, his bones scoured by a strange wind and bleached under a foreign sun, nourishing the soil of an enemy land. Besides, escape was out of the question while his plane and papers were in enemy hands. His *chu*, that lifelong obligation to the emperor, demanded that before anything else, those must be destroyed.

Nishikaichi reached into his flight jacket and fingered the thousand-stitch belt around his waist. He thought of the nervous swoosh of breath that had swept the deck as each man on his aircraft carrier had tied his on, some stumbling as the sea rolled their huge aircraft carrier, others struggling with anxious hands to subdue the batting strand of cloth in the high wind so that it sounded as if hundreds of birds were taking flight, wings flapping madly. Some of the *senninbari* knots had been stitched by loved ones, and these lucky men boasted about it. They named women who waited for them back home with eager arms, and Nishikaichi had dreamed with them, though he knew it was mostly lies. Nishikaichi's *senninbari* had been, like most, sewed only by strangers, and as he fingered each red knot (surprised by its knurled heft, its sturdiness), he imagined that one had been tied by the fishmonger's daughter in an auspicious coincidence that would later, he imagined, bring him to her door in gratitude. On the carrier he had written her a letter. He had held it in his hand for a long time, as if weighing its chances. At the last moment he had sent only the one to his parents; hers he had ripped up and cast into the sea. When the pieces had flown back onto his outstretched arm like small butterflies, he had taken this as a good sign that she would come to him after all.

There was a noise outside. Nishikaichi got up quietly, stiff from the night on the ground. He walked in awkward steps to the wall and squinted through a crack. In the dawn light he could see the dark shapes of his guards. The large one was turning over, muttering, his huge bulk shaking the wooden slats against Nishikaichi's cheek. The other two slept soundly, the ghostly outlines of their shovels like haphazard limbs nearby. Who were these strange tribal people? He had been startled by their resemblance to him (the black, almond-shaped eyes, the blunt nose, the darker skin), and not to the American that he had been briefed on: that pink barbarian who ritually ate raw meat for the taste of its fresh blood, who snorted more than talked, who had mucus running from his nose in floods, and nails grown long to disembowel enemies. Instead these people had shown little aggression; they were good-natured and gentle; natives, he supposed, who had escaped the Americans' rapacious ways. He had heard of Hawaiians, and how they had been wiped out by white disease—but here they were, intact. It was amazing, and for him, fortuitous. It would buy him much needed time.

Though the Japanese couple had assured him that the islanders would have no way of knowing that a war was on, because there were no telephones or newspapers and only one radio, at their Main House, the crooked-toothed man had told these men to stay with him all night. Perhaps the pilot had been too insistent about the papers, and the man had become suspicious. Perhaps—as the Japanese man had told him—he just followed the rules of the pink barbarian who oversaw them, some man named Robinson-san. Either way, he reminded himself, he would have to be more careful. These people might be ignorant, but they were not stupid.

He thought again of the fishmonger's daughter. She had carefully combed black hair and small teeth and, he had noticed, a short, white scar on the soft place above her thumb. Perhaps she'd cut herself with her own paring knife when her concentration had flickered away from a customer's fish to—what? He wished he knew. Perhaps she thought of a sunny afternoon in a boat on the nearby lake. Perhaps she dreamed of children at her feet, pulling the hem of her dress. Perhaps she thought of him, or someone like him, since he had never dared to say a word to her beyond asking for the fish his mother requested. If he ever returned he would speak to her, something precise and wonderful. What would that be? He had no idea. He would make his war friends laugh with tales of how tall and wide the men on this dusty island were, of how rotten their teeth, of how strange their native language sounded. He would tell them how badly it smelled in the shed he had to sleep in, of dead meat and flies. But none of that would be right for her. Nevertheless, he saw his mouth moving and her answering, glance-away smile. He would take her home to his parents, he thought, and they would not mind that she was the fishmonger's daughter.

He fingered the thousand-stitch belt again. He was unsure

whether its luck had worked for him. It was that last moment, he thought, when things went awry, after he had raised his fist like a young, undisciplined boy. So overtly pleased with himself. Such shameful hubris—that had been his downfall. Then, his unspeakable cowardice, his keening need to live. He should have crashed his plane in the ocean, he knew that. It was one of the mandates in the *Senjinkun*, the war manual from the emperor—never surrender yourself or your possessions to the inferior enemy. Not that it was necessary to read something like this in a manual—this kind of obligation was as much a part of him as his skin. He dropped his head as shame swept over him again like a wind; now he was not among his navy brothers in the honorable realms of the dead, but surrounded by strange-looking people, weighted down by his unresolved *chu*.

They had squinted at the cut on his face, and finally an old woman, short in stature, but with a broad, blocky body, and hair frizzed like dried grass, had thrust a poultice toward him. He had reflexively tried to hit her—his military training had taken over—but at the last moment he had seen his own grandmother, dead now, in her face. The poultice had smelled like leaves and something else; fish, he thought, though this he put down to his dreams of the fishmonger's daughter. Nevertheless it was a good sign, so he'd relented. The old woman's fingers had latticed his cheek; she'd pressed the strange ingredients to his skin. He had suddenly smelled honey, it was unmistakable. He had closed his eyes for a moment before he'd remembered that he had to remain on his guard and opened them again, just as the woman reached for his cupped hand and gently lifted it upward. He thought she might clasp it to her own wrinkled cheek, and he had almost smiled gratefully, but she had put it up to his head instead. She'd wanted him to hold the poultice in place.

The heat had been terrible; sweat muddied the blood on his

face, darkened his brown collar. He'd strained to understand the conversation as he ate, keeping his eyes down carefully. Though his English was poor, he had studied enough at the military academy to know that these people were speaking another language entirely. The sounds darted and flitted in a singsong manner; and finally he surmised that this must be Hawaiian, the tongue of the people of these islands.

As the afternoon wore on, exhaustion had prickled the back of the pilot's neck, had quietly forced his shoulders to sag, had urged his forearms to relax. When the crooked-toothed man brought out a ukelele and the crowd sang Hawaiian songs for his benefit, the pilot caught himself tapping one foot. He'd even cleared his throat when the milling crowd finally quieted, and tried to express his thanks for their hospitality, feeling it would be a useful tactic at least, in case their mood changed. Unable to find the right gestures, he instead sang the first few lines of an old Japanese folk song. The sounds came out hesitant and his voice wavered, but the villagers did not seem to notice. They hushed, their delight evident, so that the pilot, forgetting all the words for this one, continued into another that he knew better, and soon the notes stopped quivering, and he felt, to his surprise, that he was enjoying himself. Only after he'd stopped and thought of the Japanese couple, who had long since disappeared, did his unease slowly return.

He had not noticed the wife at first; she was hiding behind her husband's large back and clutching a child. It was only when she stepped sideways to hear his story better in the din of the room that he saw her. She did not look directly at him, but stared at an indefinable place on the table as he spoke, her body so still and her face so expressionless that he might have believed she was a statue, except that once or twice she lifted a hand to wipe invisible hair off the child's cheek. She was small, and as pretty as her husband was handsome; they made a striking couple. But it had quickly become clear that they didn't have an allegiance to their real country of Japan, as he had hoped. Or did they? Even as the man foolishly insisted they were American citizens, he seemed to hesitate at the words, as if he himself wasn't too sure. But he hadn't liked the request to retrieve the papers from the crooked-toothed man—clearly there was some bond between him and the villagers. Then they'd left abruptly. Well, he knew he would see the Japanese man today; he would have to plan how to win him to his side. With this, Nishikaichi sat back down on his haunches. He wanted to wash himself with water, but there was none; instead he ran his hands over his face. He could smell the pig fat on his fingers, and the gasoline of his downed plane in his hair. He thought of the fishmonger's daughter and her thin white scar. There would be no witty words to her, no smile from his parents. There was only the paper and the plane and his own honorable death. He clapped his hands once in the tradition of Shinto, and then he prayed to his emperor, Son of Heaven, for the successful completion of this one final mission.

Near dawn Yoshio sat up and gasped, unable to breathe. He jerked sideways, pushed away the sheets tangled at his shins, and almost fell from the small single mattress. On the edge of the bed, he waited for his heart to slow down, and untangled his clenched fists from themselves. Irene, in the next bed, was just a small shadow, sleeping soundly. Yoshio got up and walked outside.

He stood by the corner of the house, listening to the thud of his own urine. Tomorrow the sun would bake it and Irene would scold him, but he didn't have the strength to make his way to the outhouse, as she insisted. When he was done he knew he didn't want to go back into the dark room. He walked to the apiary.

With each step he remembered the evening before as if it had been a dream: the pilot's voice speaking to them in the language of his parents, saying terrifying things. The plane stretched out on the field like a burn. Taeko slipping from his hands like sand and marching toward the plane; he, frozen and ineffectual once again. The cut on his wife's foot, which she refused to let him tend. Then he and Irene, hunched in front of the radio that the old foreman had previously owned and which Irene turned on every night as one of her small pleasures, flicking past the Hawaiian music and the sports scores until she heard the triumphant hoot of the trumpets and knew she had landed on the big-band station. But last night there had been none of that lifting of her spirits, that slight foot tapping and small smile as she let herself be carried away from this island and its monotony. There had only been her tears and his own shock and horror. They had known that tensions were high with Japan—after all, it was impossible not to hear the news once the radio was on. But their neighbors, radioless, without phones or newspapers, knew nothing, and the Haradas never mentioned it aloud to anyone else on the island. Still, they were not prepared for this. It was true, all of what the pilot had said, worse even, perhaps, because now came the numbers and the devastating descriptions of death and dismemberment. In his mind Yoshio saw the mound of gray, metallic dust that had once been the Pacific Fleet, the black smoke that rose as if from a volcano, the flames. He heard the echoing cries of the men still trapped within the groaning, broken hulls, the twisted remains. He hated the pilot for what he had done, and for landing here, on Niihau.

He reached out a hand, and walked down the rows and rows of wooden hives, laying his fingertips on each one, as if greeting it, or trying to feel some deep internal hum within. Each one was painted white, and they sat side by side under a large tin roof also painted white (everything on the island was painted white, Yoshio had long ago decided). Irene did not like the bees, and though Yoshio told her often that they were gentle creatures, she did not believe him, and stood at the edge of the apiary only, and something in Yoshio did not mind this. He liked her fear, he knew, and the way she watched him point out the layers of each wooden hive—here's the lower deep for the brood chamber, the upper deep for honey, here the shallow super for surplus honey, here, the queen excluder—with a mixture of awe and trepidation. She didn't understand the words, but he knew she saw his excitement, his momentary mastery. It was, he would tell her, a perfectly run society. Perfectly run perhaps, she would reply from the distance, which never got closer over the years, but perfect? In the end someone wanted more than what he had, and he would sting for it too. He would laugh. *No, no, not the honeybee.*

Yoshio heard Irene approach but did not turn. He wanted to hear the breathing of the workers, finally at rest. The mating season was long over, and those drones who had not managed to mate (whereupon they died) had been expelled. Only the queen and her sisters were left. They would be tightly clustered against the cooler night air, some with ragged wings, at the end of their short lives, others bright and robust. It would be months before the hive would be fully roused by spring, when the queen would be fed her royal jelly and stimulated to lay eggs. But Yoshio loved to peer inside during the still, winter days, blinking at the undulating mass, amazed by how the hive was at once one and many parts. Now, so early in the morning, it was too dark to see, but he imagined their minute embraces, their peace.

He knew she would come no farther than that invisible boundary where her fear got the better of her. For a few moments he did not turn, said nothing to indicate that he had heard her. Finally he murmured,

-Soon this will all be over. Mr. Robinson will take charge.

The two were silent for another long while. Yoshio could hear his own breathing and the low crack of his knees when, once or twice, he shifted slightly. Finally, she said,

-Do you think Kauai has been invaded yet?

-No, no, *kachan*. The radio last night said only Pearl Harbor.

-It could be a trick.

Yoshio shrugged.

-Perhaps.

-We didn't tell the Niihauans the truth, she said. We could have told them, right there at Howard's kitchen table.

-They can't handle the truth, said Yoshio.

-You sound like Mr. Robinson.

Yoshio did not respond. He kept his eyes on the beehive, as if waiting for something inside to give him advice.

-We wanted it a little, don't you think? said Irene softly.

-What?

-We thought, for a moment, Let them come! Take over and give us a home where we can buy land, and our children can marry who they want. Where we aren't treated as outsiders, even though we are as much a citizen as anyone else. Imagine, with the Japanese troops here, how people will look at us with respect. Not just sizing us up for our use, like horses.

-Don't talk like that. It's treason.

-Yoshio, listen to me. We have no country. At least our neighbors have Niihau and Robinson. We have no one but ourselves.

-We're American.

Irene said nothing to this, just pursed her lips and clicked her tongue. He knew what she was thinking: We aren't treated as American, that's for certain.

Yoshio turned and walked to Irene, his expression indecipherable in the low light. She reached forward and put two fingers lightly on his bare chest. For a moment he thought she would push him away. He knew that sometimes, when he was like this, soft and vulnerable as a child, she fought the twin urges of love and contempt. He caught the hardness in her eye, but then she put her arms around him and murmured something. Together they walked back to the house. The light had risen quickly and he was due at the boat dock today.

When they got to the door, they both stopped, knowing that once they tiptoed inside they would have to be quiet for Taeko's sake.

-If Kauai's been taken, we're our family's only hope, Irene whispered. My sister, with her babies. Your mother.

-We can't help them, said Yoshio. They might as well be on another planet now.

-We have the pilot. Maybe we can strike a deal. If we help him . . .

-Help a man who destroyed Pearl Harbor? Yoshio's voice rose. I don't understand you!

-And what about us here? Taeko, your little girl? When the Japanese army comes to Niihau, we'll be shot along with our neighbors, unless we've shown that we—that we're Japanese.

-There's no proof that they're coming. Perhaps our troops have held them back, perhaps—

-You heard the radio! It's chaos out there. A sneak attack that got the better of us. Our boats are in ruins, Oahu is on fire. There's nothing to protect us!

-Please, Irene. We'll let Mr. Robinson handle this. Yoshio lowered his voice again, took a deep breath. He'll know more.

-It's time you came through, she hissed.

There was a sudden glint of the whites of his eyes, as if something shone from within momentarily. He ducked his head and with a slap his hands came together. Of course, she would never forgive him. Never. They stood, silent, and each thought about their first child's birth, a long and difficult delivery in the heat of a Hawaiian summer. He imagined the weight of the washcloth on her forehead and the tang of the herbal concoction the midwife pushed under her nose; he once again heard the high-pitched call of her sister through the sugarcane. There was not much time, she had told him breathlessly. Irene was weak and the birth was not going well.

But he could not muster the courage to ask the *luna*—a small man with scarred skin and a tendency to use the whip at his side—if he could leave the fields to be with a wife in labor. When the sun dropped, and all hands were ordered to leave the field, he had run with all his strength. He'd bartered his only sunhat for a ride on a cart. But he was too late to see his child breathe his first and last breath, and too late to repair the wound left on Irene long after the others had healed. He had cried and cursed California, where his courage had seeped out of him like blood, but it would not bring his child back.

Yoshio pulled his hands apart with two distinct jerks, as if they clung together of their own accord and fought him, and worried his fingers against the porch banister. The smell of salt tightened in his nose. Had the sea breeze suddenly come up, or was that his own sweat?

-It's time to dress, Irene said, and turned abruptly into the house.

9

The plane gathered dust quickly. By dawn on the second day—Monday, December 8—its lustrous flanks had dimmed, its hard skin had become minutely pitted. The morning wind blew its shattered glass aside and irreverently spun the amputated front wheel. Insects scurried across the knobs and buttons, now white with the droppings of curious birds. The sun began to rise. Soon it beat down mercilessly and the seats wilted. The stick grip became soft. With enough time, the plane would melt into the red soil and eventually disappear. But if it were like all the other foreigners who came to this island, it would never vanish completely.

Howard had not slept well and his head ached. The plane was on his mind, sprawled in his backyard like a hammerhead. All night he thought he'd heard a phlegmy, snorting exhale from its direction, as if it were alive and breathing. He'd been glad when dawn finally broke. But instead of heading to meet Mr. Harada and the strange pilot as planned, Howard walked toward the plane. At one point he stopped to comb his hair and catch his breath. The large, leaden creature did not stir. Still, *something* had been disturbed on Niihau. Howard could feel it. He was a Christian, so he shoved aside the sneaky feeling that his ancestors' spirits had been upset. It was the devil, he said to himself, which tiptoed across these dry fields.

He stepped quickly now. As he drew alongside the scattered wreckage, a glint of metal half buried in the sand caught his eye. He stopped and squatted, peering closely. He was reminded suddenly of the sugarcane grown on the dunes and pushed horizontal by the wind, so that you had to lean down and swab the sand away to free it. Other islands called this Niihauan sugarcane *Ko eli lima o halalii*, or Sugarcane Dug by Hand, but to the Niihauans it was simply the normal adaptation of life on a weatherbeaten island. Now Howard saw a movement on the bright surface—his own shadow. Slowly he brushed away the soil. The piece was flat and squarish, with sharp metal edges where it had been torn from its original home. Perhaps it fit on the wheel somehow. Or it was part of the propeller, a mechanical wonder he had seen while on Kauai. As a boy he had liked to sit at the dock and watch the flat-bottomed ferry throw up a large spray of water and gasoline as it left its moorings. Onboard, large-hatted white ladies clutched their throats with one hand and waved their handkerchiefs in the other, while their men stood against the rails with self-satisfied smiles on their faces, but Howard and his friends had eyes only for the heaving, spinning propeller. The sound was one that every little boy loved—angry, aggressive, embattled. He would feel its reverberations in his stomach, at the tips of his fingers. Often his friends would cover their ears and laugh but he would not. He watched with his hands at his sides and his mouth pitched half open in awe so that he tasted the bitter edge of gasoline for hours afterward.

The piece was not as heavy as he expected. It was shaped haphazardly, as if hit by a lightning bolt. Perhaps he could cut it into an ornament for his hatband or fashion it into a bauble for his wife, Mabel. He turned the square over. Cut right, it might make a good blade handle.

What else could the plane offer? It had not occurred to him to take anything when he had first seen it. But now he felt a strange yearning. For what? There was nothing he needed. He put the piece into his pocket anyway, and fought the urge to touch the plane itself. The thing was bad luck—*kapu* even. It was from the modern world, and nothing good could come of that.

Ella arrived at the plane later. She stood a few yards off and looked around. No one else was there. The screech of a mynah bird startled her; she took a moment to pray against whatever made her so jumpy. It was already hot and she knew that she should be back at her house. But no, she was here, and it wouldn't hurt to investigate further. She edged closer.

The plane was bigger than she'd imagined, and not at all as commonplace as her husband, Ben, had told her last night, when he would only let her gaze at it from afar, telling her there was nothing much to see. She had imagined something fierce, and it was, but after a moment, when the plane did not growl or spring up to bite her, she made her way to the wing, which she reached out and touched. Reddish dust sparkled on its leading edge; a gash like a mouth grinned at her from one side.

How could something this large and ponderous make its way across the sky? It baffled her. She tried to imagine how her home would look from so far up in the air, near where she supposed heaven was. She knew it would seem small, but she wondered further if it would be insignificant, the way an insect is not just small but insignificant, so much so that you don't feel bad about giving it a good stomp, don't think about it at all really. And she wondered at how hitting the line of the horizon must spin you back the other way, so that you circled endlessly, like an ant yourself, in the blue. What did flying feel like? It would be like a long, flat-out run on a horse, she decided, that moment when the horse switched from a canter to a gallop and only one leg instead of two touched the ground at once, and you knew it, even though you weren't quite sure how you did. She rarely galloped these days; that was for ranch hands and children. But the few times she allowed herself to, she loved the exhilaration, the freedom. And what would happen when the plane hit a cloud? Would you float even more? Ella sighed. For once she marveled at how much she did not know. It had never occurred to her before, but then why should it? She was wise in the ways of the island—how to string shells into a lei, when the *imu* was hot enough for cooking, what it meant when a child cried for so long in that certain way. She knew everything she needed to, and that was all there was, until now. Now something had come from outside, and it brought up odd, discomfiting feelings. She dropped her hand from the hot metal and stepped back.

She wondered what her ancestors would have done with this sudden intruder. Her family had hosted Captain Cook, but they'd learned quickly that not all the gifts that the explorer brought were good for the island. Even the missionaries had made disruptive changes, though of course they had brought God, and for that Ella was grateful.

Ella's ancestors had latched onto Christianity quickly. Only a year before the missionaries' arrival on the Sandwich Islands, as they were then called, the ancient Hawaiian religious doctrines—the Kapu—had been abolished by King Kamehameha. Nothing had been offered to replace them. Suddenly, without warning, the Hawaiians were spiritually adrift, their lives unstructured, their gods meaningless. It was into this void that Christianity landed, by fortuitous luck or, as the missionaries would later claim, divine intent, in the unlikely form of a boatload of wan, seasick, petrified New England Christians seeking to spread their Word.

Within the year, Christianity drummed and thrummed on all of the Sandwich Islands. Those first emissaries of the 1820s did not initially make their home on outlying Niihau. But every now and then they braved the difficult crossing to ensure that God's word was still firmly planted in the red, dusty soil. The changes everywhere were swift, like a sudden rainstorm on thirsty, waiting soil. Willing rivulets were carved, then streams, then rushing rivers. The Puritan missionaries waved and shouted, whispered and moaned, rolled their eyes to the heavens. They decreed new lifestyles for the savage Hawaiians, beginning with the very structures they lived in. Homes were to be not just shelter, but hearths of religious and social purity, a place of gathering for the family. The well-insulated grass huts with cool dirt floors were replaced by small wooden structures. Women were expected to stay at home and manage the children instead of wandering to other villages for days at a time, showing a distasteful independence. *Malos*, men's loincloths, were replaced by pants and white shirts; the women were quickly covered by long, heavy *mu'umu'us* or fitted *holokus*. There was to be no more sexual openness. Surfing (naked bodies on wood and steep waves) and sliding (naked buttocks placed on large tropical leaves down steep hillsides) were frowned upon. The sacred Makahiki festival, a weeks-long sporting celebration, was abolished. But even though Hawaiians, and especially Niihauans, converted at a fast rate, the missionaries were distraught over their insufficient piety. Secretly, they fretted that the islanders mimicked Christian rites but remained heathen in spirit.

What the good Christians must have reluctantly realized was that what appealed most to the Hawaiians was not the ideals of their religion, but its ritual nature, and so its proximity to the old Kapu worship. Bells, hymns, and parables of the fantastic—a man who rose from the dead, fishes multiplied magically to feed thousands—these were the things that Hawaiians could relate to. The rest of it—long sermons, no dancing during worship, restrictive clothing in hot weather, a ban on sports, severe punishments and shame for certain sexual liaisons, suppression of the *kahuna* healers—was obeyed but not embraced.

Soon Hawaiians were dying of foreign diseases. Ella's own grandmother had taken only a few days to expire from a strange and devilish sickness. She had raved incoherently at the end, finally drowning in the fluid that bubbled from her insides. So died much of the Hawaiian culture, quickly, painfully, an asphyxiation without recourse. With each death from smallpox, measles, or influenza, the Old Ways slipped away. Foreigners took root and spread their habits, their language. It was hardly more than a century later now, and much of the true Hawaii was lost. Only on Niihau, it was agreed among the people who admired the Robinsons, were Hawaiians protected.

Ella turned away suddenly, and left quickly.

Back in her Puuwai house, Ella sat at her kitchen table and stared at her hands. The strange machine scared her. A foreigner was on the island, and though he had not been aggressive and Mr. Kaleohano was handling the particulars of his sudden arrival, things were not right. Mr. Robinson would arrive today, but it would not hurt to pray. She brought her palms together and closed her eyes, even as the plane leaped up in her imagination and took wing into the morning sky.

10

The cart trundled along the rough dirt trail. Howard flicked the reins lightly but repeatedly against the horse's neck. Now and then Yoshio glanced over his shoulder to see that the pilot had not been bounced out by an especially large rut and sometimes Howard looked back too, but otherwise there was little movement beyond what each man needed to keep his balance in the violent hiccupping of the cart.

It would take a few hours to reach the winter boat dock of Kii, fifteen miles away on the other, eastern side of the island. The Nonopapa dock was much closer, on the western side, but suitable only during the calmer summer months, when the full force of the Pacific dwindled to friendly slaps on the shore. Yoshio had always liked the ride to Kii, but today he could not enjoy the sparse landscape, the increasing rocks and scrub as they moved farther from Puuwai and the ranch house, where the acreage had been partially tamed into grazing ground and orchards, and now gave way to Niihau's true, raw self. Yoshio loved that the island adapted to its owners by offering up part of its soil for their use, but never relinquished its wilder side. But today the desolation reminded him of death; the quiet, of the impending storm. The sky was clear and blue, but at any moment it might darken with hundreds more

Japanese planes, all ready to land on Niihau. The tension was unbearable. He wished the miles between them and the boat dock where Robinson would arrive would crease under their wheels, throwing them there in an instant, and this was new to him because though he respected Mr. Robinson, he never enjoyed his visits the way the Niihauans did. Instead, they made him nervous and brought him back, reflexively, to his other interactions with *haoles* over the years. Mr. Robinson may have been a different kind of white man, but he was still a white man.

-This visitor's not our doing, Howard said suddenly, over the rumble of the cart. *Malahini* don't know the rules, that's not our problem.

-Yes, Yoshio said. His voice was squashed by the wrenching wheels and the loud snorts of the horse. He repeated himself louder. Yes. Mr. Robinson handles this. Not to worry.

-He left a huge mess of metal and wheel parts in a field. He's not disinfected. He certainly wasn't invited. Howard flipped one hand behind him in disgust. Mr. Robinson can't be angry with us for that. Not our fault. What do you think, Mr. Harada? The boy drops in like a flying fish, what can we do?

-These things happen, agreed Yoshio.

Of course, this was patently untrue. These things, these sudden visitors, did not just happen. There had been, Yoshio had heard, a redheaded man who had washed ashore after a shipwreck, but that was more than a century ago. Captain Cook, the famous white man pictured as tall and handsome and kind in all the schoolbooks, came too, but that was also long before the Robinsons had the island. Except for the outbreak of measles more than a decade ago, little since the Robinsons' arrival had been unplanned.

-It'll be fine, said Howard.

-Of course, said Yoshio.

But he did not believe this. All morning his imagination had been crowded with terrible visions: Robinson stepping off the boat with a contingent of Japanese military men prodding bayonets into his back, Robinson handcuffed and slouched beside a fierce Japanese commander barking orders to execute them all, Robinson floating faceup in the water, his wide blue eyes staring all-knowingly at Yoshio. Robinson, forgiving nothing. Not that Yoshio had done anything. But Irene was right, he'd thought about it. And he had deliberately withheld information, though it was information that surely was of little use to his neighbors. He repeated to himself that he had made no direct move to help the pilot and that the Niihauans had always been protected from the outside world, but his hands maintained a vise grip on the muscles above his knee bones.

For a while they traveled in silence, both men listening to the creak of the axles over the rutted ground, the surf and snort of the horse's breath. The pilot made no sound behind them, and when each glanced to see whether he'd fallen out or fled they saw him clutching the sideboard and staring out to sea.

Homesick, Yoshio heard Howard mutter. But he knew better. Submarine, he thought.

The dirt path wound quickly above steep cliffs and Yoshio could see the corner of a beach below. He had heard that there were caves all along the stone precipices, but the Niihauans had never shown him where. There were springs around the island too, but these were closely guarded secrets as well, from the days when water was not kept in thousand-gallon tanks or piped from cistern to cistern. Even Mr. Robinson had no idea where this precious resource bubbled from the ground into small, muddy pools, a fact that Yoshio liked. He had even hoped, upon hearing this, that one day the Niihauans would show him where they were. Now he knew that this was vain and ill-deserved; he was keeping secrets from his neighbors just as they kept secrets from him.

-Harada-san, said a voice loudly by his ear. Something touched him on the shoulder. He jumped; the pilot raised his hands to show he meant no harm.

-Tell me, he said, what is this emperor we're going to meet like?

-Mr. Robinson? He's not the emperor. He owns this island.

-Does he come with many men?

-Not usually. But don't try anything funny out here. There's no water, you'll die within hours.

-I'm not afraid to die, Harada-san. The pilot smiled calmly. But I do have a job to do, which is to destroy my plane and my papers. So I'm not going anywhere. The papers are with this crooked-toothed man here and I need to get them back, so I thought it would be best to do what he says until I understand where he put them. Also I get a chance to talk to you.

-We have nothing to talk about. Yoshio abruptly turned his back.

-But we do. The pilot tapped him on the shoulder again.

-No. Yoshio refused to look around.

He fixed his eyes on the undulating hills scraped with rock outcrops, brown against the heavily blue sky. The pilot's openness startled him, his willing divulgence of his plans made Yoshio uneasy. Did he think that Yoshio was an ally? Yoshio felt angry then, and almost turned to Howard. *He wants to destroy his plane and papers and then all of us,* he tried to shout. But he didn't. Of course he didn't. He wasn't sure of what to do, as usual. He only pressed his hands together and stayed quiet.

Howard spoke incessantly of horses, of honey production, of surfing, of the impending drought. Yoshio tried to be interested.

Howard was a talker, and what he said came out impossibly exaggerated, but he was in other ways a sincere man. He had taught Yoshio to ride an especially high-spirited Arabian. He'd shown him how to herd sheep and cattle, keeping the ornery ones in line and the laggards from getting lost. And though he regaled him with fanciful riding tales that inevitably had himself at the center, his teaching was sound. Most times Yoshio liked to hear Howard's stories of bravado and danger. The man had a grand sense of showmanship that Yoshio enjoyed because it was so unlike the way his parents spoke. Their stories had always been carefully modulated and short; Howard's were overlong and inevitably ended dramatically, with the light of God helping him make the right decision and Jesus holding his hand while he did whatever that decision demanded. But now Yoshio couldn't listen; he wanted only to arrive quickly at the Kii boat landing and hand the pilot over to Robinson's care.

But the boat was not there. Howard stopped the wagon and stretched his arms for effect. When the three got off, each tried to cover his disappointment; Yoshio knelt and began to dig absently in the dirt, Nishikaichi stood with his feet planted wide and continued to stare out at the ocean, Howard walked out onto the dock as if testing its seaworthiness. Finally, when each had turned his head surreptitiously toward Kauai a few more times, Howard pointed out it was early enough yet and that they would wait in the old storehouse that faced the beach.

They left the door open so that they could sit and watch, but the pilot indicated he needed to stretch his legs and walked slowly around the dilapidated interior. Yoshio watched him assess the place with a keen eye. There were empty crates piled on one side, and a bench that looked as if it might fall over if someone sat on it. Light fell through the slats like clutching fingers, and the place was stuffy with heat and dust. Above the entrance and to the left was a crudely made cross of heavy wood. It was balanced on one of the joists. Of all the things in the warehouse, this was the most cared for. It looked less dusty, its edges were smooth, and it was perfectly perpendicular to the floor, as if it had been fussed over recently. Yoshio wondered briefly if it would serve as a viable club in the pilot's hands, knocking both Howard and him down with one brutal and ironic blow. But the pilot sat down without so much as a glance at it, and seemed to nod off. Yoshio cleared his throat.

-Don't you want to take that thing off? It'll be more comfortable. He waved his hand at the pilot's flight suit. Despite the heat, it was still buttoned to the chin, and the sleeves had not once been pushed to the elbow. Only the flight hat had been removed in a small concession to the sun, thrown in the corner of the cart and left there.

Nishikaichi opened his eyes and shook his head; Yoshio shrugged. He opened his mouth to say something else, but decided against it. He leaned against the wall on the far side and from the corner of his eye watched Howard, who hummed a Christian song and ran a small comb through his hair in short, hard strokes, as if he was digging an especially deep hole in difficult soil. The comb was metal, so it flashed periodically in the sunlight that fell through the walls and made small circles of light dance on beams above him; behind Howard's back the villagers often made fun of this small vanity. It was an old electric comb, with its small battery no longer around, and it had been given to him by a shopkeeper on Kauai because he couldn't sell it like that and not, as Howard thought, as a sign of his high esteem.

Presently all three men sat against the far wall, spaced apart from each other, but each with a good view through the lopsided doorway of the dock and the ocean beyond. The warehouse remained mercifully dark at the edges, though the light bled in with the strength of a powerful searchlight, so that the dust hung like millions of orbiting stars. It seemed as if hours passed, and that perhaps they slept. Without any of the usual chores to mark the day, time slowed, as if melting in the heat.

Howard got up and stretched noisily. Yoshio opened his own eyes rapidly and saw that Nishikaichi stared through the open doorway, his face rigid. Yoshio followed his gaze to the ocean, where a shape curved above the surface like the dark side of a quarter moon, and vanished. It rose again, black and shiny and metallic. Then it was under once more.

Dolphins, Yoshio thought. He had no idea what the word would be in Japanese, but there would be no need; he saw disappointment quickly stretch the pilot's features and that he touched something white near his collar, under the flight suit. Neither man knew that in fact the sub captain would never come; he had instead been redirected from his mission to search for downed airmen and told to head to the mouth of Pearl Harbor.

Howard sat down again and reached into his pocket, unaware of the dolphins or the pilot's momentary hope or its ultimate futility. He laid a small square of paper on the dirt floor. He glanced once at Yoshio, but the man's eyes were closed and his mind far away. Still, Howard felt sheepish. While his neighbors tolerated his small indiscretion, attributing it to the fact that he had been polluted by growing up in the outside world, they did not wholly approve. The cowboys looked away pointedly, as if a mere glance would tempt them, and the women openly frowned, but still he could not resist the pull, and anyway Yoshio was a kind man, and a forgiving one, not to mention that he too had grown up off-island and must have a sense of just how weak a man could be, how strong corrupting influences. Anyway, Mabel wasn't around, and he should take his chances while he could.

Howard drew tobacco quietly from a small leather pouch.

He looked again at Yoshio, who had not made a sign he had heard the rustle of the shirt or the just perceptible crackle of the dried plant between fingertips. He sprinkled the tobacco into a neat line on the paper and with prim concentration began to knead it between his thumb and forefinger. For a long time he did this, rolling it back and forth, back and forth. Finally he licked the paper carefully, sealed it, and seeing the pilot staring at it, grinned (he had lost a lot of his embarrassment by now), and proffered it in an outstretched hand. Nishikaichi shook his head. Howard frowned slightly and motioned again with the cigarette, jabbing it in his direction.

-What's he keep fiddling with in there, Mr. Harada? That a pack of cigarettes he's hiding?

-No, said Yoshio. It's, I think, his shirt.

-It's cigarettes. Tell him to show to me. I've never seen Japanese cigarettes.

Yoshio waved him off.

-It's nothing.

-Okay, said Howard, rising from his place by the wall. I'll just—

Yoshio scrambled to his feet.

-You'll just scare him, he said. I'll go ask.

Yoshio paused until Howard had sat back down, and then walked slowly to the pilot. He thought about squatting next to him but decided to continue to stand. He looked down at the pilot.

-What do you have there, Nishikaichi-san?

-Nothing.

-Don't make Howard suspicious. Show me.

Nishikaichi pushed opened the collar a little more, so that Yoshio could see a pattern of small red dots.

-We're not going to steal it, said Yoshio. Howard just wants to know what it is.

-It's a good-luck charm. A thousand knots sewn by a thousand people. To bless us in our mission.

-A thousand? said Yoshio. Nishikaichi nodded.

Yoshio leaned in and stared at the cloth that the pilot wore hanging from his shoulders. He glanced at Nishikaichi's face, then back down at the red-dotted sash. He wanted to touch it but couldn't bring himself to ask.

-Not exactly a thousand, he said instead. Stitches, I mean. Probably less.

-Of course it is, snorted Nishikaichi. One thousand exactly. I'd let you count it but you've insulted our samurai tradition.

-I didn't mean— He sighed. I didn't mean it like that. It's just that people lie about these things.

-In this country perhaps, but not in Japan.

-Okay, okay, not in Japan. I get it. So tell me, samurai—and here he lowered his voice—when are your people going to land here?

He said "your people" deliberately, to separate himself, to show the young pilot that he was no friend of his, that he did not forget that he had bombed his country, his Pearl Harbor.

Nishikaichi blinked. He took in Yoshio's intent face, his pale, uncertain frown.

-Land? he said. The submarine?

-Take over. The whole troop, not just the sub. On Kauai, here. When do you expect them?

Nishikaichi paused. He was only a pilot, and not privy to the grand will of his emperor, or even of his unit commanders. He did as he was told, and, like the rest of his squadron, never fully understood why he was attacking what, then, just that it was important that he do so. This operation against Pearl Harbor had been especially secretive. But he was fairly sure—through gossip among the ranks, and from things his immediate superior had said—that there were no plans to take over the Hawaiian Islands. Japanese interest was in one thing only these days: fuel. The United States had led international sanctions against Japan for the past few years, and now fuel, a precious resource for a nation with ambition, was scarce. Military operations in China and elsewhere were threatened, and living conditions in his homeland had deteriorated rapidly. Of course, the people were happy to practice austerity for the emperor. Still, there were fuel reserves scattered about the Orient, which the Japanese nation deserved.

The Son of Heaven had rightly decided to decimate the Pacific Fleet, based in Pearl Harbor, knowing that once these battleships and fighter planes were out of the way, the eastern oil ports would be easily taken. Hong Kong, Thailand, the Philippines, these were the targets Nishikaichi had heard about. But clearly this man Yoshio understood none of that. He'd heard of Pearl Harbor's devastation and destruction and logically thought that this island was next.

There was a moment's hesitation as the pilot stared at the Japanese man in front of him. Then he slowly shook his head and lowered his eyes and took a deep breath.

Then he lied.

-They should arrive any day, he said. To make this island Japanese. If you are to fare well in that, you must help me in my mission.

Yoshio inhaled sharply and felt his skin prickle. *Any day?* He opened his mouth to speak, but Howard interrupted from the far corner.

-What's he got there? He squinted and leaned forward, as if to get a better view in the dim light.

Yoshio straightened. His mind was racing ahead to put together what the pilot had said. Any day, soldiers were arriving. He fought the urge to run out of the warehouse and crane his neck at the sky, listening for the drone of bombers and the high-pitched victory cry his old neighbor on Kauai used to imitate when he was drunk and nostalgic for his days in Japan.

-What's he got there? repeated Howard, louder now, breaking Yoshio's reverie.

-He's got, it's a . . .

Yoshio stopped, realizing that he couldn't tell Howard without explaining what "mission" the pilot had been on, why he needed a good-luck charm in the first place.

-Nothing, he finally said. Just part of his shirt.

Howard rearranged his cigarette so that it hung precariously (and, Howard himself thought, charmingly) from the corner of his mouth, a skill he had secretly perfected after he had seen a movie, on his only trip to Oahu, many years ago, in which the hero spoke every line with a cigarette dangling from his lips.

-Well, tell him to stop itching and scratching, he said. I'll wager my hat, dirty as it is, that Mr. Robinson'll be here soon enough.

11

The white emperor, the pink barbarian, the Old Lord, this *Ka Haku Makua*—by whatever name he was called—still, he did not appear. The men sat in their hunched positions, each against his own warehouse wall. Nishikaichi, himself hunched now, his military bearing softening under the heat, wondered if this was a good or a bad thing. After the adrenaline of the initial crash, alertness had given way to bafflement at how to proceed. He had never made his own decisions before, he realized. Always, he had been guided: by his parents, his military superiors, the *Senjinkun*. He was given orders and he followed them with the exactness of a tailor, as if the orders were measurements and he the scissors with which to cut a fine coat; for this he was considered a good Japanese man and a gifted pilot. But now he was on his own. What would he do if the pink barbarian, this White Emperor Robinson-san, arrived and knew all about Pearl Harbor? If he was combative and cruel, unlike these islanders? Nishikaichi accepted, even welcomed, death, but not the capture of his plane and papers. There was little time now: he must convince the Japanese man to destroy the plane and papers with or even without him. He would need the nervous man's help, no matter what, that one thing was clear.

The pilot watched his hosts from half-closed lids. For a while he focused on the native man, wondering where he might have hidden the papers, how to effect their return without arousing more ire or suspicion. It seemed useless to keep insisting directly, because the man acted as he thought his emperor would want him to, and a strange intruder would not change that. Nishikaichi understood, even admired this. He also admired the way the man smiled so heartily, despite his awful teeth, and moved with compressed excitement, as if the world was constantly new and interesting to him. True, he spoke too much, thought Nishikaichi, but the melody of his strange language was beautiful, and brought to mind birds soaring on the flanks of Mount Fuji, or sometimes, when the man was really excited, the pillowy building of a thunder cloud. Nishikaichi didn't need to know the words. The curve and bend of them, the way they swung in the air, reminded him of haiku. It was, he thought, close to the sound of his love for the fishmonger's daughter, if he dared to make that sound out loud: lyrical, joyous, never ending.

Finally Nishikaichi flickered his eyes to the Japanese man. Harada-san was larger than anyone he knew back home, as if American excesses puffed and elongated a normal Asian body. The man had broad shoulders and long fingers which, Nishikaichi noticed, held his legs as if he worried they would collapse into a pile of bones and tendons otherwise. At first glance he had the lifted chin and direct gaze of a military man, but his habit of squeezing his hands together nervously betrayed the fact that he was not a soldier. Nishikaichi puzzled over what his next move would be with Harada-san. He knew that he couldn't get the papers back without some assistance. Worse, without gasoline on the island, it would be difficult to destroy his plane. He needed him, and it was best if he could convince Harada-san that this need was reciprocal. He had clearly become unnerved when Nishikaichi had convincingly agreed that the Japanese military were coming, and this, thought Nishikaichi, was good. Disorienting a man was the first step toward his pliability, something Nishikaichi knew from the old boastings of a drunken military officer who, with enough rice wine, would tell lengthy and gruesome anecdotes of interrogations. Nishikaichi had never liked these stories and dismissed the most horrific of them as tall tales, impossible, against the tenets of Bushido, not the doings of the emperor's people. Still, he'd gleaned that a man's greatest vulnerability was his mind, not his body. Hadn't he been overwhelmed by it himself as he tried to sacrifice his plane and himself to the ocean? He winced again at the memory. If he had acted like a true son of Japan, he would not be here, in a hot, dark warehouse, with a slice of the brilliant day bleeding in through a tilted wooden door, and his eyes fixed on that opening as if it were a last meal, or the doorway through which the Son of Heaven himself would step. He would instead be dead, and the letter announcing this sacrifice would soon be opened slowly by his parents, and read with commingled joy and sadness.

-Harada-san, he called out, his voice raspy.

Yoshio did not move.

-Harada-san, he said more loudly.

The man's head jerked up as if he had been stung by a bee. Howard looked over with interest.

-Harada-san, my bladder is bursting.

Yoshio blinked as if not understanding.

-I have to pee, repeated the pilot.

Still, Yoshio did not react.

-Should I go out on my own?

-No, no, said Yoshio hurriedly. He put up his hand and began to speak to Howard.

-You come, interrupted the pilot. We need to talk. About the soldiers.

Howard was beginning to rise, brushing off his denim pants, pulling his sweated shirt from his chest.

-I know you're acting calm on the outside for the sake of your neighbor here, insisted the pilot. But inside you're shaking because you know the terribleness of what I'm saying. Our soldiers are angry and determined. It's time to talk, really.

Howard was stretching his arms.

-I can make sure that the commander knows—

Yoshio scrambled to his own feet suddenly.

-Be quiet, he said to the pilot sharply. Then he addressed Howard, who shrugged and sat back down against the wall.

-Well, make sure he has a good, long piss. And try to get him to take off that gosh-darn flight suit, Mr. Harada. I don't want a dead guest when the Old Lord arrives.

Yoshio flinched at the word "dead" and then forced himself to smile.

-A good piss it'll be, Mr. Kaleohano, he said.

They walked to the scrub behind the beach and stood in silence. The pilot unzipped the angulated fly of his flight suit and Yoshio took a few steps back. The pilot urinated without a word, letting Yoshio's tension build, in no hurry to speak first. Feeling the man's anxious presence just a few feet away, he casually cased his surroundings in full, looking one way and the other, taking in the beach in its entirety. When he was done he zipped and turned, surveying the inland flats. Scrubby trees he did not recognize fizzed from hard, red soil. The land rose and fell gently, like a line of easy waves. It was then that the pilot realized he no longer thought of the island as desolate and ugly. The sparse simplicity moved him, the hues of brown against the blue sky lifted his heart. It was, in a distinctly Japanese way, beautiful.

He looked at Yoshio. He bowed slightly.

-Harada-san, you are the elder of us. You know the ways of the world with far more intelligence than I. But I know the ways of the military. Things will go better if you help. There's a sub looking for me and angry Japanese warriors on the way. I'll make sure no harm comes to any of you on this island; I can *talk* to the commanders who land. Should I even tell you what China looked like after we were through with her? No, I won't, it was a terrible thing.

-If you'll just get in it and row away quietly, Yoshio responded roughly, I'll see what I can do about a boat. But I can't help you with your papers and your plane.

Nishikaichi stared at him.

-Those must be destroyed, he said. You understand. I am a warrior for the emperor and I have a duty. It is my imperial *on*. Don't you understand *on*?

-Then we are at an impasse. Yoshio turned away.

The pilot sighed and shook his head.

-Harada-san, he said. You're more Japanese than you admit. Your loyalty to your neighbors, your concern for your family. You understand *on* perfectly. Perhaps you'll think about this for a while and we'll talk later. For now, thank you for accompanying me.

He bowed again, nodded solemnly, and without another word began to walk back to the warehouse.

-And what of your submarine, Nishikaichi-san? Yoshio called out.

Nishikaichi stopped.

-She'll come.

-Then you won't need me.

-But then it will be too late for the island. If you don't help me now . . .

The pilot let the sentence trail off.

Yoshio shook his head, and followed the pilot.

12

Aylmer Robinson squinted down the beach. He could see men stumbling in the heavy sand, and every now and then a curse floated toward him. He thought he would immediately know which men were his, but from where he sat, on his horse, with one hand over his eyes to shield them from the low-hanging sun, there was no telling who came from the next plantation, who was the local storekeeper, who the bank clerk—even the pastor was said to be there. From Robinson's vantage point, the men—and even some women—had fused into one strange land creature pinwheeling across the sand. Grunting and snuffling and snorting, it was an amalgam of pale, pudgy shoulders and brown, muscled ones, bare feet and loafers and boots all working to string a long barbed-wire fence along the beach before the Japanese military emerged like walking fish from the sea. For a moment Robinson thought he should strip off his own shirt and trudge toward the creature; without a doubt this was what his father would have done. The old man would have eschewed the paperwork, the tête-à-têtes with the local muckety-mucks, and instead picked up a shovel and joined the rabble out there in the hot sun. How many times did he tell Aylmer about the long days building houses and barns on Niihau, how with enough hammer strokes a man could transform not just the land but himself—didn't the Bible itself say so? (Aylmer had looked, but couldn't find it.) But Aylmer wasn't the showy man his father had been, knew that the ruckus caused by the old man peeling off his shirt to show his skinny white chest and stringy forearms was what the man would've been partially after, the need always to prove himself above and beyond what everyone thought he could do, even at the end when he had the houseboy read the Bible nonstop while he knelt and prayed, coughing up blood the whole time.

Aylmer reminded himself that he was needed in town, and wheeled his horse onto the dirt road. At a canter he passed a group of men who clutched pellet guns and pitchforks, heading to the bridges, and when he got to the one and only streetlight on the island, he saw a few children with stones in their hands. Their faces were set in what they took to be serious expressions, mouths turned down like the adults, brows hunched together. They looked him up and down before becoming distracted by a lizard flushed out by the dust and noise and which had made the fatal mistake of dodging onto the road. Even women carried shovels or knives, ready to slit a yellow throat if necessary. It occurred to Robinson suddenly that it was Monday, December 8, and he was due on Niihau today.

At least the Niihauans won't hear what's going on, Robinson thought. The news was devastating, almost unimaginable. More than two thousand Americans had died in an inferno of fire and explosions. Many were still trapped in overturned ships, knocking frantically in hopes of rescue. Hundreds of aircraft strafed. Hangars bombed. Buildings collapsed. Yesterday KGMB kept intoning, *This is the real McCoy. The Japanese have attacked Pearl Harbor. This is the real McCoy,* until its signal was shut down for fear that a new wave of Japanese fliers would navigate by it. Only KTOH kept broadcasting intermittently throughout the night, mistakenly overlooked by the government, until just hours ago it too finally went silent. What he would give to be on Niihau right now, Robinson thought, to ride the plateau past the merino sheep and the star-apple trees, far from the guns and radios, the shock and the fear, shielded from the world and its discontents.

At the Piggly Wiggly, Robinson dismounted and entered. The place was jammed with people desperate to pick up emergency supplies and trade the latest rumors. They scooped up batteries and canned food and talked under their breath, as if they didn't know who might be listening: *They'll come by sea, they'll poison the water supply, they'll knock out the electricity towers*. None of it was confirmed, but people drank from the streams anyway and took up posts along the high-tide mark, lying flat on the sand, using anything as a weapon. Here at the Piggly Wiggly items like garden rakes, which wouldn't sell for half price last week, were reimagined as swords and now flew off the shelves into defiant hands.

-Any news? Robinson yelled to the storekeeper, who was himself yelling something at his young son over the bedlam. The Japs getting to Kauai?

-They've been here for years, that's the problem, the man cried. He waved a hand at the emptying shelves. Grab what you can, Mr. Robinson. We'll be out of everything by nightfall.

But Robinson hadn't come for food or batteries, just reliable information, which he now realized was in short supply too. He pushed his way outside and remounted his horse. He'd head to the hospital and see if his brother Lester's wife was there. He was sure she was; she had her hands full with two young sons, but everyone was pitching in, in whatever way they could. He felt partially responsible for her, because Lester himself was on the mainland, arranging sales of the Makeweli Ranch sugar yield. He would know what had happened to the islands, and be sick with worry.

Of Kauai's 35,000 citizens, half were of Japanese descent. As Robinson rode up to the hospital, all of them seemed to be there, in a silent line that stretched from the front door and around the corner to the sugar field beyond. He tipped his hat mechanically but they glanced away without speaking. He wasn't sure what he thought of the local Japanese now, and they weren't sure either. He'd always admired the nisei's discipline and reserve. That's why he'd hired young Mr. Matsuda to oversee the feed supplies here at Makeweli and why he'd asked the Haradas to take care of his house on Niihau, and eventually run the small store out of one of the sheds. His only complaint had been that the nisei weren't Christian. This would come in time, he'd thought. Heathens everywhere were flocking to the Lord, and Kauai would be no different. But after Pearl Harbor his heart was heavy, his fist clenched in anger. He'd prayed over and over to rid himself of this devilish fury, but still, last night he'd woken in a sweat, his heart pounding, his tongue dry, his throat tight. And he'd heard about *things* in the past twenty-four hours—Japanese men dragged from their homes, Japanese women—well, he wasn't sure what had happened. The island was tense, that's all he knew. Jaws were set and eyes were clamped on the horizon.

Robinson stopped his horse next to a man he recognized who worked with his turkeys.

-Mr. Komichi, he said. What's going on here?

-Blood, Mr. Robinson, the man said. He lifted his arm briefly and twisted at his sleeve. To give to our soldiers.

For a moment Robinson wondered if a big cache of enemy Japanese had been caught and were for some reason being resuscitated by the blood of their expat countrymen and -women. Then he realized that Mr. Komichi was talking about *our* soldiers, as in American ones, and it took Robinson a minute to process this.

Robinson finally nodded. He knew that the nisei had been

abruptly banned from much of daily life, or at least that which included gun carrying and war planning, which was most of what was going on. But yesterday he'd seen them in small, quiet groups of their own, towing abandoned cars to block the airstrips from Japanese planes, clearing *kiawe* for American military vehicles. Now here, giving blood.

Robinson rested his hands on the pommel of the saddle and scanned the line, finally lighting on three white women standing just apart from the rest. Their faces were shadowed by hats perched like mongooses on their heads, their stiff postures radiated discontent. They had come to give blood, yes, but had not wanted to stand so close to the nisei, who had always been disdained and were now downright dangerous. He tried to acknowledge the women with a touch of his hat, but they were turned in profile toward each other, clutching, as if to keep their balance on a swaying ship. One woman held her lips together so tightly they overlapped, as if she was telling the world that even she herself did not believe the ends she would go to for duty.

Just then Shanagan galloped up with a gun on his shoulder.

-I'm hearing we'll be switching the crops away from sugar and back to foodstuff for the troops.

-If necessary, Robinson said. News?

-The usual blarney. Subs offshore, Japs under every tree, waiting to slit your throat.

He brought a big hand to his face and wiped the sweat from his brow. For a moment the two men were silent, busy fiddling with their reins, their hats. Shanagan patted his shirt pocket and looked at the sky. Finally he said,

-I was thinking, sir, about the band I was hearing the night before this all happened. The radio had the navy boys playing against each other, boat against boat. You know, the *California* against the *Arizona* against the *Pennsylvania* and all that. The whole lot of us got up and danced, twisting the knobs on that radio as high as they'd go. Well, the *Pennsylvania* won, and that was all right, but the *Arizona* should've taken it, I tell you.

He shifted in his saddle. Robinson could hear the clickety-click of his throat swallowing.

-See, they're all dead, sir. Every one of those jitterbug-playing boys. Gone. They're saying the *Arizona* took the worst of it, no one had a chance. I can't believe it. Mind-doogling, it is. He spat on the ground, and pressed a hand to his eyes. And this. He jerked his chin at the crowd. Don't think it's a good idea, this. Nisei probably poisoned their own blood on orders of their emperor. Sly devils, these Japs. Let 'em live here and now it's coming around to bite us in the arse, 'scuse my French.

He didn't lower his voice when he said this, but kept staring down the line at the men and women who stood without a word, their heads turned pointedly away or looking at the ground. He shifted his gun from one hand to the other and spat again.

-Well, I'll be taking a turn guarding the electricity plant, Mr. Robinson, unless you'll be needing me for something else. Word's out that there's saboteurs about, see—and here he lowered his voice and flicked his eyes meaningfully to the line of people and back. But every good man's got a gun, so they won't be taking Kauai without a brawl.

-That's fine, Mr. Shanagan, said Robinson. No boats allowed on the water anyway, so I won't be going to Niihau right now. When I do, you come back and take care of Makeweli Ranch. Until then, go where you're needed, and Godspeed.

Robinson nicked the brim of his hat with his forefingers and turned his horse away. He was tired and suddenly uneasy about missing his monthly visit to Niihau. It'll be fine, he thought. Just fine. That island's protected by God, if any are.

13

In the late afternoon, they left Kii. Even Howard had lost his good humor. He cursed quietly at the horse and combed his hair only once. The sun condensed from blinding yellow to a tight orange ball and began to sink below the horizon. The pilot was quiet. Yoshio ignored them both and stared silently at the water, thinking of the submarine. What would the Hawaiian sharks think when they saw that dark, silent shadow? Legend said that the large *mano* protected the island in an ancient pact bartered by the Niihauans' ancestors. And it was true, no shark attacks had ever been recorded on Niihau, though men swam through infested waters often. Could the *mano* spirits protect them against this deadly man-made machine? Yoshio did not think so.

The radio was about the size of a small pig. It was wood paneled, with a dial on the right side that spun a thick metal shaft in a circle to catch the radio stations. The only identifying mark was the word "Supreme" etched in a copper plate on one corner, which Irene supposed was the silly, boastful name of a mainland radio company.

She always marveled at the good reception, despite the distance from the other islands. She imagined the radio waves slowing in the heat, perhaps dragging a long trail of red dust as they dropped down the chimney and squeezed through the cracks in the walls, finally alighting on her machine and wiggling inside. It was a miracle really, and a miracle too that Robinson had not removed what Howard Kaleohano had once called, in English, "a modern conniption," after the white foreman had died. Mr. Robinson had not been happy that the old man had wanted a radio, but had relented, only after making him promise that the natives would not come over to the house and listen to the frivolity that burst from its wooden ribs. The old foreman had agreed, but sometimes the cowboys heard its melodies anyway, drifting to the *wiliwili* in the back field when they were tending the Arabians, or carried by the afternoon wind toward Puuwai. At first the radio had been a thing of mild interest, and the few who caught a glimpse of it told tales of mysterious gurgling and hissing inside a wooden crate. But no one understood the language that came out of it, and the music itself was strange and tinny—not nearly as nice as a live Niihauan voice and a ukulele—and it was easy to forget about because soon enough Mr. Robinson scolded the foreman and he was more careful to keep the music down. But the Haradas were glad for the "conniption," and Irene was vigilant about putting it away when Robinson came around, to make sure she never lost her only connection to the world beyond Niihau.

Irene spent most of the day heaving the radio from place to place in the house, trying to pick up some news from outside. But there was only an insectlike hum; broadcasting had stopped completely except for an occasional voice that came on, clearing its throat in strangled bursts and saying in a high, nervous tone, *Be calm, be calm*. In the background Irene could hear the scraping of furniture in what she imagined was a fortress being quickly erected. The radio station that was the only link the world had to itself was barricading itself in, and that could not be good.

Behind the quick, repeated two-word pronouncement *(Be calm, be calm)* she caught the indecipherable shuffle of other voices, high and low, falling out as they moved too far from the microphone, wafting back in, disappearing again. Then, after only a few moments, the radio would return to its hiss and static. She swung the dial first with the careful precision of a sniper taking aim, then with abandon, trying to pluck the airwaves from the sky. She did not know that all over the Hawaiian Islands, radio broadcasts had dropped out hours ago. The broadcasters dared to come on only infrequently, for just a few seconds, lest enemy Zeros navigate by their signal. Irene was not the only one fiddling anxiously with the buttons, waiting in vain for news of what was happening in the outside world. Everyone in the Hawaiian Islands was. But she was the one most isolated. She imagined people on Kauai and Maui and Oahu walking to their neighbors, then clustering on porches or slouching around kitchen tables. There they would trade rumor and fact, not knowing which was which, but still comforted by each other and news, any news. Not Irene. The almost complete silence from the world outside was like being lost on a mountain and peering into a dark night for a light that had flickered once in the distance and then had disappeared. What was going on out there? Was it all over? Had the Japanese invaded, or was the United States military right now dropping bombs on Tokyo? How could she and Yoshio know what to do with the pilot if there was no clue from outside about the war and its combatants? Irene felt again her anger against Mr. Robinson and his silly, vain need to keep the island cut off from everything.

As she listened throughout the day, though, she pieced the fragmented words into a fuller story: Enemy parachutists had landed near King Street. Nisei citizens had been rounded up for questioning and detention. There were reports, then retractions, of Kauai being invaded by Japanese frogmen. As Monday afternoon gave way to Monday evening and Yoshio still had not returned, Irene's panic level rose. The reception wandered in and out with fickle abandon, but Irene, her ear pressed against the ribbed amplifier as if listening for a heartbeat, had heard enough to understand. Japanese Americans were being forcibly taken from their Oahu homes by police and military. There were shots in the street. People attacked Japanese businesses and, in a few cases, beat up Japanese men. Police were being sent to investigate "suspicious" Japanese locals. Who qualified as suspicious? Irene wondered. Who called these suspicions in?

It was well past sundown when Irene turned the radio off and checked on Taeko. Irene dropped her face to her child's tiny hands. In the dark, resting on her plump chest, the fists looked like small, perfect shells. Her musty, milky smell, ubiquitous to small children, hit Irene's nostrils. She breathed it in and thought instantly of her younger sister. Perhaps she was right now, *at this moment*, being rounded up and pushed into some dark jail cell. Her oldest nephew had probably signed up hastily for military service at the Kauai airbase. He was that kind of boy, foolish and sincere. She fought the urge to pick Taeko up and press her to her breast and run to the boat dock to see why Yoshio still had not returned. It occurred to her how furious she was that she had ever agreed to come to Niihau.

She woke to Yoshio slipping into the single bed, next to her. He put a hand on her shoulder but she did not move. He pulled his hand away, rose, and went to his own bed.

-Everything okay with Mr. Robinson? she finally said. He didn't reply for a long time.

-He didn't come, he said finally.

-They're rounding up Japanese on the other islands, she said.

There was a pause.

-Robinson comes tomorrow. Yoshio's voice was muffled under the sheets.

-Yoshio, for all we know he's dead. They say the Imperial Navy is sneaking up on the beaches as we speak. She sat up and looked at his prone form. It's time to help the pilot.

-No, he said after a long pause. And when it was clear she was not going to lie back down, he added, Wives don't disobey their husbands.

After a moment she whispered a response.

-Husbands protect their families.

He didn't answer. Somewhere the wind swung a board against a shed. The scrub outside the house rustled. The island, thought Irene, creaked and swayed like a ship at anchor, and it wouldn't take much for the chain to snap and set them all adrift on a dark, endless sea.

14

In the morning, Tuesday, December 9, Irene prepared Yoshio's tea without a word. It was still dark. Yoshio sat down to drink it, his wife a dark, slight shadow in the graying light.

-You're sure the Japanese have landed, Yoshio finally said. You heard for certain.

Well, she had heard for certain. Panicked reports of parachutists landing on King Street, those frogmen in Kauai. Warnings of sabotage by local issei, first-generation immigrants, and nisei, their American offspring. The information was unreliable of course, and it had come only briefly every few hours. She had also heard the opposite: intermittent appeals for calm, assurances that the islands were now secure.

Abruptly, she flung herself down on her knees. She held her hands forward in a dramatic gesture of supplication. Her hair fell from behind her ears onto her face and she made no effort to remove it.

-You see for yourself that Robinson does not arrive! We must be practical, Yoshio, my love, or we die! We must help this pilot, don't you understand, we have no choice. The Japanese have destroyed all the ships in Pearl Harbor. Next they'll take over the islands, or else why would they do such a thing? It's time we were on the winning side, Yoshio. The white Americans have no love for us, it's all over the radio what they're doing. But when the Japanese come, who will we be? In the eyes of the United States, we're not American, why would you want the Japanese navy to think so? If we're not American and we're not Japanese, who are we? Please, for your child's sake, if not for mine, we must make a deal with the pilot!

Yoshio reared back momentarily, shocked by his wife's sudden outburst. Then he leaned forward and touched her forehead, but she pulled away like a wild animal.

-And the Niihauans? Yoshio cried, dropping his arm. We just side with the pilot and forget about them?

-Your family! She rocked forward. With both of her small hands, she squeezed his face with a sudden and surprising force. Do you really think that the Niihauans love us as you say? We'll always be outsiders, Yoshio. Even old Shintani, as long as he's been here, is ultimately called Japanese Man by his neighbors. And look at Howard, even though he taught you to ride, you can tell he comes here and steps into the kitchen and the first thing he wonders is why he, the most educated Hawaiian on Niihau, wasn't picked to run the ranch for Mr. Robinson. You see it too, the way he flicks at those teeth with his tongue. Before he even greets us with the traditional *Hele mai ai*, he's thinking to himself, *Why aren't I in charge of the Old Lord's house?* Mr. Robinson loves his Hawaiians, no doubt about that, but it's the love one has for small children. One day they will know this, and his paradise will be gone!

Yoshio pulled back from his wife, and drummed the table with one thumb. His cheeks were red from Irene's fingers, his ears rang with her pleas. She was right, he knew. After all, didn't he understand? He had often been passed over for a job position that was instead given to a white man, and ironically, as bad as things got for the Japanese Americans, things were sometimes worse for the Hawaiians. All over the islands they were treated as a vanquished people would be, with a kind of pity and condescension, while at least the nisei inspired fear and some respect because of their obvious education and their sheer numbers. Somewhere in there was the Negro, but he had met so few he had no idea where to put him. Also, the Portuguese, the Filipino, the Chinese, the Korean—the list would go on, each a rung in a steep and unforgiving ladder the *haoles* had successfully built, themselves perched smack on the top, looking down with large, fixed smiles and angry, fearful eyes.

Yoshio pushed his tea away, and stood up.

-You don't think we can trust our neighbors. That's what you're saying.

-Who treat Mr. Robinson as a god! You really think we can depend upon a people who deify a *haole*?

Yoshio ran one hand across his eyes. He felt tired and older than his thirty-seven years. He hated the hollow cast of his wife's eyes, the disgust at him implicit in her voice. Perhaps she was right. There was no reason to think that the Niihauans would be good allies, that they would rise above the anti-Japanese hysteria of the other islands. They were, after all, willing minions to an eccentric white man. He put a hand on Irene's shoulder.

-If Mr. Robinson doesn't come today, I'll ask that the pilot stay with us tonight. We will talk to him frankly and decide what's best to do.

They rode by cart again to Kii, and waited in the warehouse. Sometimes Howard walked out onto the sand as if the reason Robinson did not arrive was simply a matter of the right vantage point. He returned each time and wagged a finger in the air to indicate that the boat's arrival was not imminent, but impending nonetheless. Yoshio said little and studiously avoided Nishikaichi's gaze.

Howard called his name.

-Do you want a swim? It's hot enough to roast a pig. I could throw a *popola* on the sand and we'd eat in ten minutes. How about it, a swim?

He pointed to the ocean and then back at himself and then at Nishikaichi. When Nishikaichi did not respond, he prodded Yoshio.

-Tell our guest what I'm asking. A swim! Do they do that where he comes from? Or does a machine swim for him? He chuckled, not unkindly, at his joke.

Yoshio watched the cigarette jump up and down on Howard's lips like a dying fish. A swim? It seemed inappropriate, but then Howard did not know all the circumstances surrounding the strange pilot.

-Swim? said Yoshio to Nishikaichi. He jerked his head toward the ocean and then, unsure whether he had chosen the correct Japanese word, raised his arms and grabbed at the air, closing his mouth and squinting his eyes against a cool, imaginary wave.

Nishikaichi jerked his head with a sudden rushing smile.

Yoshio was an excellent swimmer, but today he waded in only to his knees and slapped his hands at the surface, cooling himself. After a while he removed his white shirt and scrubbed its underarms, thinking how Irene would be pleased. When he was done he laid the shirt flat on the water and let it float in front of him, a jellyfish of cloth. He glanced once at Nishikaichi. The boy was clearly enjoying himself; he made large, splashing noises when he surfaced and held his breath with his cheeks puffed out, like a child. He was not a good swimmer and Yoshio was disappointed by this; part of him hoped that the young man would just up and breaststroke away, that he would disappear from their lives like a receding wave.

Today Robinson would again not arrive. Yoshio knew this because the sun was beginning its downward descent into the horizon and there was still no speck on the ocean, and because in his heart of hearts he knew that what had happened was bigger than Robinson. Pearl Harbor, gone. America, at war. Even if he told the Niihauans the truth, they would refuse to believe this; Robinson was the Old Lord, after all, and only God could keep him from Niihau. War? Not something that would get in the way of *Ka Haku Makua*. Yoshio sighed and folded his arms. He stared out at the small splash of Howard's kick and, beyond that, to Kauai's leaning parapets. Perhaps Irene was right. Perhaps Kauai had been invaded and Robinson was at this moment being interrogated by Japanese soldiers. The thought made his throat constrict. It would be only a matter of time before they came to Niihau and did what victorious armies did—loot, pillage, torture, rape, shoot.

Underwater, Nishikaichi watched his flight suit billow like loose skin in the water. Momentarily he let himself forget that he was racing against time, beholden to his *chu*. Instead, he was relaxed and, finally, cool. He held his stinging eyes open so that the swirling underwater colors blurred together—the green flight suit, his silvery hands, the beige sand, the turquoise sky. He was for a moment indistinct from the world, part of the silt he disturbed as he floated by.

When small, orbiting diamonds rose from his exhaling mouth, he thought of a night flight he had once taken over the China Sea. The sky had been moonless, and the thicket of stars made way for him and his plane as if they were gods. His gauges had risen fast—altimeter, engine, oil temperature—as his stomach had dropped with the beauty of it. Now, underwater, he felt just as glorious. Miraculously cool and heavy on his body, the ocean had the thick but calming embrace he could liken only to his one encounter with a whore when he had been stationed on the outskirts of Shanghai. He had been young, just seventeen, and depressed by the destruction all around him, the dull-eyed women, the dirty, half-dressed children with plundered gazes, the smell of burning rice paper and wood, the endless hiccup of random artillery fired by bored, homesick soldiers. He had gone to the brothel because his flying unit had insisted on it. He was afraid that the woman would be young and recently brutalized, so he chose an old one, her face plastered with bright color, so fat and heavy breasted that, midpleasure, he thought he might suffocate. But there was no doubt that the interaction did what it was supposed to—transported him momentarily away from there. He felt as if he were in the hold of some dark, listing ship that smelled of mold and chalk, bound for somewhere far, far off. Now, for an unguarded moment as he pedaled through the water, he wondered what he'd ever seen in his life as a soldier, the drone of days waiting for a conflict, the mindless destruction. Even flying had its downside. Yes, the sudden thrill of loosing free of the ground and the dizzying spirals and sudden climbs of combat suited him, as did those beautiful views of the whirling, tilting ground. But once in a while, when there was nothing but cavernous sky and a straight compass bearing to the carrier, he felt a pure and weary loneliness. It mingled with the g-force-induced nausea and the hammer of the engine in his ears. He inhaled it with the smell of gasoline and leather so strong it watered his eyes. It pulsed through him like blood. When he landed and whatever hormones and secretions that surged in combat flight (endorphins, adrenaline) had receded, a small part of this loneliness remained, whirring and clacking through his bloodstream like a broken piece of machinery. He had wanted to ask other pilots about this, whether they felt it too, this certainty that each human is ultimately alone. *Like islands,* he'd wanted to say. But he had never found that kind of bravery.

Finally out of breath he scrabbled his arms and legs to the surface. He swam (if one could have called it swimming) as if through a thunderhead, buffeted and churned by the wash of his own windmilling limbs. He could have just touched the bottom and straightened up—he had not gone out of his depth—but he wanted to remain as long as possible part of this pelagic world. As he broke the surface, one hand swatted the water from his eyes; the bright, shimmering day came harshly into focus. Blue sky, yellow land, red rocks, and pounding heat all jockeyed to copilot his senses. He didn't want to think about his mission, or try to summon up the energy to talk to Harada-san and convince him of a new allegiance. He wanted to go back underwater.

The pilot shook as if suddenly cold, but already the sun heated the back of his neck, the cloth on his arms. Yoshio thought how he looked more boyish than ever; only two days on Niihau and already he had unknowingly molted. His wet flight suit clung to a thin frame, and his skin, rosied from the sun and now clean, had lost any of the fierceness that dried blood and dirt may have given it. Yoshio wanted to steer as clear of the pilot as possible until Irene was present, but at this moment he looked so harmless, he decided it would not hurt to find out a little more now.

He nodded at the boy, who waded toward him and then stopped and turned wordlessly to face the ocean. For a while they both watched Howard swim. Then Yoshio cleared his throat.

-There's something that doesn't make sense with you. If your people are coming, why do you need to destroy your plane and papers? You keep pestering me about that, but it's not adding up.

Nishikaichi looked at him solemnly.

-*Meiyo*, Harada-san. Honor.

-You mean if the American army lands here instead of the Japanese Imperial Navy.

-I mean that . . .

He stopped and frowned. He didn't really have a good answer for this. He had just convinced Harada-san that his troops were coming, and this meant that his plane would not need to be destroyed. He bit his lip and hoped his insincerity would not show through.

-To tell you the truth, Harada-san, my commander's a son of a dog. He'd disapprove if he saw my plane intact. Once it's been crash-landed, it's my job to destroy it, even though we both know it won't ever fall into enemy hands. He's a stickler for things like that. I would be shamed, and so would my unit, even my family.

Shame. *Haji*. Yoshio shrugged, as if the word meant little to him, but he felt the skin on his face grow hot. His hands flew together and began to clench. He thought he heard a man's whisper. *Yellow sissy*, it said, twice. But no, he was here on Niihau, next to a young Japanese pilot, and no one was speaking, especially not English. He looked down at his writhing hands with disgust. Quit it, he admonished himself.

Nishikaichi glanced at Yoshio's grasping hands, then up at his face.

There was silence for a while. Howard was headed back to shore. Nishikaichi pointed.

-He's like a fish in the water. He must be someone who stands on the waves too.

Yoshio did not understand at first, but then the young man spread his arms out and bent his knees. Yoshio nodded.

-You mean surfing.

-We saw so many pictures. Men on wood, like flocks of strange birds! When we flew into Pearl Harbor, I thought I'd see hundreds like that. But perhaps I'll see some here.

Yoshio turned away. The mention of Pearl Harbor made his stomach curl up.

-Do you walk on water, Harada-san?

Yoshio exhaled and then glared.

-We have nothing to talk about any longer, Airman Nishikaichi. You and your compatriots have bombed my country, and I do not forget that.

-Harada-san, perhaps *you* don't understand. With all due respect to your age and experience, how can I explain? He frowned. Last year, he said, on leave from my duties, I went to Mount Aso, our beautiful national park. Have you been there?

Yoshio had never been to Japan. Not like Irene, who had gone and always talked about it as if it held something special.

-My squadron and I went for a hike. While on the mountain we saw a fox and he saw us. He watched us for a while but ran when we tried to get close. He was smart. He knew who should run and who should not, that his mountain had changed now that we were on it.

Howard was closer now. They could see the sun flash on his face when he lifted his head to breathe.

-Perhaps you are the small fox here, Yoshio finally said. His voice was quiet, heavy. We are the army. If all of us on Niihau get together against you, you will run.

-Perhaps. But there is a reason you haven't told your neighbors about Pearl Harbor and that they haven't lined up against me. Look, Harada-san, you don't want to be a second-class citizen again.

-Again?

-America is not kind, Harada-san. We know this in Japan. In the newspapers we read of respected citizens who come here to work, to find only slave labor and misery.

-Your newspapers profit from exaggeration, pal.

-Perhaps. But here no one knows their place. In Japan we do.

-Fix your plane and leave, Yoshio responded quietly. I won't stop you.

-If only it was that simple. Nishikaichi laughed. It's not as if I can flap the wings like a bird and leave the earth with a worm in my mouth. The plane is dead, and now I must dispose of its body properly. I won't leave before it is completely destroyed.

Yoshio tried to imagine Nishikaichi lifting a hammer to the ruined plane, its long, already broken body coming off in chunks under his blows. He couldn't see it, something so powerful giving in so easily. Even in pieces as it was, it was so clearly a plane. What could he do to alter it? He would need to grind it so far down, he supposed, that whoever finally took the island would see only a pile of black dust.

-We know you're not allowed in the same movie theaters as Americans, Harada-san.

-I keep telling you, I *am* American. For goodness' sake. He frowned. Anyway, it's whites. We're separated from them. Not the whole theater. Just the sections. We sit in different sections.

-Like the Africans.

Yoshio shrugged.

-Why do you accept that? Do you think that's your rightful place?

-Who said I accepted it? Yoshio's voice was suddenly tight. He heard a sound to his right that could have been the shore break, or was it in his head? His fists jammed together. He felt the back of his neck prickle as if with cold, but the day was still blazingly hot. Then it was too late: he was back in a theater in California. A young man, on a date, and he had mistakenly sat in the reserved section. The next thing he knew he was being pulled at by large, exuberant ushers. The girl he was with screamed as the men came at him with open hands and leering grins, enjoying the break in their usual tedious work. Their square hats had tilted with the effort of the extrication, though he had not fought at all. All he could remember was the rhythmic sway of their yellow usher epaulets as they dragged him, stunned and unmoving, from the theater. The silly uniform gave a certain military authority to the situation; even Yoshio felt the hollow thud of shame in his stomach, as if he had truly done something terribly wrong. The girl's scream (what was her name; he could not remember) had disappeared abruptly when the theater's doors to the street swung closed behind them. The three men dropped him in the gutter, and one had, after an extra push on Yoshio's limp shoulder with one shiny black usher shoe, slapped his hands together in a washing motion. That sound, the susurration of what Yoshio could only describe as a kind of *contented violence*, reverberated in his head for years. Even after the screams of the girl had finally faded from his memory, this did not. That sudden, mocking swish-swish, half applause, half gleeful hand rubbing—even now he sometimes heard it in the hum of the surf, or in the first clickety-clack as Irene pushed denims under the sewing machine. It stopped him dead in his tracks and his heart would begin to thump wildly. Of course, he had worse memories. And there it was, that voice again.

Yellow sissy, it whispered.

-No disrespect meant, Harada-san. But in Japan there is a right place for everyone. Surely a Japanese man like you would never bow so deeply to others.

Yoshio came out of his reverie and saw Nishikaichi staring at him. He forced his hands loose and slapped at the water. Then he put his palms on his hips, as if afraid the fingers would come together again, and glared at Nishikaichi.

-You're the prisoner here, not me.

Nishikaichi looked at him with squint-eyed concentration.

-You deserve more, Harada-san, that's all, he finally said, bowing his head.

-We wait for Mr. Robinson, Yoshio said quietly.

-Harada-san, I'll make sure no one here on Niihau gets hurt. If you help.

Yoshio blinked at the water. For a moment it seemed as if he would nod in agreement.

-Here comes Howard, he said instead.

When the sun was a palm's width from the horizon, Howard announced that they would stay the night instead of making the long, fifteen-mile journey back to Puuwai. Yoshio felt a surge of relief. Irene would be disappointed and frustrated that the pilot would not be at their house. But he was glad for the short reprieve.

Yoshio motioned that he would be back soon, and made his way to the end of the beach where the cliffs plummeted to the ocean and a stand of *kiawe* withstood the onshore wind. There he stopped and exhaled. He wanted to scream or cry, he did not know which. Instead, he turned and stared at the horizon.

He was not looking one last time for Robinson, but for the Huna Motu, sacred and mysterious islands that the ranch hands sometimes mentioned. In 1778 Captain Cook reported that he saw them, naming them Moonapapa in his journals, and returning to Niihau twice with high hopes of sailing toward them, but they never appeared again. Irene had laughed and said it was all ignorance. But when the *unulau* wind blew, some of the villagers, unbeknownst to Robinson, headed to the old volcano Kaiwoha on the eastern tip of Niihau to catch a glimpse of one of the Huna Motu chain, the island Unulani, which burst with fruit, animals, and houses. Right before dawn it appeared for seconds, they said, and disappeared again with the sun. Yoshio had pushed to hear more about it, but the men had shut up then, and turned to peeling their fruit with sudden earnestness. Perhaps the islands would appear for him now, even though it was dusk. Yoshio raised his arms. What was he doing? he wondered. All he knew was that he needed a sign and anything would do, a disappearing island, a shark spirit, Jesus Christ himself.

15

As Nishikaichi settled onto the hard floor for the night, he was strangely calm. In the cooling air the warehouse smelled of old wood and dust and reminded him of the temple near his home in the Shikoku prefecture, where the pilgrims came and lit candles and left offerings, and where the rooms were ghostly with ancient things, as if all the candles ever lit, all the whispered prayers ever exhaled, all the fruit ever offered had left their scents in the grain of the walls. But as he turned on his back to get comfortable on the dirt (the other men put their heads on the tight balls of their dusty shirts, but Nishikaichi would still not allow himself to remove his flight suit), he caught sight of the Christian cross on the wall. It reminded him of the Zero, its wings outstretched uselessly, tilted on the rocky ground, abandoned. His heart clenched then, but he closed his eyes to feign sleep, though he would not sleep, not now, when his mission was so far from completion and dishonor pushed down on his shoulders like a weight. When the sub came—it would come, wouldn't it?—he wouldn't need Harada-san anymore. The sub's crew would blow the plane up. He would watch as the sheared metal heaved toward the blue sky in one last effort to take flight.

His anxiety did not last long. The hum of the shore break was soothing, the wind, which had picked up, whistled quietly. Nishikaichi had begun to see why Harada-san was still loyal to this island. There was a serenity here that Nishikaichi could not explain. Perhaps it was the lack of machines. Perhaps it was just the heat, relentless, sapping. He would have to be careful that he did not let his guard down too much, get carried away by this loosening of his limbs.

As he drifted off to sleep, the pilot thought of the white scar of the fishmonger's daughter. It moved like a wave, beckoning him. He lifted his arms and, still breathing deeply, began to swim toward it.

Nishikaichi woke the morning of Wednesday, December 10, with a headache. He'd had disturbing, incoherent dreams of a plane come alive. It walked on its back tail and flapped large wings menacingly. Which was why, despite the steely nerve that had been drilled into him as a soldier, the sight of Howard looming over him startled him so much.

-*Ohana,* the Hawaiian man said. Nishikaichi got to his feet, thinking that perhaps the emperor's boat had come, but then Howard stopped a few feet outside the door and kicked some rocks out of the way. Then he went carefully to his knees. He raised folded hands to the lightening sky. After a moment Nishikaichi heard a strange bleating sound and realized that Howard had begun to sing. His voice quickly gathered momentum and soon it was loud and exuberant. Despite his tightened bladder, Nishikaichi did not move from the warehouse. He was not sure what to make of this sudden, unabashed worship, but he knew he did not want to disturb it. He slowly sat back on the ground, crossed his own legs, and lay the backs of his hands on his knees. He closed his eyes. Within a moment he had forgotten his own need to urinate. He blanked his mind in a quick rush of what he could only describe as wind and felt the familiar lightness that came with the meditative prayer he had learned as a boy. He chanted in a voice that came silently from the crown of his head. While the voice repeated the sacred words, his heart opened slowly, like the mouth of a cave seems to do when the sun hits. His heart spoke then, without words, asking the great forces to allow him to see the fishmonger's daughter one more time, to miraculously destroy his plane and papers, to protect his parents, and to keep the war from this lonely island. He wondered if this was blasphemous, communing with Lord Buddha against the backdrop of Jesus. It didn't feel like it; it felt organic and whole. The more powerful Howard's singing became, the more the white light behind his eyes shone, the more his scalp glowed. When the singing stopped, Nishikaichi opened his eyes quickly. He was letting his guard down too much, much too much.

No one said anything during the breakfast of leftover yams, not even Howard. When the sun was well above the horizon, Nishikaichi walked to the water's edge, but he no longer wanted to swim. The Niihauan emperor had not arrived, and this was Nishikaichi's third day with no sign of a rescuing submarine. The sub was not coming, he would have to face that. Now something had to change here, he knew. He waited for Yoshio to join him so that he could begin to talk in earnest to him, but the man stayed in the warehouse, a tormented look on his face, and so Nishikaichi stared out to sea alone.

16

Late that morning three children rode up on horses. The two younger ones rode together—a round, wide-smiling girl and another more serious one on a handsome young piebald. The boy skidded up on a horse of his own. He was older, perhaps sixteen or so. At the sound of the arriving horses, each man perked up slightly. Howard stood and stubbed out his cigarette with haste, his shame returning momentarily so that he shoved the remainder in his pocket too roughly and waved at the smoke as if punching the air. Yoshio raised his head for only a moment before putting his hands together and lowering it again.

-Mr. Kaleohano! called the boy, one hand raised in greeting.

-Ah, my friend, Kahuna Pule. Little Preacher. Howard coughed, looked from side to side anxiously, and then shook the young man's hand with vigor.

-My father wants to light the emergency signals on Mount Paniau, Little Preacher said, glancing at the pilot.

Howard paused, looking alarmed, and then his face broke out into his crooked-toothed smile. He waved one hand.

-Hanaiki worries too much. He'll be like the old man Ben Kanahele if he doesn't stop!

He kept smiling, but inside he thought how it was no good that the people were losing faith in Robinson, and that it was his job to stop that. He leaned toward Little Preacher and dropped his voice

-The Old Lord comes today, Little Preacher, he intoned. I assure you, by the rump of my chestnut horse, that he'll pull up any minute now. I think I even see a speck out there. Look.

-You sure?

-Sure.

-And if no?

-If no, by early afternoon, then okay, go tell your father to light the lamps. But not until then. Mr. Robinson, he'll come, not to worry. Stay for a while now, swim. Or just cool yourself in the warehouse. And tell the *keiki* to stop sneaking around out there.

With this last comment Howard jerked his head to the wall behind him.

There was a loud shuffle. A few seconds later the two girls appeared at the side of the door, looking solemn and sheepish.

The serious girl gave something to Howard and then approached Nishikaichi, avoiding his eyes, holding out a strange fruit, which he took and examined. It was heavy. It had thick, spiny skin. Leaves sprayed out from one end. He shook it. No sound. Holding on to one of its stiff leaves, he put his nose close and sniffed.

-*Halakahiki*, the girl said. Pineapple.

With two quick arcs of his knife, Howard cut his, the pieces falling away like petals. Yoshio watched the pilot stare at the flashing knife. Was he going to lunge for it? And if he did, what would Yoshio do?

Nishikaichi made his move then, but it was not what Yoshio expected. He voraciously jammed his teeth against the skin of the fruit in his hand. He bit hard and deep and Yoshio flinched from the sting he knew his gums would feel from the stiff, unforgiving rind. Yoshio watched as the young man tried to clamp his jaw shut and tear a bite away, but the fruit would not give. He heard a sound between a gasp and a giggle; the girls stared at the pilot with wide-eyed amazement.

-Skin isn't for eating, said Yoshio gruffly.

The pilot shook his teeth free and then let the thing fall to the ground, where it thudded loudly and kicked up dust. Then he spat a few times and smiled sheepishly.

-No *halakahiki* in Japan, I see. Howard guffawed and continued to cut his fruit into pieces.

Little Preacher stood with his arms folded. His nickname came from his earnest pronouncement at a young age that he would be a minister, and he had grown into a serious young man, as anyone who had taken all the biblical stories of scourges and plagues too much to heart was bound to be. He didn't find anything particularly funny in the stranger spitting out pineapple on the floor. In fact the stranger meant little to him at all. He had disliked the large, broken carcass of metal and rubber left in the Niihau field. Its charred smell and dark frame had reminded him of the devil himself, and it had spooked Little Preacher to stand guard next to it. Though he had originally been as intrigued as anyone else about the stranger who had fallen from the sky, now he couldn't look at the stranded pilot without thinking of the archangel Gabriel tumbling through the clouds as he was banished from heaven. The sooner the man left the island the better, Little Preacher thought, turning from Howard to watch with the rest of them as the girls ran laughing into the water.

Nishikaichi said nothing until they were out of his sight. His face was flushed.

-I scared them, he said to Yoshio.

-Don't worry, he responded. They don't know any better.

Yoshio's voice was nonchalant but inside his stomach had jumped. The sight of those children laughing, the way their hands flew up to their faces as shields and dismissive waves at once—it reminded him of days in California when children smirked at the sight of him, or backed away when he dared to smile. Once, in his first few days there, a small girl had asked him if he really ate the boys before the girls, and he had first thought it was a joke, but she had been solemn and unsmiling. He thought suddenly of Taeko, on the floor with shells under her tiny fingers, Irene nearby, her *holoku* swirling around her thin frame as she turned to look at him. What was the look? Accusatory? Pleading? He heard more laughter on the shoreline, and from the open door he could see the two girls slouched toward each other, arms akimbo, flailing with hilarity or mockery, he could not tell which.

Abruptly Yoshio turned to Howard. Be back, he said. He tried to keep his legs steady under him as he moved fast in the posture of someone heading to the bush to urinate, but it was all he could do to keep from falling to his knees. He stumbled into the bright sunlight. He turned left, to distance himself from the girls, needing to escape from their sound, needing to go far away, needing to have this whole thing be over, but knowing that it was up to him to make a decision, soon. At a clump of scrub beyond the wagon, he stopped and put his hands on his thighs to catch his breath. He wanted to vomit, and wondered if it would make him feel better. Instead, he walked unsteadily to the wagon and then lay in its stingy shade. He closed his eyes, hoping to block out California's insistent, mocking roar.

People on Kauai had looked at him differently when he returned. He had lost weight and he spoke little and drank too much. They knew something had happened over there in California. Yoshio wanted to tell them that it was the endless march of small humiliations that cracked a man. But in his case, this was only partly true. There had been one final moment, as dark and narrow as an alley, as unforgettable as a kick in the ribs—*yellow sissy*—that had ultimately crushed him. Without this moment his sense of self would have been crimped and pockmarked by the ceaseless rain of stifled laughs, sideways looks, and spit, but even in pieces it would still be there. Instead, a whole part of him had fled. This was why he loved Niihau so much. She was eroded by constant winds, pounded by a merciless sun, trampled by cows and sheep. But she held up, always the same island every dawn, no matter how badly Mother Nature had treated her. Nonchalant, even scornful. Confident. But if the Japanese came? Perhaps it would be her own terrible moment, and he would see how she would endure.

He allowed himself a few more minutes under the wagon. Then he pulled himself up and leaned against its wooden sides. He would have to go back to the warehouse soon, he didn't want to arouse suspicion. As he straightened and wiped the sweat from his brow, something caught his eye at the far end of the wagon. It was small and dark: the pilot's flying cap.

It had stiffened in the sun, and one earflap had curled. Yoshio held it for a few moments; his fingers pressed the cracks of the leather, his eyes squinted at the decorative seams. He guessed the pelt that lined the inside was made of rabbit, but he couldn't be sure. On its front he noticed a raised circle of leather, inside which was a small, five-pointed star. He ran a finger over it carefully, as if the sharp points might cut him. Then he dropped the flight hat on his fingertips and held it upward to get a better view, as it might look on a man's head, allowing the earflaps to fall around his thumbs. Hung like this the cap seemed to exude power and certainty. It was the mantle of a man with a purpose. Yoshio glanced right and left, and then toward the warehouse. Well, no one would see him, and it wouldn't hurt. He squatted behind one wheel and with a deft movement pulled the cap on his head.

He only let it rest there a little while. He wished he had a mirror, but wearing it was enough. When he reluctantly withdrew it from his head, his hands were no longer shaking. He left it where he had found it, and walked back to the warehouse, his step quicker and firmer than it had been, and something beginning to take hold in his heart.

17

They rode harder than they usually did. The bridles clanged, and sweat gathered around the cinches like foam on waves. The two kerosene lamps, which would be used with the reflectors to transmit the emergency signal, made the saddlebags bulge. The three men, Ben, Hanaiki Niau, and his son Little Preacher, talked low and kept impassive faces, unwilling to show one another their excitement, but the horses felt it anyway and strained against the bits and flicked their heads to and fro. Despite this and even though it was late afternoon, they wouldn't keep this pace for long. Ultimately the men slowed their mounts to trots with murmurs and tightened reins. They knew that up ahead there was a spring where they would stop, and then the long, steady climb of Mount Paniau.

The horses drank first, their necks extended, their nostrils flared. Then the men, flat on their stomachs, using their hands as scoops. Except Hanaiki Niau, whose bulk needed room on the embankment and who waited with his head turned away, as if he didn't care much.

Ben Kanahele—Ella's husband—rose to his feet first and wiped his mouth. He looked up the scrubby slope with its thickets of *kiawe* and *wiliwili*. He didn't like to light the lamps, for fear of a fire, but it had to be done, he knew. He hadn't meant to stare at Hanaiki's saddle. But as he had turned from the mountain with a small twinge of worry in his stomach, the leather had glinted like a star.

-What's this? he asked, pointing below the pommel, to something bright and round, recently riveted into the saddle.

Hanaiki had finally lowered himself to the spring and he wasn't about to turn and look, not now, when the cool water was at his mouth and it felt so good to drink.

-Wait, he grunted. He splashed his face and arms with care. He took a final sip. Then he pushed himself slowly to his feet.

Ben pointed, Hanaiki shrugged.

-Came from the plane, he said.

-Sure it isn't bad luck?

-It's metal, that's all.

It was thick and beautiful, a deep gray color that reminded Ben of a sky that promised rain.

-Mr. Robinson won't like it, Mr. Niau. Could bring disease.

He said this gruffly, despite the fact that he had already run his palms down the plane's flank more than once and had even reached below the instrument panel to touch what he did not know were the rudder pedals, twisted and now useless. He too had felt the urge to take something, though he had no idea what he specifically needed. Almost everything on the island was provided—free taro root, free fruit, and as much milk as one needed from any cow. The rocks at low tide were covered with *opiki*, which were easily pulled off and then picked nimbly from their shells. The fish were plentiful. Wild boar roamed the island. And though each worker paid rent, the houses had been sturdily built with wood shipped in by the Robinson boat, with Robinson money. The ranch hands were outfitted with work clothes for a fair price, often handed down from other cowboys, yes, but sturdy and useful. There was even the store his wife, Ella, liked to visit for extra things like flour or beans. His salary of $1.50 a day (par with or even a little better than the pay of other plantation workers on other islands) left enough for these luxuries. In sum, Ben had never felt before the lack he'd felt as he rummaged in the cockpit pushing and pulling at strange buttons and flat stirrups and small leather-covered chairs. He had none of these things in his life, and though he knew that on the one hand he wanted nothing to do with a machine that flew in the sky, he also knew that it represented a whole world he did not know and, worse, could not comprehend. Before this, he had never wanted to comprehend it, agreeing with the Old Lord that the best things were simple and godly. But faced with it, in the form of this downed plane, he felt an odd, inexplicable pull. Not to mention the high emotions it had sparked in Ella. She was ornery to begin with, but she never defied him. Yesterday, though, she had argued that she wanted to visit the plane despite his stern prohibition. He had been angered by her impudence, but in many ways he understood that the plane had a strange effect on everyone. Now as he stared at the bright, jagged ornament on Hanaiki's saddle, he wished he too had taken something when he'd had a chance.

-What's it good for, there on the saddle? muttered Ben, shaking his head.

Hanaiki shrugged amiably.

-No use. I just like it.

They said no more after that, and slowed their horses to a walk.

As they neared the top, the brush got scrubbier and the soil began to show its molten beginnings. The fine red beads crunched like bones under the horses' hooves.

-Why has he forsaken us? asked Little Preacher suddenly. The young boy rarely spoke in the presence of his father, Hanaiki, so Ben was startled.

-God? said Ben. God is all around us, He hasn't—

-Mr. Robinson, the boy interrupted. It's been three days and he hasn't come.

-Son, we know he's got good reason. He's an important man, with important things to do. He doesn't know yet that we have a stranger here. After we signal, he'll launch a boat immediately, I guarantee it.

Little Preacher looked doubtful. He shook his head.

-Everybody's getting worried. I heard Mrs. Kaleohano say that it's a bad sign, the Old Lord late, and a foreigner we don't know what to do with.

-Hush, boy, said his father. No sense talking about bad luck. That's superstition, and God would not approve.

-Yes, agreed Ben. You'll learn as you get older, Little Preacher, that listening to the women can get you in trouble. Isn't that right, Mr. Niau?

The men laughed. Little Preacher smiled uncertainly, looked up the mountain. By now, they could see the ocean on three sides. They rode on in silence. Only a few hundred feet from the summit, Ben frowned.

"*Aoa*," he said simply. Hanaiki looked over at him and nodded. Yes, the wind was coming strongly from Hanapepe, Kauai, an *aoa* wind, perfect for a crossing. Usually this was cause for celebration, but today it was an ominous sign. It would have been one thing if there had been *kiu-kulepe*, a fierce wind, or even the typical *lehua*, afternoon northeastern trade wind. That would explain the Old Lord's tardiness. But the wind yesterday and today had been a steady east wind, the water ruffled but easily manageable by the large boat. There was no reason for him to be late.

The wind brought many things to Niihau, depending on its direction. Rain clouds lumbered over from Kauai. Birds glided in from the open sea. The first Niihauans may have been blown here by a whimsy of the weather. So it was no wonder that the Niihauans had given the wind so many names—*kiu-pekekeu* for light, cold winds; *kiu-koolau*, moderate cold winds; *kiu-mana*, a cold wind from Kauai; *unulau,* a wind from the northeast that brings rain and a vision of the mysterious island, to name only a few. Ben realized that this wind was *aoa,* but in his bones he felt suddenly another wind, *kiu-peapea,* the cross wind that brings with it war, strife, and disharmony. He wanted to stop his horse and double-check by swiveling his cheek in all directions, but he did not want to alarm his neighbors more than they already were. That was all they needed: Robinson not here and an omen like that. It would be too much. Ben said nothing.

The final few minutes upslope they sat a little taller, pushed their heels tighter to urge their tired mounts a little faster, and when they finally got to the summit, dismounted quickly, without looking around too much, to unpack the lanterns and kick clear a place in the red-black soil upon which to set them.

Ben finally raised his head to check the view. He did not come up here often—when was the last time?—and he had forgotten how much one could see. The small dock at Kii stretched out like a stick at Kaunuopou Point, and though he thought he could make out the buildings, he could not spot Howard, who was no doubt moping a little because the Old Lord still had not come, and was perhaps on his way back to Puuwai. Just above that, along the shore, he could see a clearing in the brush that would be the remains of Pahau, once the place to which unlucky lepers were sent, and beyond that the nearest *heiau.* There were many of these sacred temples on the island, built by the ancients for the gods they had believed in, and though the Nihauans now knew that there was only one God, the *heiaus* were secretly deemed important in their way. Even the Old Lord had not been told where all of them were; Ben suspected that he knew this, though he probably did not like it. Ben turned in the direction of Puuwai; he could not make out any houses, but finally, after staring for a long time, he saw the white glint of the beloved church.

The clatter of the lanterns stilled. Hanaiki and his son straightened to look. They stood in reverent silence for a few moments, hearing only the whistle of the wind and the intermittent snort of the horses nuzzling at the brush. Then they continued their work, and when it was done, sat and waited for dark.

They began at dusk, arguing a little about whether they should have a steady light or try to attract attention with an intermittent beam. Ben had been told once by Howard that there was an actual flickering system that signaled certain things, like letters in the air, but the other two looked at him blankly.

-We'll get the light trained on Kauai and then we'll pray, said Little Preacher. This was self-evident, that God would transmit the actual message.

And so the three men went slowly, carefully, to their knees. After a while Little Preacher began to sing, low at first. The hymn was his favorite, one that he hummed when he was afraid or angry or when powerful, embarrassing feelings came over him, like when he was near Mrs. Keale's daughter. When he was done he peeked through lowered eyelids at the lantern light, which, it seemed to him, shone brighter and steadier than ever. Buoyed, he went through every hymn in their Hawaiian Bible and then back through them again as darkness came quickly and the light narrowed the world to just what fell within its large cylindrical beam. Insects, fooled into thinking the moon was nearby, whirled and glimmered like sudden stars as they flailed across its path. Sometimes Ben and Hanaiki joined in with the singing but mostly they stared up at the night sky, and thought of the plane, and of the Old Lord, and why he had not yet come.

18

Imperceptibly, the plane had begun to disappear. A piece here, placed by the *imu.* A piece there, dropped in a pocket and jangled every so often for good luck. In the Kelly household hung the sinew of electric cable across the corner of a bed, ostensibly for decoration but also because there had been a rumor that the blue and green and red held some key to amorous powers. The tire, whose saltatory dance upon impact left it far from the axle it had once belonged to, was gone from its place near the fence post, which itself now lay flat against the sand, mistaken for the island sugarcane by curious gulls. Ella thought she saw the rubber jutting from the Kaleohano outhouse, but Mabel shook her head fiercely and denied it. Ella couldn't pursue it, for then there would be questions about why she was there in the first place, near the plane and thus with a clear view of the outhouse. Ella had of course *very good reason* for being there, and she practiced saying it aloud in case someone asked. *Walking the long way to the beach.* But of course she wasn't going to the beach at all, because it was midday on Wednesday, December 10, and everyone who was smart was either in her house or on a horse fanning himself with a cowboy hat under the shade of a *wiliwili.*

She had never wanted to know much about the outside

world—it had seemed enough to push out her five squalling babies and then care for them in the heat and dust; life somewhere else couldn't have been much different from where she was. Years ago, before the measles epidemic and the current drought, when more people had been allowed to leave the island and then return, freely, she had heard stories of the outer islands. Those stories made it clear that beyond a few more churches and a few more *haoles*, the outside world was not much different from Niihau. But now that the plane had crashed into their island, she was suddenly intrigued. She had questions: How does this fly and why? Who are the people who thought such a thing up? What other machines have they made? What is it like to live a life full of metal? The questions disturbed and animated her—she had asked them of her husband, Ben, but he had only looked at her, alarmed. Women weren't supposed to ask things like that, he said. Then, for the first time since the beginning of their marriage, she had defied him. She had agreed not to go back there again and then she had blurted out that of course she was going, it was as much her plane as anybody else's here on Niihau, and besides, Mrs. Niau said that Hanaiki's saddle looked like a crown from a picture book, so much silver and jewels from the plane were now on it, and Ella wanted some for herself, after all. Ben had blinked at her and turned red. Later he'd complained that his hip, the one damaged in the horse accident, hurt, and she had soothed him, but there was still that rift between them.

So now she was back to find out what had seeped into her blood so suddenly, with fervor not unlike the way her first child fell quickly to a strange disease that later someone called *influenza*. The stranger himself, pale, just a boy, did not interest her—and anyway, it was unseemly for a Christian woman to show too much interest in a male guest. But the plane, its calligraphic strewing of shiny knobs and metal planks, glass, and rubber tires, was trying to speak to her. And what it spoke, now in a whisper, now in an insistent, clear shout, was of the outside world, strange, mysterious, and forbidden.

The sun sprayed its leaden heat, the flies, numerous and persistent, lighted on her arms and legs, humming angry disapproval. Ella waved away dust (resigned to the flies), and remonstrated with herself to turn around and go home, that there were shells to be organized and food to prepare. But at each house, she continued to the next until she was by the church. Hot and thirsty and in need of some guidance, she stood to one side and debated whether to enter.

It would have struck Ella as ironic to know that the church itself was a composite of strewn parts—stained glass brought around Cape Horn, benches hewn from Pacific Northwest trees, nails and metal brackets torn from a home on Oahu razed to make way for a military base at a place once called Puuloa, then renamed Fair Haven, and finally christened Pearl Harbor. The church's tin roof had been thrown into the *Noio*, the Robinsons' private boat, alongside cattle and sheep and some of the thousands of ironweed trees planted each year. It had been ceremoniously hoisted into place by many hands and blessed by the preacher of the time, Moses W. Kaaneikawahaale Keale. Also blessed were twenty-five stone plaques that were laid alongside the church walls, naming the head of each family on Niihau in that year of 1912, when the church was finished. Ella walked over to the stones now. They were hot to the touch, but she wedged the large, rough tips of her fingers into a few of the letters anyway. She was illiterate, but she knew the names of the families by heart, and she used to pretend to read them off the stones to her children, mixing it up each time, but naming all twenty-five without pause: Kahale, Niau, Lawai,

Kalalua, Niheu—the names still thrived today. Ella thought of how that made Niihau as fine a place to be as any, if not finer—this long lineage of families who extended back into the past and would continue reaching into the future. She nodded her head in respect to the twelve stones on this side of the church and then pushed the front door open.

It was not cooler inside, but it was darker because all the windows were shuttered, and this tricked the body into believing (such deception being unseemly, Ella would in a few moments think, for a good Christian church) that the temperature had dropped with the light. Soon Ella would be sweating again but now she lifted her head and walked, slightly refreshed, to the back pew. She knew just how stooped she was getting when the space between being seated and standing to sing the hymn got smaller and smaller, until she wondered if she should bother to stand at all. But today there was no service, and so she sat with no intention of bobbing up and down but to stay seated like this, shoulders pitched forward, head down in what was finally, in her old age, the perfect meeting of comfort and worship. Here was some quiet time for her to sit and think. She glanced around to see if anyone else was there, hunched perhaps in one of the pews before her, like a solemn *he'e nalu* on some dark shore-bound wave. Satisfied she was alone, she let the floating figure of Jesus on the cross above the lectern come slowly into view, first as a thin, rising cumulonimbus cloud, then as a misshapen, ragged-winged gull, and finally as the doomed Son himself, bleeding from the waist and the wrists and the feet. Though this she couldn't see in the dusk of the interior, she knew the blood drops by heart, so fascinated was she as a child by this stiff reenactment of a violent end and the careful, loving rendering of the blood spots, complete, upon closer inspection, with errant brush hairs.

It was unusual to have a crucifix in a Protestant church; this particular Jesus had been acquired from a Catholic parish on Kauai, back when "popery," as Eliza Sinclair had called it, had a bigger hold on the islands. Mrs. Sinclair had disliked the drama of Catholic worship, which bordered, she'd thought, on pagan ritual. All those robes. That swinging incense. The foreign incantations. She especially didn't approve of the way the savage nature of Jesus's death was exclaimed on walls and in stained-glass windows. But she had been a practical woman. She'd realized that if the predominantly Catholic Niihauans were to convert easily under her new ownership, she would have to make some concessions. She bought the wooden crucifix for more money than she liked, from a priest who'd found it in the basement of his church. Catholicism was scrabbling for a foothold on the islands and badly needed the cash, and Mrs. Sinclair regretted that she might be funding its spread. But she threw a burlap sack over the crucifix so she didn't have to look at it, and at the first opportunity it was boated across the channel and then nailed to the old church wall without fuss. Every so often the wooden Jesus was carefully painted, the blood drops renewed, the beard darkened. His skin was also redone with care, but at some point over the years, the paint color went from its pinkish brown to a startling white, so that He glowed incandescent at times when the light was right. The color had been used on the outsides of old farmhouses in the East, picked for practical reasons rather than aesthetic ones: it was cheap. It was the kind of white not qualified by any adjectives in the paint store: off white, white oak, bone. This was simply white white, and it had been imported by the Old Lord's father for exterior walls. In an unconscious, perhaps divine, symmetry, Jesus actually matched the outside of the church and all the apiaries and houses on Niihau. Unbeknownst to His followers He was also guaranteed to weather well under the unfortunate but unlikely scenario that He was left in the open for any length of time. The Robinsons said nothing about the ongoing care of the Catholic symbol. Quietly, imperceptibly, the bloody crucifix became part of spiritual life here, and the plan to dispense with it when the time came, in favor of a simple cross perhaps, was put aside or just forgotten.

Below Jesus was the lectern, a small shelf nailed onto a thick plank and used at an earlier date as a ship's navigation table (something that, if Ella had known, she would have approved of, feeling that Christianity was a sextant on seas that got rougher and higher as one aged), and now only a dark shadow. The pew itself was cushionless, and when Ella went to her knees on Sundays, it was sometimes with the padding of her husband's hat. Otherwise the pews were comforting without being comfortable; even in the dim light she knew that each one was shiny with the constant sway and shift of her neighbors' buttocks over the years, bright with the sheen of hot fiddling hands. Now she put her palms together and brought them to her forehead, simultaneously rapping prayers awake and taking her familiar place among Christians everywhere.

Ask and you shall receive. She knew this to be true, but it was as if the plane had scooted her head clear of everything but a whirling, heaving *koolau* wind. What sins did she need to have cleansed because of the plane? Covetousness? Disobeying her husband? Worshiping false idols? Greed? This last one appealed to her, it sounded right. She was greedy, not just for the baubles of the plane but for its secrets. She asked the Lord to forgive her for this and to guide her thoughts elsewhere.

And yet there they hovered, like one of Niihau's insistent flies, above the twitching plane (in her mind it was always moving, or about to move), which looked less threatening now, less strange.

God, she assured herself, would not have let such a thing drop onto their peaceful island if it was something bad. She raised her head slightly to look at Jesus again, who always seemed in an eternal state of bafflement himself, as if his naive, trusting heart couldn't quite believe he had been trussed up on the cross by his flock. But it wasn't Jesus up above the lectern, it was the outline of the plane itself, and the image gave her such a fright she cried out and then slapped her hand against her mouth as the shape became Jesus again, emaciated, drooping, covered in blood.

She hurried out of the church. The door shut with a derisive hoot, and this spooked her even more, as owls had been holy beings for ancient Niihauans. She was receiving signs everywhere, but she had no idea how to interpret them. There was only one thing to do and she did it now: she headed for the plane itself.

She made a wide circle around the Kaleohano house and approached the plane from its far side, so that Puuwai showed up behind, with its houses like sparse, mangy trees, the lava walls around each dark shadows, the cereus blooms that crawled up their sides just visible as tiny blood spots (another sign). Even in the full light of midafternoon the area around the plane itself gave the unmistakable impression of a graveyard, its headstones fallen and in disarray. Even with the red-brown dust softening the dark metal skin, the sharply angled, toothlike edges where parts had been violently sheared off upon impact or, she thought, by the intrepid sawing of one of her neighbors' knives, were frightening. And though the plane as a whole sagged into the ground, it was less the posture of a relaxed guest next to an *imu* than that of a predator animal snugged and motionless, ready to move in for the kill. The diaspora of parts was silting over too, so that it seemed as if they would melt right into the ground, and Ella thought that if the rains didn't come this year, the bits and pieces would surely disappear completely, claimed by the mythic Pele for her very own. Pele's first step on the Hawaiian Islands had been here on Niihau, and it was said that she built her fire pits from Kaluakawila to Puulama, and though she eventually went to Kauai, and then on to the island of Hawaii, her spirit, the elders said, always remained here on Niihau; it would not be beneath her to snatch such strange and lovely gifts from the island that was first her home.

The red circle on the plane's side, which had earlier been bursting with color, was now dull and faded. This was what Ella wanted to touch first, and she was picking her way toward it when suddenly a movement by the *kiawe* tree startled her. She froze and instantly forgot her practiced excuse, the auguries and omens that had led her here, the red circle itself. But it was only a mynah bird, which squawked its familiar greeting and cocked its head at her. She tried to shoo it away. When it did not leave, she squatted and watched the plane carefully. Then she shuffled one hand in the pocket of her *mu'umu'u*. She carefully pulled something from its depth and looked around quickly to make sure that no one was watching. Slowly, she put a cigarette to her lips.

She didn't smoke much, and what she did smoke was often the remains of what Howard Kaleohano carelessly left behind when he talked in the yard with Ben. She had only been curious at first, but then found she actually liked it—the way the tobacco calmed her even as it sharpened her focus, the ritual of taking the butt from her mouth and blowing into the air. Once or twice she smoked with Mabel, who sometimes confiscated a cigarette from her husband when she was angry, and the two of them shared it over gossip and shell sorting. Mabel was no good at smoking, though. She coughed violently upon inhalation, and usually just let it burn down between her fingers. Now Ella squinted at the plane through her smoke, watching that red circle. When the butt was too small to hold any longer, she kicked sand over it and stood up. She glanced once at the mynah bird, which had not moved.

-Keep watch, little friend, she said, and walked toward the plane.

Later that afternoon Ella ran into Mabel and Hanaiki Niau's wife, Hannah, on the way to the Main House and the store that Irene Harada ran there. Hannah was the schoolteacher, known for keeping a pencil in her pocket at all times, as if writing things down was a common practice on the island. When she saw that Ella was pale and breathless, she asked what was wrong. Ella waved her hands and said nothing.

Mr. Robinson had not wanted a store on the island. The Niihauans have all they need, he insisted. But Irene was quietly, vehemently persistent; the women waited too long for thread and there had been talk about canned goods after one had found its way from another island a few years before, unbeknownst to the Old Lord.

-Possessions take us further from Him, Robinson had huffed.

-And Makeweli Ranch? Irene asked innocently. None of the people there have access to such things?

Mr. Robinson had turned beet red then, caught in his own hypocrisy. Of course they had such things: his workers had access to the Piggly Wiggly and sometimes the airfield canteen. Even he shopped at the Piggly Wiggly, though he disliked doing so. But it was convenient. Finally, he'd grudgingly relented.

The store had been an immediate success. One shelf was lined neatly with cans of green beans. The second contained short, squat containers of condensed milk. On the floor was a barrel of flour and another of rice. Sometimes Irene even managed to get candy. The hard, round sweets fared the best, but even these suffered in the Niihauan heat; they stuck together so that you had to hit the tin a few times against a wall to separate the pieces. But no one seemed to mind this extra effort. Long after the candies were gone, the pretty tins remained, full of sewing thread and needles or in one case baby teeth, perched on the corner shelves in some of the Puuwai houses. They were dented at the edges but still shiny, as if the women often took them down to look at them.

Shoppers were eager to show Irene that they were grateful for all the supplies she got for them. An item would go down the line of curious hands like a new baby and inevitably end up on the far side of the store from where it had been originally placed, cock-eyed, on a different shelf. Irene would pick up the object carefully, and with a grim set to her mouth, return it to its rightful place, which the Hawaiian women thought might mean that she wanted them to examine it again, which they then did. It was Ella who had figured out that they were actually annoying the young woman, and though now they kept a respectful distance, Irene was never the friendliest person. Still, the women wanted her to feel at home and often burst into the store laughing and greeting her loudly, whereupon she seemed to shrink into a far corner, nod her head, and smile faintly.

Today the beans had been pushed together to make room for Christmas ornaments—winged angels, large tin stars, red balls. The three women entered, the red dust shimmering in the air and then falling behind them.

-*Aloha*, they greeted her. *Hele mai ai.*

One by one they blinked at the shiny glint on the upper shelf.

-Ooh, cooed Mabel. She squinted and leaned forward to get a better fix on the source of the brightness.

-So pretty, said Hannah.

-Christmas nonsense, said Ella gruffly, pleased. There had never been such a display before, the store's hot wooden room now alight with color. Irene smiled shyly at her neighbors' pleasure.

-Two cents for each ball, she said. The stars are three cents.

-You've outdone yourself, Mrs. Harada, Ella said. And the boatman didn't break any?

-A few. But I told him they were eggs, so he was extra careful, though I think he thought I was crazy.

The women laughed. There were chickens for every family here on Niihau; eggs were the last thing they would ever ship in.

Later, after each woman had held a few of the ornaments in her hand, Mabel spoke:

-Look, she said.

She shuffled around in the bosom of her *mu'umu'u* and then withdrew, with squinting concentration, a shiny, silver bauble. It could have been one of the Christmas ornaments for all its gleam, except that it was as small as a cowry shell. She held it pinched between two of her large fingers, as if it were the neck of some temporarily subdued but dangerous creature, and the other women leaned in close to see.

-What is it? asked Ella. She reached with her fingers as if to touch it, but lost her nerve and left them lingering in the air near Mabel's elbow.

-Comes from the plane.

Every woman suddenly reared back, as if the small, metal animal had lunged.

-Plane? Hannah clucked and frowned. Nervously she withdrew the pencil from her pocket and began to lace it through her fingers.

-It came from the . . . place with the chair. Where all the *maka* were. Mr. Kaleohano brought it home for me. Looks like *onohi*. Eyes. Like *haoles*', round and made of silver. Must be the way the plane sees its way across the sky.

-No, said Irene. That's an *instrument panel*. She said the last two words in English, not knowing the Hawaiian translation. The *kaula waha*. Reins of a horse. The driver pushes and pulls the buttons to get across the sky.

She didn't know how she knew *instrument panel*. Living on Kauai, she supposed that military jargon had seeped into her vocabulary. Also, she had seen the dashboard of a car, which had buttons that looked similar.

-You should put it back. Bad luck, said Ella slowly.

-Bad luck? It landed on our island, so it's a gift, insisted Mabel.

Hannah looked back and forth between the two women. Since she was the schoolteacher on the island, she was used to arguments among the children, and she began to prepare to intercede. She knew that Ella was easily irritated and that though the two women liked each other, they scrapped like siblings. She pursed her lips and raised her pencil.

-A *mea ka ʻaine ʻe* boat dumped a casket of bad water into an island harbor one hundred years ago and with it came the mosquito. Just because it arrives doesn't mean that it's a gift, Mrs. Kaleohano. But, Mrs. Kanahele, surely it doesn't hurt for her to get a small souvenir.

Ella puffed up her chest and put her hands on her hips. Her chin stuck out and her eyes narrowed. The women leaned back slightly.

-That plane has disturbed the spirits, she said loudly. See how it lies like a big hammerhead on the sand? I had a vision when I returned to it this morning and approached the wings.

-You approached the wings?

Ella blushed.

-Yes. And I had a vision, she continued, but with less vigor. That plane is evil.

Mabel nodded, but her mouth was set in an angry line. She looked away to the Christmas ornaments.

-Throw it in the sea, advised Ella.

-For the spirits, Mrs. Kanahele? said Mabel. That's ancient nonsense. I wouldn't want Mr. Robinson to hear you talking like that, it's downright heathen. Well, I'll talk to my husband. He walks to that plane a lot. So it's his to make right, to your shark goddess or to your plane.

Ella flinched and forced herself to remain quiet. If it was not a vision from the spirits that she'd had that afternoon, surely it was a very bad case of the willies. It had started when the mynah bird would not leave, its dark, raggedy shadow jerking in her peripheral vision. Nevertheless, Ella had climbed carefully on the plane's wing and peered into the cockpit. She had touched the leather seats, but they were too hot to explore for long, so she pulled free a long, canvas strap with a metal ring on the end. The ring was dull with red dust, but a few swipes against her dress began to bring out its old gleam. By now the skin on her spine had tightened and begun to prickle. She ignored it. She rubbed the ring a little more but a few dark places remained. Stubbornly, she continued to rub it, determined to restore the ring to its original luster. Still the dark stain persisted. Finally, she spat on it. The cloth of her dress went dark red, and she realized what she was cleaning off—blood. She dropped the ring onto the seat, her heart pounding. Then she caught sight of the machine gun's spidery legs. It was too much, seeing that. Ella thought of herself as a peaceable woman, a Christian, averse to violence in any form. She lowered herself from the wing quickly and took a few steps back, staring at the plane. Suddenly it was clear to her—the way her skin jumped, the way her stomach dropped—that the spirits were profoundly disturbed here. She had fled as fast as her fallen arches allowed her to.

Now, in the small ranch store, Ella knew that Mabel would not put her bauble back. They all understood its power, how everyone had quickly looked away from the bright red Christmas ornament to the shiny glow in her hand. Ella imagined that Mabel had polished it carefully and had soon been able to see, when she peered in close, a small, distorted reflection of herself in its face. The blue sky became a line of azure, the white of her house behind her a halo around her head. It took in the world, like a divine hole that only special people stepped into. No, Mabel would keep this on her shelf in the firm belief that it would protect her and her family against bad luck and the jealous stares of her neighbors.

-Anyway, said Hannah, happy to divert the conversation from the plane, which seemed to arouse high emotions in her neighbors and even, she disliked admitting, in herself. My husband has gone to signal tonight. To Mr. Robinson. Everyone's so nervous that he's late like this.

-What? Irene took a step back, alarmed.

-Oh, Mrs. Harada, it's nothing to be afraid of. It's just so strange that he hasn't come, or sent the boatman with a message. So we signal to the Old Lord's Kauai ranch from the mountain. Emergency lights.

Irene's hand flew to her mouth.

-Something wrong, Mrs. Harada? asked Mabel. The Old Lord should know he's needed here. The last time we used them was when the sickness came. He was here by the next day.

-It's just that . . . She blinked rapidly and hesitated.

-Yes, Mrs. Harada? Hannah looked at her as if worried she might faint.

- I just, you see, didn't think it had come to this, lighting emergency signals. She laughed in a stuttered, high-pitched way. Isn't that a bit much, for a mere boy who had the misfortune to crash his plane?

You're signaling the Japanese, she wanted to say. Shake each by the shoulder, and tell them the truth. Cry out for their help and forgiveness, at once.

-But, Mrs. Harada, we'd like to get the visitor off the island, said Mabel. He's not supposed to be here, you know. But we want Mr. Robinson to handle it.

-Of course, said Irene. *No,* she thought. *NO.*

The four women looked away from one another. Hannah coughed once, Mabel noisily pushed the bright ornament from the plane back into her *mu'umu'u.*

-I'm a good Christian, and don't you think otherwise, Ella finally barked. She sniffed and held her head up. Only that plane would make me think of spirits. The good Lord's telling us something, that we should get rid of it as soon as we can, so that this island can go back to normal again. Mr. Kanahele hasn't been able to look after the cattle all afternoon because of this pilot. And, Mabel, I know your husband has been at the boat dock for three days now. The sooner Mr. Robinson comes, the better. Now, it's cooling down out there, so let's take the cart back. Thank you, Mrs. Harada.

Ella nodded at Irene and gathered her ornaments carefully. The other two women followed her out. Once on the pathway, Ella, feeling sheepish about her bad temper, turned to wave to Irene, but she was not in sight. There were only her ornaments, glinting, colorful, in unnoticed disarray on the counter.

19

On the late afternoon of Wednesday, December 10, Howard had consented to the emergency signal. He had also agreed, reluctantly, to return to the village for a large meal and a restful sleep. And when Yoshio told him that it would be best if the pilot stayed with his family and out of everyone else's way, Howard agreed to that too.

Nishikaichi entered the Haradas' small, neat house and sat down on the simple handmade chair Yoshio nervously offered him.

The Keo twins shuffled in the doorway. They were typical of Niihauan youth, solid boys with hair yellowed by the sun and faces dirtied by the dust. The twin on the left (Yoshio could not tell them apart) held the round *kakalaioa* seeds in one hand. Later, he would hear the murmurs of the *kini kini* marble game in progress near the store's shed. Now he handed them long, twisted strips of salted pork, which they accepted with diffident smiles, stuffing them into their denim pockets to eat on the ground near the horses where, as guards, they had been told by Mr. Kaleohano to sleep.

Yoshio sat down next to the pilot. They said nothing, just stared at their hands as Irene prepared their dinner.

Irene put plates of *poi* and salted pork in front of them. On another plate lay pieces of fruit.

-Eat, she said to the pilot softly, gesturing with the back of her hand in a scooting motion. She described the food carefully, practicing the language of her parents with each noun. Then she looked at him expectantly. He nodded.

-*Arigato*. You remember your native tongue well.

She bowed.

-No. Only a little.

Yoshio noticed that she blushed as she turned back to the food. He felt something in him suddenly thicken. Was he jealous? The pilot did look dashing, despite the fact that his skin was now burned a reddish brown and his hair stood churlishly on end, stiff with dust and salt. He was handsome, yes, but it was more than that. The uniform, for one. Even though it was blotted with dust and sweat, it was an impressive piece of clothing: hemmed and pocketed and riveted and seamed for every eventuality. He wanted to tear it suddenly from the pilot and put it on himself, as he had done with the hat. Instead, he anxiously wound his fingers together and watched his wife hover nearby. What should he say to the pilot? Was bargaining really the right thing to do? Once or twice he saw his wife glance at him, or perhaps at the pilot, he couldn't tell.

Irene gestured and walked to the front door.

-Come with me for a moment, Yoshio.

He hesitated and then followed her outside.

-They've lit a signal, she whispered, though they spoke in English, which neither the pilot nor the Keo boys understood.

I know, he said. It's all right. If he's still alive, he'll come. If not, we're no worse off than before.

-But the Japanese! They will see the light and come to investigate! If they're on Kauai like we think, they'll be the ones the villagers are signaling to, not Mr. Robinson. Yoshio, can't you see? We have so little time.

-Well, then, we must tell our neighbors why he's here. It's no good trying to do all this ourselves.

-Are you crazy? We'll be blamed for everything! They'll wonder why we didn't speak up earlier!

-Shh. Please. Look, we'll tell them that the pilot didn't say.

-And you think they'll believe us? Yoshio, I was at the store today and do you know what I smelled?

-I don't—

-I smelled tobacco. It was as clear as if someone had blown it in my face. Well, not immediately. At first it was just like any other day, the women coming in and they loved my ornaments and that was so nice and I almost felt like telling them all about this, bringing them to our side, getting their help. It was hard to order those decorations without Mr. Robinson knowing, but I felt the women deserved them, that I could do this for the island. And they appreciated it and for a moment there was—well, I was happy. But then this smell. Sour. At first I thought it was that old bitterness of mine—here she laughed—leaking out into the air, but then I realized that it came from one of the women. It was in her hair. It was tobacco, Yoshio. Ella Kanahele smokes cigarettes!

-It doesn't matter, said Yoshio. I mean, it's just tobacco. Howard smokes like an *imu*. All day, all night. I know women don't usually, but . . . He shrugged.

-You don't understand, Yoshio. Would you ever have thought she smoked? An old lady like that? Of course not. And what else don't we know? Perhaps the islanders don't like us as you think. Perhaps the second they hear that Pearl Harbor has been bombed by the Japanese, they'll blame us too, and then where will we be? Unable to save ourselves, and then the Japanese come and we don't belong to them either. We're shot with the rest of the villagers and the pilot goes free.

Yoshio turned away.

-All this because of a cigarette? He tried to keep his voice low, so that he found he was hissing. We've been here two years and when can you think of a single instance where we've been openly wronged? You're being hysterical, *kachan,* I mean it.

-Am I? Or am I the only one here who can make a decision?

With that she walked back into the house, past the pilot and into the back room where Taeko napped.

Yoshio sat back down at the kitchen table and tried to appear unflustered. Perhaps his wife was right. It was time to make a decision.

-I should wash your flight suit, he said. The pilot looked up from his food.

-It smells? the pilot asked. It was half a question and half an apology.

-After a while, everything here smells.

-They didn't tell us about this heat.

-I will bring you some of my clothes. They'll be big, but all right.

-I don't think so.

-If you're asking us to trust you, you should at least trust us.

-It's not that. It's— He pushed his plate to one side. Okay then, he said.

Yoshio told Irene to fetch clean clothes, and though she refused to meet his eyes, she did not hesitate to return to their room to rummage among his things as he'd asked. He ignored his need to apologize or touch her shoulder, and instead decided that he would walk to the apiary while the young pilot dressed. There was no pressing need to visit the bees; nectar gathering was over, honey no longer available. The hive was hunkered down for the winter. But

Yoshio still liked to hover nearby, doing nothing much really, but feeling his inchoate part in the whole. After a while, feeling calmer, he returned to the house the long way, walking past the pasture with the six Arabian horses Mr. Robinson so loved and entrusted to his care, past the honey shed. When he got to the house, he peered into the window.

Nishikaichi looked younger than ever, the too-big shirt and the pants, though cinched with a belt, perched just above his flat buttocks. He stood on the far side of the room. Yoshio watched as he raised his hands in front of his face and held them there, palms inward. Then he lifted them and began to pat his hair flat. This last gesture was so awkward, so boyish, that Yoshio turned away as if he had mistakenly interrupted him at an intimate moment of pure nakedness. When he looked back in again, the pilot was at the table, sitting quietly, his hands in his lap. He thought for a moment that this was a ruse; surely the pilot would prowl around the house in these spare moments, picking up small carvings, opening the few drawers. Yoshio watched him for a few more moments, feeling powerful and ashamed simultaneously, then walked quickly to the porch. There, to his surprise, was Irene, Taeko asleep in her arms.

Yoshio didn't want to startle his wife; she looked so relaxed, leaning against the balustrade, perhaps asleep. Now her eyes fluttered open. For a second she looked almost beatific, then he saw a wisp of disappointment slide across her features. He couldn't say why he knew this, exactly what her eyes or mouth did to signal this, but his own heart sank. The next thing he said came out of his mouth in a whispered rush, as if he could blow the look off her face with the wind of his words.

-We'll help, *kachan.* It's the right thing to do for everyone. It's the only way to keep peace on the island. He's just a boy, but there are his fellow soldiers to think about. We'll destroy his papers and plane and figure it out from there.

And her features transformed then, and he saw her dark eyes widen and her small triangular face lift and open with relief and joy and something unknowable. He felt better then, better than he had in a long time, and when he walked back into the house he buried his dread with a quick nod of his head.

-Nishikaichi-san, he said. We must talk now.

20

The Burns Airfield sentry burst into the wooden barracks where First Lieutenant Jack Mizuha stabbed at a typewriter. It was an old typewriter and a bad one; the *k* didn't work well, an especially unfortunate happenstance for an air base in Hawaii, where the names of so many streets and towns started with that letter. The young private saluted hurriedly, then dropped a bundle of papers on Mizuha's desk. He left quickly, swinging his arms like an overwound top. Everyone on Kauai was in motion—digging trenches, marching around bridges, waving in the newest cargo planes sent from the mainland. Still, no reason to behave sloppily, thought Mizuha. He was in a nervous mood himself. He blamed the typewriter, with its ornery keys.

The office was crowded with two desks, two chairs, and a surplus of file cabinets pushed together so that they only opened when their neighbors were nudged away. There was a conspicuous lack of shiny medallions or framed diplomas on the walls, though someone had hastily tacked a poster of a large-breasted white woman half dressed in sailor wear, which upon closer inspection of the edges had been torn recently from another location, most likely from the wall of a drinking establishment. But the disarray was hard to see in the dim light; windows were taped tightly according to the strict blackout rules even though it was daytime, so that Mizuha squinted over a small, weak lamp that made the dust motes in the air shine but little else. Mizuha's other office, the spacious one that until only recently had contained pictures of the Mizuha family smiling from a bright green background courtesy of Waimea's Family Photography Shop, with framed diplomas and pictures of airplanes on the walls, and his habitually neat stack of papers on the left side of his desk, was now occupied by a white man who had only a few days ago been of lower rank. Mizuha, an American citizen, had been the commander at Burns Airfield. But he was of Japanese descent, which meant his demotion had been swift and efficient. He was now an executive officer in a makeshift office.

He'd never met Aylmer Robinson, but everyone on Kauai knew Makeweli. It was the biggest ranch on the island. He'd heard Robinson was an eccentric man, devout, a loner, unmarried, perhaps even celibate. Despite the interesting fact that there were distress signals coming from Robinson's island of Niihau, Mizuha stopped reading the report the sentry had unceremoniously dumped on his desk before he was even halfway down the page. There was no point in continuing; boats were not allowed on the water, and that was that. It was understandable that Mr. Robinson was concerned, but he would have to wait. As powerful as he was, the military was now more powerful.

Robinson did not know what to make of the flashes of light he saw from across the channel. He cursed himself for not using pigeons to communicate, as his brother Lester had suggested a few years before. Things could happen, Lester had insisted, but Aylmer couldn't imagine what. Besides, Lester was not interested in Niihau; it was an affront to his acute business sense. Ranching that arid island lost money, lots of it. So he preferred to let Aylmer run its day-to-day affairs, though he was peculiarly insistent on this matter of carrier pigeons. Aylmer had scoffed. Niihauans had been living without that kind of speedy communication for centuries. He'd refused his brother, pointing out that one just never knew what disease the birds would bring on their feet and feathers. When Lester had looked unconvinced—many birds traveled to Niihau from other places, he argued—Aylmer had pressed; there was something spooky about messages dispatched by winged creatures—it brought to mind the devil's hand. Furthermore, he added, it would just lead to frivolous contact with the outside world, messages to family members or friends on other islands. Besides, the Niihauans were mostly illiterate. Their schooling on the island didn't go past fourth grade, if that. Education, in Aylmer's mind, was for certain people, with certain temperaments. He was a Harvard man himself, and he knew that knowledge brought a responsibility for which some people did not have the constitution. This was not prejudice, just good sense. On Niihau, being undereducated meant that the people remained incurious about the world, and so protected from it, in Aylmer's view. He was plain about this, and told everyone who asked with a defiant lift of his narrow chin, and even a quote from the Bible, whatever applied, a shepherd and sheep allegory, or something about the meek ultimately inheriting the earth. But he was not so eager to discuss the other obvious benefit, that a flimsy education ensured a ready workforce: by the age of sixteen, the boys were suited only to be ranch hands, the girls suited only to marry them, making shell leis and keeping a good Christian house along the way. No, there was no need for reading and writing. He sometimes rued his own education, which had foisted such responsibilities on him. He *knew* the evils of the world. No one protected him from its temptations.

Now he walked from the air base, past men in stiffly pressed uniforms with blank expressions and unnatural postures, and the incessant noise of planes landing and taking off, with a sinking feeling in his stomach. The brothers had ultimately compromised, deciding on a signal system using lanterns and reflectors. But now there was no way to know what the problem was. The Niihauans would learn to write a little more, he vowed, and they'd go to the carrier pigeon idea, once things had returned to normal.

Back at the Makeweli Ranch, he sent for his dinner. It was early yet, but he would go to the beach once the sun had set. He wanted to see the lights again. Perhaps if he stared long enough, he could discern their meaning. He sat at his wooden kitchen table—there was a grand dining room, but that was used only for entertaining, which, as he hit his fifties, was something he liked less and less—and stared out the picture windows. The sinking sensation in his stomach had not been hunger, he realized, but fear.

He cut his meat slowly and ate without relish. Again he glanced outside. The clouds rosied at the edges. They lost their billowed look, fanning out as the afternoon wind and heat lessened. He asked his manservant, a small, quiet Hawaiian who liked, inexplicably, to salute, to fetch Mr. Shanagan.

A rock wall surrounded the back area of the house and what had once been Great-grandmother Sinclair's beloved garden. It had been carefully planted with her own hand but was now, Robinson noted, tended by strangers. There was a fountain she would not recognize and flowers imported from the mainland whose names she could not have pronounced. And it wasn't just the garden; the idea of two Great Wars only thirty years apart would have stymied her. She'd befriended the Maoris in New Zealand and the Hawaiians here; she would see no reason why the great governments couldn't get along as the Lord commanded.

From the direction of his brother's home, a large but plain ranch house fifty yards to the left, Aylmer thought he heard the hesitant plunk of a piano. He wondered if one of his nephews was at it again, and whether the abrupt sound, not unlike the barks of an embattled dog, had startled the finches that now sprang from the rim of the fountain and flew off. It was the same piano his great-grandmother, in that curious mix of irrational stubbornness and brilliant foresight so peculiar to his family, had brought over on the long sea voyage from New Zealand. Then Mr. Shanagan appeared at the gate. Aylmer watched him as he stopped to press down his shirt with his hands and began to lope toward the house.

He entered the room in his dark socks, his boots removed in the tradition of the islands. He doffed his wide-brimmed hat and squinted at Aylmer.

-Can I do fer ya, Mr. Robinson? He rubbed his sunburned chin. There was a low whirring sound as his hand wended back and forth on the uneven whiskers.

-Tell the boatman we'll be heading to Niihau soon.

-They're letting boats by, eh?

-Soon enough, he said.

-You know, when I came here from Ireland, Mr. Robinson—and here he lowered his voice to a whisper—I'd never seen so many Orientals. It was like they multiplied like fleas. Seemed like it wasn't a good idea, so many of them here.

-The mysterious ways in which God works, we can't always understand, Robinson said, and he went back to staring out the window, so Shanagan thought he might be talking about the sunset, which was spraying the sky with pink and orange.

-'Tis a godly sky, he offered hesitantly.

Robinson frowned and waved his fork in his direction.

-The issei work hard and know their place. They don't talk

back, they don't argue. And they're not greedy, they don't need a large wage. See, the good Lord's shut out of the places they come from. It's His way of sending the unlucky to a good Christian land, to learn His ways. Everyone deserves a chance at a Christian life, Mr. Shanagan.

-'Tis true, sir. He's the way to heaven and everyone gets a chance, I'll agree with you there. Even Pearl Harbor, which's a living hell, if you'll excuse me using the word, has a meaning somewhere, though I tell you, I can't figure it out right now.

-It all comes down to faith, Mr. Shanagan. Don't ask for answers. Just have faith. He pushed back from the table and nodded at the sky, which was streaked with the last rays of the sun. Saddle me a horse. I'll be riding to the point now.

The signal continued for a long time. Sometimes it was just a steady light, sometimes it seemed to flicker on and off. Sometimes it appeared to wander slightly across the darkness, as if someone had hoisted up the lantern and rode it across Mount Paniau's wide summit. On another day, to anyone else, this kind of signal would have been insignificant. But any light from Niihau, which had none of the modern conveniences, was a dire message in itself. Horse and rider stood still on the dark beach, watching. In front of them crisscrossed the hastily laid barbed-wire fence that, as Robinson approached, looked like a long, jagged bush of thorns. He hadn't expected it to change the look of the once beautiful beach quite so much.

Should he have warned the Niihauans about the war? Just two months ago he had asked the men to furrow the open, fallow fields, on orders from the government. But he had not explained that everyone on the islands was doing it in order to discourage enemy planes from landing in the event that American relations with

Japan broke down beyond repair. He had told them it was a new method of windbreak, and they had, of course, believed him. Should he have instead come clean, explained to them that the island air bases had taken to lining up their planes wingtip to wingtip and out in the open, to discourage the Japanese-American saboteurs they were sure would attack first? This prejudice had ironically ensured the squadron's almost complete and utter destruction when the Imperial Navy had attacked instead, from the air. Or should he have long ago explained to the Niihauans that people were anxiously following news from Europe, where the world was slowly falling to a rapacious German leader? That thousands were dying, and that there seemed to be no way to stop it?

Robinson's horse snorted restlessly and pawed at the ground. Robinson patted his flinching withers, keeping his eyes on the light, as if by staring hard enough he could divine what it meant. No, he said to himself. It was right that he had said nothing. Niihau was now the last place on earth that did not understand the turmoil the world was in, and that in itself was a blessing from God. Everyone needed a paradise, a respite from the terrors of the world. Niihau was his homage to a more perfect place, one where the good Lord Himself would find relief when He finally came down to earth again. There had been no need to tell the Niihauans about the outside world; he himself wished he did not have to know. This signal was just a panicky response to his tardiness. Or perhaps someone had fallen off a horse and needed a hospital. It was something that could wait, he reassured himself.

He patted his horse again, and exhaled slowly. They were out past curfew, and though he doubted it mattered much, it wouldn't do to alert a jumpy soldier. He listened. The wind crackled through the palm leaves. The surf, unreachable beyond the barbed wire, maintained a quiet, rhythmic mutter against the sand. He tried to read the hands of his pocket watch and, when he couldn't, guessed by the movement of the stars that he had been watching those desperate lights for almost an hour. He used to ride at night often, just happy to be in the saddle and away from people, enveloped in the warm evening breezes and darkness, protected. But that was in his youth—these past few decades he was usually in bed by now, reading, or even asleep. How swiftly life passed. If he had looked forward from one of those nights on his horse, back when he was fresh out of Harvard and new to the world, he would never have imagined himself here, on the same Kauai beach, head of his family's business. At the time he had actually believed that life opened like a flower, from a narrow stem outward, that he was bound for far-off places and exotic people. He had wanted to be a missionary in the strictest sense of the word, sent on a ship to spread His word to the most heathen of places, the bowels of Africa or the searing plains of Persia. Instead life was like a funnel, where moments thrown in the mouth converged into a tight, predictable trajectory. His father had let him think that upon his graduation, the world was his, but in effect had always known he would be back to run the business. Sons followed the word of their fathers, he'd said, knowing that the metaphor with God would hit home. And so Aylmer had returned. It was only the first years that were hard, when the imprint of the world (or more likely, since Aylmer had not traveled beyond Cambridge, Massachusetts, its promise) lingered like a sharp, metallic aftertaste. And then, like all aftertastes, it had gone and things had become easier.

He sat for a while longer. His horse stamped nervously now and then but quieted under the pressure of his hand. The warm breeze and the rhythm of the incoming surf lulled him and he almost forgot, in the beauty of the night, that the world was at war. The flashes had become part of the night sky, a bright, undulating star on the horizon, beckoning, Robinson thought, much like the guiding light of Jesus' birth.

He dismounted as quietly as he knew how. His horse nuzzled the dune grass, disinterested. The sand was deep and Robinson broke into a sweat quickly, though it wasn't a far walk. The Japs would have a time getting up this beach, he thought with satisfaction. At the barbed wire he stopped. It looked flimsy, thin ligaments stretching from post to post. He reached out to push on it carefully, twanging the wire like a ukulele. It had little flex. He felt a surge of pride; his men, and the others of course, had dug deep. Still, barbed wire was for cattle, not men with guns and savvy. He reached out and pressed down on one of the barbs, harder than he meant to, and pulled away as the edge punctured his skin. He thought with surprise how it hurt and put the finger in his mouth, the blood sharp on his tongue. Perhaps it'll slow them down at least. Give us all a few minutes to grab a gun and defend ourselves.

Finally he heard voices skittering on the wind. He couldn't see from whom or whence they came, so he crouched to be safe, and on his hands and knees, a little embarrassed by the indignity of crawling at his age, he scuttled back to where he had come. He led his horse to the trees. He stood there a long time before he made out two hunched figures and the small orange flare of their cigarettes along the shoreline. He heard the boastful staccato of young men but could not make out their words. Japanese? Finally he heard one speak.

So then this horse's ass of a guy stands on his bar stool, and takes off his shirt to show us. There was a snorting laugh. *Says he got it from Italy, the Battle of fucking Ravioli or something.* Another laugh, and the words faded again. Robinson mounted and rode back to Makeweli. It was Wednesday night, December 10. He was already three days overdue on Niihau.

21

Before dawn on Thursday, December 11, Ella rose from her bed and lit a lantern. She pushed her graying hair back and made a small fire. This morning she and Ben did not talk much; they prayed together and she made sure that food was on the table for him to eat. Then she left for the beach.

Niihau had once been famous for its *makaloa* mats, woven from a unique sedge grass that was soft and colorful. But the sedge could not survive the grazing sheep that Robinson's family brought in, and by the end of the 1800s, it was gone. Now Niihau was known for its beautiful shells, which winter surf scooped up in large amounts and threw unbroken and still brilliant with color on the Niihau shores. Some mornings the sand was brittle with its new gifts, other mornings there were fewer to choose from. Still, Niihau was blessed with a certain current and a particular seafloor, so that no other island in Hawaii experienced such a surfeit of intact and glowing *pupus*. They were collected before dawn by the women and children, who raced by lantern light to beat the rising sun. They scuttled like crabs along the sand, and when the bleaching rays finally reached over the horizon, wrapped their cache up and started for home. A few villagers stayed longer, greedy for as many shells as possible, knowing that when it came time to string them, more than half would not survive the process. But Ella never stayed. She only wanted to string those with the brightest of God's colors.

Ella ran into Irene just as the path met the beach. There was an awkward silence. The small storekeeper shifted the child on her back and looked down.

-I don't usually see you here, Mrs. Harada, Ella said. She was glad for a chance to prove that she didn't really believe in spirits, as she'd said at the store. Plus, she liked Irene. Though she wasn't a friendly woman, Ella sensed that she was good, like a piece of wood was good. Hard, practical, adaptable within reason.

-I couldn't really sleep. The heat, you know. I don't know if I'll ever get used to it.

-Yes, well, said Ella. You've come at the right time anyway; I ran into Mrs. Niau and she says there's a new crop of shells on the beach. *Uliuli* and *kahakaha,* lots of them.

Irene nodded and smiled politely, but clearly she did not understand the significance. These were rare shells that never came in the winter months. Ella was excited, and wanted to say so, though she didn't know whether this mysterious event was a good or a bad sign. Instead she put out her hand and touched Irene's wrist.

-Would you like to accompany me, Mrs. Harada?

Irene nodded, and for a moment Ella thought her eyes widened with some sudden emotion and then blinked. But it was too dark to tell for sure, and the lantern tended to distort things. Ella stepped carefully down the path, with Irene behind her.

Many women were already there and it was true, the beach was coated with a thick layer of brilliant new shells. Ella put her lantern close to the ground and leaned over and even she could not suppress a small cry. The sand was a kaleidoscope beneath them—full of *momiokai* and *laiki,* but also the blue and gold winking of the *uliuli* and *kahakaha,* usually found only in the beginning of the summer, and then even rarely, and now miraculously here, in the early winter months. Ella stooped and put a hand on the sand. She held a shell to the watery kerosene light and stared. Its blue was so bright that she was sure it lit her face the color of the sky. It would wake Irene's child with its glare. After a moment more, she dropped the shell into her basket. She suddenly felt scared. This abundance under her feet felt as magical and impossible as the plane that had fallen from the sky. What else would arrive on this tiny island?

Ella looked up to find Irene staring at her.

-Very beautiful, she said gruffly. God's with us these days, child.

Then Ella lowered herself slowly to her stomach and began to sweep her hands across the nap of colors. Niihauan shell picking was done best like this, flat on the belly, chin to the sand, so nothing was missed and little was damaged. But next to her Irene tucked her knees under her, Japanese style, and darted at the ground with her fingers like a beak. Ella wanted to tell her how much easier it was the Niihauan way, but knew that Irene might take offense. Ella suspected the shopkeeper often went home with the tips of her fingers scratched and a cramp in her back.

-You must come and string all these beauties with us, Mrs. Harada. Ella did not stop picking shells, but from her prone position glanced over at Irene, who seemed to have frozen.

-When the time comes, I mean. There's nothing that gets me in a worse mood than hours of all this necklace nonsense and no one but Mabel Kaleohano to talk with. You didn't come at all last year. We thought maybe you'd forgotten how to drive the cart.

-Oh, well, Irene said, and shifted on her haunches. With the store, it's—there's just so little time.

-There's always time for enjoying life. Our Creator wants us to. You'll begin to understand, the longer you're here.

-Well, thank you. I'll, yes, I'll try to come.

As both women knew, this morning's shell picking was only the beginning of the lei process. The *pupus* had to be sorted into used bean cans and old honey jars by type, color, and size. When the time came to string them—usually in midsummer, when fewer and fewer shells were found on the beaches—each shell was held up for inspection. They were tiny, no more than two rice grains across, and Ella's fingers always hurt with the effort of pinching them just right as she scanned for imperfections. Sand was then carefully removed with a needle and short, sharp exhalations of her own hot breath. Any irregular tips were shaved smooth. Finally, a stringing hole was made by poking the *pupu* just right with a sharp-pointed iron cowl—this was when the shell most often broke. It would disintegrate against the whorls of her fingers with a tiny clap of calciferous thunder. Her heart would jump with disappointment. But then she would flick the shards to one side and start again with another shell, her eyes folded into a squint, mouth sighing. After hundreds of shells had been peered at and poked, it was time to prepare for their stringing. She would put a tiny dab of beeswax on the tip of green fishing-net string and roll it under her fingers until it came to a fine, hard point. The readied shells were threaded—more squinting, more finger aches—so that they fell against each other in a particular pattern, depending on the necklace. Finally the lei was finished with a beetle-sized cowry shell at one end. Into this the other end of the green thread was pushed. It held because a warm, pliable wad of beeswax was remolded onto the tip and, once pushed into the cowry shell, it hardened into a permanent fastener. It was important not to disturb the lei as the beeswax dried, but sometimes Ella picked up one end, just to feel the silky swoop of all those small shells, and hear their distant companionable chatter.

* * *

Now, pink tendrils floated across the sky. Hurry, hurry, before the sun comes up. The beach crackled under swift, probing hands. Ella heard Mabel Kaleohano chide her son. A few yards away, seagulls fought over a fish.

-Do you feel something? In the air, I mean. Something . . . cold, Irene suddenly said. Ella could see her halved by the lantern, her features sharpened into shadows. Something like your spirits, she said. She stared intently at Ella.

-There are no spirits here, dear. Ella lowered her voice conspiratorially. It's just God.

Irene nodded and sat back on her heels, staring at the ocean. Ella looked to see if something had risen from the waves, but there was nothing.

-Mr. Robinson would insist that Mr. Jesus Christ himself get permission before coming here, Irene said slowly. We're so shut off from the world, it's like we're floating up in the sky, like the moon. The end of the world would happen and we'd never know it.

-Mr. Robinson would tell us, Ella said.

Irene looked at her.

-Where is he now, then?

Ella hesitated. Where was he? People were getting worried. The weather was fine, yet even the boatman did not appear with news.

-Mrs. Harada, she said, shaking off her own unease. It's a beautiful morning for shells and Mr. Robinson will come when he can. God watches over us here on Niihau, there's nothing to worry about.

They were quiet for a while. Taeko snuffled now and then, and to keep her sleeping Ella began to sing "Onward Christian Soldiers." When the song was over, she stopped picking up shells and turned her head to Irene.

-Queen Liliuokalani came here once, she said. She came to this beach, to see the shells. I was young, only ten years old, but I remember that she found the most beautiful *onikiniki*. She wouldn't keep it, though, saying that it belonged to Niihau. Only a few years later, the *haole* deposed her. I don't know much about what goes on outside, but that's something I'll never forget. My father cried the day we heard. Even old Mr. Robinson was sad, though he never spoke much about it. And she was our last queen, Mrs. Harada. I don't even know who rules the islands now.

-It's President Roosevelt, said Irene.

-What?

-I said it's— Irene hesitated. Never mind. There's no need to know. Everything we need is here, on Niihau.

-I feel that way too, Ella said. Now hurry, the sun is almost up. Pack the shells you have, we'll walk home.

-Thank you, but I think I'll stay and walk the beach. But thank you, thank you. You've been—kind.

-Protect the shells, then, Ella said, waving her hand at her. Remember to come when it's time to start stringing. Make a lei with us old girls.

Irene turned away without saying anything, and Ella thought she saw her shoulders roll forward while her head dropped. She's a funny woman, she thought, and then picked up her basket and headed for the path.

22

On Thursday morning, December 11, Old Shintani shuffled to the large apiary at the edge of the village. The hives sat side by side, tall, hand-built casements over which a sturdy roof had been erected for shade. To the uninitiated there was no hint that each of the casements was home to sixty thousand bees that produced eighty tons of honey annually, a few tons of beeswax, and a little bit of royal jelly reserved for Mr. Robinson alone. They looked like upright armoires, perhaps from a bedroom on Oahu. But a sweet floral smell pervaded the air around them. Nearby were shallow water stands. If a newcomer, still puzzled about where he was, decided to peer into one of these stands he would finally see, perhaps jumping backward with a small cry, stout-bodied yellow-and-black-striped *Apis melliferas,* perched on carefully placed rocks, drinking.

Ishimatsu Shintani had been born in Japan and had come to Hawaii in 1900 in search of a better life. He was just one of his many countrymen encouraged by *haoles* to immigrate during that time. Cheap labor! Cheap labor! Cheap labor!—that was the urgent cry, essential to the Hawaiian economy of sugarcane and pineapple. Plantation owners realized early on that, at the rate the native Hawaiians were dying from *haole* disease, workers would have to be found elsewhere. Initially, men arrived from China in great numbers. But by 1886 their immigration was limited, for fear they would soon unite and demand better working conditions. Plantation owners turned to Japan to dilute the Chinese and bolster the workforce.

Eventually, this meant new problems and questions. Queen Liliuokalani, the native monarch, had been overthrown, and the businessmen who now ran the Republic of Hawaii wanted closer ties with the United States, their main trading partner. The most powerful of these businessmen wanted Hawaii to become a territory of the United States; it would mean reduced tariffs and expanded business opportunities. But the United States was wary of a country overrun with Orientals. Pointed discussions of what constituted a proper "American" ensued, with many *haoles* from both countries agreeing that they qualified, but that Asians most certainly did not.

Meanwhile Japan had begun to assert itself in the Pacific, and some saw the Hawaiian Islands as at a crossroads. With eerie prescience some pointed out that Hawaii, with its proximity to the East and its fine naval harbor, was an important bulwark against an increasingly aggressive Japan; detractors cried that Hawaii was a noncontiguous landmass, too hard to defend in time of war, and that annexation meant the start of unwieldy, unnecessary imperialism for the United States.

Ultimately, in 1898, Hawaii became a territory of the United States. Every person born on its soil would become an American citizen.

Shintani immigrated to the newly Americanized island of Oahu, but he soon went to Niihau, hired to tend Mr. Aubrey Robinson's burgeoning honey business there. Granted permission to stay, Shintani married Malia Lelela, who then had to give up her American citizenship because she had married a Japanese national. But the Shintanis were unfazed; Niihau was their country, and the confiscated American citizenship only a vague concept. In fact, Shintani had never minded the feudal system on Niihau, though when he had first come to Hawaii even he had been taken aback by the disparity between the plantation owner and the worker, which rivaled that of the local lord and the peasant in Japan. Once on Niihau, though, Mr. Aubrey Robinson had been a fair, straightforward man. His son Aylmer was just as fair and straightforward, if not as charismatic. Shintani was given the responsibility of running the honeybees on the island; there were 1,615 hives under his guidance. Now, nearing the end of his life, Shintani counted himself contented, almost happy. At least, he had before last Sunday. Now he woke every morning with a pounding heart. He'd lost his appetite. The bright lights of bombs being dropped on schoolhouses shimmered in his mind's eye. Dying men screamed and pointed accusing fingers at him. He was Japanese, and the terrible prejudice he'd encountered on his first days in Hawaii rushed back in a fury; he would be implicated in this catastrophe one way or another. He had understood immediately what the pilot had told him about Pearl Harbor, but had continued to tell no one, for fear he would be blamed. Not even his wife knew. This past week Shintani had gone to church every day at noon and kneeled in the dark. On shaking knees, he'd prayed to the Christian God he had embraced when he'd first arrived and the older Robinson had said that everybody, *everybody*, goes to church daily. So far He had been a good enough God, who turned what Shintani thought was a slightly deaf ear to his supplicants, and who had at first seemed a little abrasive, with his scourges of locusts and plagues, but whose heaven was much easier to attain than satori; this last point was, to a hardworking man like Shintani, at once soothing and suspect. But for the past few days, not even He had offered solace, or a sign that he had heard Shintani's reverberating plea: *Lord, keep me out of this.* Yesterday, his nerves frayed, Shintani had erected a small shrine to Lord Buddha. He had offered small slices of fruit and a few flowers. His wife, shocked, curious, had badgered him about the queer arrangement of items on the table and the tattered picture of a strange fat man that he had withdrawn from a pouch. But this morning, when he'd heard Howard calling him, Shintani knew, with a cold shiver in his heart, that both Gods had forsaken him.

Howard stuck out one hand, which Mr. Shintani shook, his expression lost behind the netting on his head.

-Mr. Harada needs some help with the pilot. Howard patted his shirtfront and waited expectantly. Shintani shimmied his head vigorously. He had successfully steered clear of the military man for the past four days and he wanted to keep it that way.

-What for?

-He didn't say. I guess the pilot is being annoying. He keeps pestering for his papers and all that. What do you say? Give Mr. Harada a break from hosting our guest.

-My Japanese, Shintani said. It's very rusty.

Then he whacked his hands against his thighs a few times as if for emphasis, but in truth he was trying to dispel some of the anxiety that had suddenly tightened his throat and begun to whisper in his right, deaf ear, *Run, run*. Dust rose from the denim.

-Besides, I'm needed here. Mites get in the hives, the bees get sick. No bees, no honey, and Mr. Robinson is very mad.

- It's only for a little while.

- Why's Mr. Robinson not here yet?

- Wind. Boat problems. Howard shrugged.

Howard had heard from Ben about the *kiu-peapea* wind on

Mount Paniau last night. With that in mind he'd pulled the papers he'd taken from the pilot that first day from under the bed and taken a closer look. There was no question that they were maps of some sort, and though he couldn't read the Japanese writing, he saw suddenly what looked like airfields, possibly even the military base on Kauai. It was a strange feeling for him, that downward whoosh in his stomach when he realized that things might not go as smoothly as he had expected. He should have looked earlier, but the truth was, he wanted Mr. Robinson to handle this. He had willingly ignored the situation in the hope his boss would arrive and take over.

-Well, grumbled Shintani, I'm tending hives near the ranch house tomorrow morning.

-You'll see Mr. Harada then, said Howard. I'll let him know. He repositioned his cowboy hat and turned to go.

-I raised my *keikis* here, Shintani said suddenly. This is my home.

Howard squinted at the old man, puzzled.

-This is my home, Shintani repeated. We belong to Niihau.

He waggled his finger and shuffled back to the apiary.

The sands began their long, deep moan. Howard stopped his ride, thinking it was the call of a cow in pain, possibly lodged in a hole somewhere. When he understood what it really was—the singing sands of Kaluakua Beach—he fought an urge to kick his horse to a canter and turn back; the horse, sensing his sudden fear, threw her head from side to side nervously. *Shha, shha,* he hissed through his teeth to steady her under him.

The Old Lord said that the sound was simply the cumulative tumbling of grains down the steep dunes. On most days Howard liked to hear the schoolbook reasons, those explanations that only men of a certain stature or reasoning power could understand. But Howard was heading for a *heiau*, an ancient holy place, and his intellectual side had made room for something deeper within him; the *uhane*, spirits, were speaking. He had heard the legend from his neighbors, how the spirits keened their despair, how it was important to soothe them before something worse happened, and though at the time it had seemed blasphemous against the one and true God, something drew him toward it today. He listened for a few minutes more. Then he pressed his hat more firmly on his head, clicked his tongue, and urged his horse forward.

He'd picked this *heiau* for its proximity and the relative ease it took to skulk there. He'd used a tepid excuse: that he'd thought some of the turkeys had made their way in this direction and, not to worry, he'd round them up. The other ranch hands had nodded and plucked at their chins, more interested in the shade and giving no indication they found it odd that Howard would leave on his horse at such a hot time of day.

The *heiau* of the goddess Kihawahine was a large circular structure of towering stone twice the height of a man. At each end was an enclosed area where the altar had once stood; Howard imagined the large scaffolding of *kapa*-covered wood with a plank about nose high on which to place offerings, but which was now gone, having given way to the wind and the sand. The totems had also disappeared long ago, slab-tongued, wide-eyed faces of gods, and *kapua*, demigods, that had once ringed each *heiau* and could still be felt if not seen, so that Howard moved carefully and quietly in case they could be roused and angered.

Idolatrous statues, he reminded himself.

Horse and rider had approached the stone edifice from the east, knowing that this was where the entrance was, unlike most others, which faced west, toward Tahiti, from whence the *kupunas* had come on boats, navigating by stars, birds, winds, and currents. Also puzzling and unusual was the long, slab bench on the *heiau*'s exterior. This particular temple had been a Place of Refuge, where those who broke the old taboos went for sanctuary and divine forgiveness, and Howard felt a stillness in the air he took to be the weight of their sins, listing and tilting in the heat like a becalmed ship. The bench was the place where he supposed the ancients would sit, listening for their loved ones inside, or clamber upon, throwing food and words of encouragement over the wall. He wondered who of his neighbors' ancestors had broken the *kapus,* the religious laws, and had had to flee here. As was common with a Place of Refuge, the journey would have been torturous; on the run from the *alii,* desperate for water and fatigued by Niihau's heat, on foot across the dry, burning plains. If the sinner made it inside these walls, he was considered guarded by the gods, untouchable. If he (or she) didn't make it, well, it was death by strangulation or by clubbing.

Howard snugged the reins over one of the jutting stones, wondered briefly whether this was blasphemous, and then considered that he often left horses under the eaves of the church, for its small line of shade. He walked carefully inside. He realized he knew little about the goddess who lived here, and racked his brain for an old story that he might ponder. But when his mind came up blank, he walked the inner perimeter and instead studied the stacks of stone, admiring the way they fit tightly on each other, flat and reddish black. He dragged one hand along the walls' crusty, sharp surface, and when he finally made one complete circuit, pulled his hand away. He couldn't remember why he had come. Most of the old ways were forgotten, and for good reason: there was only one God now. Yet there was evidence that someone had been here in recent weeks, even days: three lopsided and dust-covered pits in the middle of the altar space, the last remains of offered mangos. Howard frowned, bent down, and flicked a finger at each one.

He fished into his denims and finally tugged out a short, bent steel cylinder studded with shiny, just polished grommets. He had found this yesterday near a wing of the plane, half buried, and it had nested like a small, dead animal in his pocket for the past twelve hours. Now it would do as a special offering. He vowed to go to church afterward and ask Him for both forgiveness and help; forgiveness for going back to the Old Ways and help in getting Robinson here safely to decide about the pilot and his strangely beckoning plane. The fight with his wife, Mabel, that morning had undone him; she had demanded the right to visit the plane as she pleased, he had told her angrily that a woman must stay home and far away from the matters of men. Ben had said that Ella had become defiant as well, as if the good Christian teachings were leaking away from the women of the island and being replaced by something else, something wicked. Howard had told Little Preacher to return to the plane for the night, though logic said that there was nothing that the silent hump of shattered machinery could really do except tempt his neighbors with its metal trimmings.

Nearly two centuries ago Captain Cook could get many days' worth of pork and yams for his whole crew in return for what his log stated was "a moderate sized nail," so eager were the Hawaiians for iron. Over the years the odd piece had washed ashore embedded in the jagged timber of some unlucky ship; otherwise, Hawaiians had never seen it. On this first trip Captain Cook was mistaken for the god Lono, who, ancient legends predicted, would arrive just as he did, on "floating islands" with "white *tapas*" (sails) during the religious Makahiki festival. His gifts of iron only solidified this reputation. It was only after Cook and his crew departed that the Hawaiians realized that their faith had been misplaced and that, among other things, a god would not have brought the horrible sickness that swept through their people. "We left a disorder among their women," lamented Captain Clerke when he returned to the islands with Cook a year later and was confronted with the natives' reserve and anger.

Howard carefully placed the hollow metal cylinder to his lips. He blew, puffing his cheeks hard and suddenly, but there was no sound except the clap of his lips and the whir of his spit. Disappointed, he tried again, but still could get nothing resembling a musical note. He examined the cylinder's curvature, the way the steel bent with no seam or wrinkle, the way the end gaped like a shell. Shrugging—there should be music with an offering—he wiped the edge and propped the curious tube carefully on the ground near the mango pits. Then he kneeled and bent his head. If only he had his ukulele, he thought.

There were many legends about the gods—and shark gods in particular—but the one that kept popping unceremoniously into his mind was one Howard had heard when he lived on Kauai. Years before, the local Hawaiians on the neighboring island of Oahu had warned builders at the military base of Pearl Harbor that a shark god lived there and would be disturbed if they continued construction on a certain lock in the far corner of the bay. The builders ignored the warnings even as their work was hampered by delays and one or two unusual tragedies, men hurt or killed during the lock's construction. And on the final day of work, it suddenly imploded. The devastation looked as if a bomb had been set off, but there was no evidence of sabotage. Timbers were split like matchsticks, the wreckage strewn about like a ship sunk by a gale. Engineers and builders alike gasped at the extent of the destruction. At a loss for an explanation, and after more urging by the local Hawaiians, who insisted that the angry shark spirit had caused the mayhem, the *haole* foremen brought a *kahuna* in to appease whatever deities were cursing the project; the lock was finished without further tragedy.

And then years later—and here Howard shivered involuntarily at the idea of it—divers found the intact skeleton of a large hammerhead buried deep in the ocean floor. The creature had been dead for thousands of years, scientists confirmed. And it was in the exact spot over which the unlucky lock had been built.

Howard had never seen Pearl Harbor, and he wasn't sure why this story came to mind. He could not even remember who had told it to him. But somehow there seemed an appropriate message in there, if he only knew how to get at it. Shark gods were buried everywhere, he thought as he knelt for a while longer.

Howard heard the sudden caterwauling of the wind, as if it had risen in response to his trepidation. Spooked, he jerked his head up. It was time to get back. His horse let out a stuttered breath beyond the wall, and he realized that he was drenched in his own midday sweat. He rose from his knees slowly, and walked to the *heiau* opening. He looked back once at his offering, which he had stuck up in the dirt so that it looked like the long neck of some under-sand creature or, unbeknownst to someone who knew little of modern war, like a submarine's periscope quietly pushed skyward from brown, filmy waters.

It was taller than any man Nishikaichi knew, and even upright in the sand, nose to the sky, it reminded him of a wing. He stood close and stared, badly wanting to lay his hand flat on the hard ebony surface, with its febrile glitter, and then pinch his fingers onto one tapered edge and let his hand drop lightly down the length. This was the way he checked his plane: squeezing, bending, pulling, patting. He felt a surge of homesickness as he blinked at the large, beautiful pillar in front of him; for a moment he thought that if he leveled it into the wind correctly, it would fly him away. He barely heard Yoshio explain that surfboards were cut from the *viri-viri* tree and many, like this one, stained black and rubbed with coconut oil. Even now, as he balanced it in front of him, Howard let one hand drop along its flank, as if buffing its shine. In its simplicity it was a thing of beauty.

-Here. Howard extended his hands and leaned the board toward Nishikaichi, who put out his fingers to grip the edges. It was heavier than Nishikaichi expected and he staggered as he took it from Howard.

-No *papa he'e nalu* in Japan? Howard said. He reached out and steadied it.

Nishikaichi regained his balance sheepishly. He glanced at the surf. What had only moments before looked like a gentle roll of seawater had, to Nishikaichi, turned into a surly line of bared, gnashing teeth.

-Lucky for you, it's tiny, said Howard. He brought the nose down deftly and the board looked light again, as if it really could fly. He swiftly tucked the thick flank under his arm and, dragging the tail in the sand, walked into the water. Nishikaichi, empty-handed, followed slowly, lifting his knees high. He was secretly glad that he had shed his flight suit—the shirt and pants, though much too big, would be a little lighter in the water. He glanced back at Yoshio, whose arms were crossed and who was rocking back on his heels as if about to belly-laugh, which he might have, so relieved did he suddenly feel. Instead he said,

-Howard won the surf contest this year.

He wanted to reassure the nervous young man, and besides that, Yoshio felt unaccountably magnanimous today, a fondness for his neighbors, a camaraderie with the pilot, an eye for the languid beauty of this dusty island, a general feeling of being right with the world. His jaw was relaxed, his throat no longer felt as if it was being strangled by some unseen hand. He took two long, deep breaths. His fingers, which had fretted all week, felt wide and powerful, as if he could shake the hand of every Niihauan and squeeze just as hard each time. That's a man, people would think as they dropped their arms reluctantly to their sides. This was what a decision could do, he decided. It settled the silt to the bottom and everything became clear. He felt light and relaxed right now and he wished suddenly that he could join the two in the waves, but he had never bothered to learn to surf, never thought about it really, just had always assumed that it was a sport of the natives and that he would look as foolish as the white man did if he tried. But now the young pilot wanted to do it and Yoshio didn't think it would be so silly after all.

Howard stood thigh deep in the water, waiting. He motioned for Nishikaichi to lie on the board and begin to paddle. Nishikaichi scooted himself warily onto the plank; for all its mass it felt suddenly tippy and delicate. The denim pants were like a million small shellfish that clung suddenly to his legs, making them heavy and stiff. With more ado than he wanted, a panicked splash or two and small strangled noises that escaped unaccountably from his throat, he was flat, and then his chin rested on the wood, his legs flayed in a wide V to stay balanced. He raked at the water in short, nervous strokes so that the board rocked from side to side and his hands sent up a large spray of water. Then the breaker rolled in, and as Howard turned in warning, it swamped him, throwing him underwater, from which he shot up sputtering, his hands pressed against his eyes to clear them. His first thought was of oxygen, and his second, in quick succession, was of the magnificent length of polished wood, which he had now lost.

But, no, Howard had it and was lying prone, one foot slightly in the air, pulling at the water in long, certain strokes. Once past the surf break he drifted, and the large black board poked slightly skyward, shimmering. Nishikaichi had retreated to knee-deep water, his feet wide apart to stay his balance as the next breaker hit, more gently now. Nishikaichi calculated the distance between himself and the board, trying more to gain an accurate measurement of his faltering courage. He thought of how many short, water-splashed breaths it would take to reach Howard's outstretched arm, assuming he outstretched it and didn't look at him with that bemused, friendly, unhelpful expression.

-Swim out, Nishikaichi-san. You'll be fine.

Yoshio had come up behind and now put a hand on Nishikaichi's moon-white wrist. Soon it would be burned by the sun if he wasn't careful, but Yoshio decided against worrying him about one more thing. Nishikaichi looked at him bitterly.

-The sea is angry.

Yoshio tried to think of something encouraging to tell the soldier, something about honor perhaps, but Nishikaichi had turned his head to Howard again, and pursed his lips in nervous concentration, swatting at his face to clear the dripping seawater. Howard himself now looked seaward and had begun, inexplicably, to paddle sideways. The ocean behind him lifted and darkened. Howard paddled harder now, and then straightened and began to windmill his arms rapidly and in cadence toward shore, and what had only seconds before been relaxed and certain began to look frantic. For a suspended moment Nishikaichi wondered if some terrible sea creature, or perhaps the submarine itself, was about to surface and Howard had seen its menacing shadow in the heave of the water as its bulk lumbered upward. The edge of the water behind him began to whiten and then to fray. Suddenly Howard was pitched forward on his board so that it looked as if he would somersault right off, and then, before Nishikaichi had a chance to exhale the breath he had pulled in sharply, Howard was standing. Standing. His arms had rocketed outward for balance and the white shirt he wore waggled in the wind like a sail. His legs, in bunched and dripping denim, were splayed as if to run, then canted drastically forward, a man tilted toward gravity and then past it, defying it. And he was skimming too, and this Nishikaichi couldn't believe, as if he had suddenly gone from man to god in the blink of an eye and had summoned the great forces of the water and the wind to lay down at his feet and obey. His face was stiff with concentration as he came swiftly toward the shore-bound men like some kind of wind-driven tree limb.

Sugoi, said Nishikaichi, his mouth agape and his eyes blinking rapidly. He had seen surfing pictures during his briefings, but nothing could've prepared him for the beauty and mystery of the real thing. Yoshio smiled. He had always liked to see his Hawaiian neighbors surf, and now, as he felt the newcomer's fascination, Howard's ride, still not over, looked especially enchanted. Part of it was the sheer illogic: how two massive components—a large man and a large tree-hewn plank—came together in a graceful synergy. Part was simply how man at once looked puny and powerful on the ocean, as if a delicate agreement had momentarily been struck with the forces of nature. And part, of course, was the balletic majesty as the surfer hydroplaned across the waves—Howard still held the glassy open chute and was zipping toward them, looking to Nishikaichi as if the white water at his tail was the churning smoke of some invisible engine and the crashing sound of the breaking wave the spit and whirl of unseen pistons. Yoshio understood suddenly why so many *heiaus*, religious temples, were built in which to pray for surf.

-I can do that? said Nishikaichi. He looked at once afraid and excited. The surfboard and Howard were close now, almost to the place where Nishikaichi had been unceremoniously dumped, and suddenly Howard dropped to his belly and slowed. The power and speed went out of his board as if a wind had suddenly died. Howard paddled again, and neared the two men. He waved to Nishikaichi and then slipped into the water entirely and stood, holding the floating board with his fingertips, checking behind him for sudden waves.

-Howard will help, Yoshio assured him. He was surprised by how it was the pilot who now lurched between confidence and fear. In turn, Yoshio seemed to have taken on his soldierly confidence. Last night he had made love to Irene with an energy he had not had in years. It had been over quickly, but still he had lain exhausted, half covering her. One hand was on her opposite elbow, where it was often carelessly slung during the rare times they slept in the same small bed, but now something new happened. His skin felt electric and he was suddenly aware of the veins, tentacular and full, running up her arms. They swung through thin slats that even in the dark he could see now—the white, porous coral of bones he had no name for. He could feel, under his own elbow, the knurls of her breast tissue, like the bark of some young, soft tree, and then the knot of her nipple, thistled with the smallest of bumps, each one precise and minute under his skin. The pleats and seams of her. The world itself a candid, geometric place, not a whirl of fog and dust in his mind, leaving him disembodied, unmoored. He had obtained suddenly what Nishikaichi clearly already had—a certainty that his life was linear and with a meaning that he could not name but still felt solid, of mass. That was what a mission did: where Nishikaichi and the rest of youth got their blundering certainty and fearlessness. Now he had it too. Narrowing his world to destroying a plane and military papers had somehow grounded him. Niihau and his family would be saved. The incoming Japanese would spare the island, and treat him as their own.

There was a chirping, twittering sound.

-Mr. Kaleohano, said one of the young children at the shoreline. Let me.

-You're too old, Lily, Howard called back.

-No! she cried, slapping the water angrily. Not too old yet.

Hawaiian women used to surf, until Christianity came along and disapproved. Those that defied Christian mores could not defy their *holokus* and *mu'umu'us,* which became stiff and binding when immersed in water, and so the women stopped surfing, and swimming too. But all the children took rides on the heavy boards. They dropped their clothes at the shoreline and begged an adult to help push them into the water. But even Howard could see that Lily was becoming a woman, and it wouldn't do for her to shed her clothes, especially not in front of the young male guest.

-Lily, move aside.

She crossed her small arms and set her mouth in the thinnest of lines. How boring it was to be a girl! And how much more boring it would be as a woman.

-You'd let your son, she said.

-That's different.

-Why? Lily had an inkling why, but she had no real words for it yet. It didn't seem right that she couldn't surf in front of the strange youth and that the young Kaleohano, who was far less coordinated than she, could.

Howard ignored her and called to Nishikaichi, who waved back and began to walk slowly into the surf. Wishing he had his flight suit back on, swallowing rapidly to tamp down the fear deep into his belly, where his chi was, he fixed his eyes on the bobbing board.

Suddenly he felt a pressure on his leg. Just as his body began to jerk back, all the fear in his throat coalescing to the muscles of his thigh in a tearing, screaming reflex, he saw the upturned face of the serious little girl. He recognized her from yesterday morning, when he had embarrassed himself with the strange fruit, spitting it on the ground and coughing. She'd waded waist deep in the water with the hem of her dress pulled up as far as was modest but which now swum around her like a cloud. Unperturbed by her now soaking *holoku*, she slipped her small hand into his. She said something, quick, earnest, businesslike, and began to match his hesitant step into the surf. He smiled stiffly. He couldn't show a little girl his fear. He stared at the top of her head, and saw, in the way that unimportant details jump out at inopportune moments, that her hair fanned out and swirled in reddish rays. She looked up at him again and pulled on his hand. He was walking too slowly and there were waves to be caught.

Howard held the board for him this time while the girl easily stayed afloat nearby, and when he was once again prone, the girl grabbed the front end of the wood and began to pull him strongly seaward. He may have been comforted to know that Lily's aunt had once jumped into stormy seas to save a ship captain who clung to the mast of his sinking ship, back when ships sailed near Niihau. The Niihauan woman had grabbed the panicked man by the scruff of his shirt and dragged him through the waves to safety, even as his tobacco-stained teeth were clamped together in a vain effort to keep out the water and his nostrils flared like wings and he fought his savior with his remaining strength, the reflexive flailing of a newborn baby. But Lily and Howard, who both knew this story well, and who now mostly saw those large schooners as small, glinting flecks on their way to somewhere else, did not tell him, so Nishikaichi was left to wonder at how he had only days before been a brave pilot in the best airplane ever made, and now was lying as if stricken by illness on a piece of wood being dragged into the sea by a small, fearless girl.

Howard surfaced nearby. He chatted with the serious girl and the two looked out at the horizon, treading water so easily they could have been touching the ocean floor except for the soft pillowing of their hands. Large flowers of water rose to the surface; Lily's dress puffed out and floated, as if it was a separate ocean being altogether. The board bobbed and Nishikaichi hit his chin once, twice, as he peered to see what the two looked at, and then Howard swiftly turned him around so that he was suddenly facing shore.

Paddle! Howard yelled, slapping at the water with one cupped hand to show him. Nishikaichi put his head down and began to swing his arms wildly while his heart ratcheted in his chest. He could see in his periphery that Howard squinted at something coming up behind, about to sink its teeth in his legs or break his plank in half. He badly wanted to turn his head and face the obvious danger, as his soldier's training had taught him, but instead, with eyes squeezed shut from the splash and the effort, he kept up his swift, panicked arm movements. And then he heard a grunt and felt a sudden push shoreward, and his legs lifted slightly and the board suddenly became at once a thing of speed and drag. His body felt pinned to the thick surface and yet he was rocketing forward with the power of a Zero at takeoff, and suddenly a long, loud howl came from somewhere near him, a sound of pure, hysterical joy, and he realized it was coming from his own mouth.

He heard the crackle of the breaking surf and remembered that at some point he was supposed to stand. He tried to push himself upward. He was awkwardly, unsteadily on his knees and grinning now, filled suddenly with the inchoate memory of his first ride on a bicycle, a large rusty thing snatched from his neighbors that his father had pushed for him and then let go of, so that he sailed smoothly right into a tree. For a moment Nishikaichi found that lightness, that thin reed of balance, once again, and then, arms wide in what Yoshio thought, as he watched from shore, was both triumph and resignation, he lost it and fell into the ocean.

For a moment there was no sign of Nishikaichi. Yoshio stiffened on the shoreline. Lily and Howard disappeared behind another small breaker that rose and obscured them, and still there was no sign of Nishikaichi. The board stayed on its lazy trajectory toward the beach—the waves really were small and harmless, Yoshio could see that. He was wondering if he should wade in or signal to Howard when a head popped up near the board, and arms flailed at its slippery edge. There was the glint of white teeth that Yoshio assumed were bared in fear and then, just as he expected a long, exhausted groan to come from the struggling pilot, he heard the sound of exuberant, gulping laughter. He began to laugh himself. Then he heard something else across the water, the squeals of young Lily, and then the roosterlike guffaws of Howard. And there it was, another perfect moment that Yoshio thought he could reach out and feel the bones of, a moment almost phosphorescent, as jeweled as the water itself, lighting the way down the path that Yoshio and Irene had now chosen (but really, had chosen that first day, though they hadn't seen it yet), a moment of pure synergy that proved, he thought foolishly, that helping the pilot was the best thing for all of Niihau.

23

That night Yoshio stood on his porch and stared at the sky. He had come out to check that the young Keo twins had settled out by the stable and not near the house, because Irene had not wanted them to be within easy hearing range; she insisted that though they would not grasp what was being discussed, they would easily understand a companionable, conspiratorial tone. No point in raising suspicions, she'd said. She was right, he thought. Still, a part of him felt banished from the room, and even after he had confirmed for himself that the dark hillocks by the barn door were indeed the sleeping young men, he did not reenter his house. He wanted to wait for the yaw of his stomach to subside, for his hands to stop squirming against each other. Only a few hours ago, he'd felt as if he owned the world. Now he was back to his old, unconfident self. Almost. Taking a deep breath, he willed his hands to fall by his side. There. That was better. He wasn't going to let go of that feeling so easily, since it had taken him so long to get to it. Years, it seemed.

He leaned against the banister and scuffed the wooden stairs with one toe. The stars were splashed against the sky like the spray of some huge, rolling wave. Something about this calmed him and he tilted his head from one horizon to the other to take it all in. If that Zero were his, he thought, he'd fly to those stars. He wouldn't bother with the petty arguments of men—he'd never touch the machine guns or engage in a dogfight. Instead, he'd aim the nose straight up, like some breaching whale. It could do that, Nishikaichi had said so. The fastest flying machine ever, he'd said. It didn't even matter if it could reach a star or not, Yoshio thought. Just as long as it took him as high as possible, so he could look back down to where he'd come from. He wanted to see how small this all was.

Soon he had to stop looking at the stars. It made him dizzy. It was like repeating the same word over and over. Suddenly you were hit by its meaninglessness, its utter abstraction.

When Yoshio reentered the house, Nishikaichi was still eating. Irene was at the counter, fiddling with some wooden bowls that did not seem to need fiddling with. She turned when Yoshio sat at the table and folded his arms across each other.

-Everything okay? she asked.

-It's a beautiful night, he said.

Nishikaichi pushed his plate away with care. He bowed his head slightly and thanked Irene for the meal.

Irene blushed. Yoshio felt something tighten in his chest. It was not jealousy of Nishikaichi—the young pilot was not interested in an older woman like Irene, after all—so he could only guess that his reaction signaled a kind of sadness. And a resolve. Soon, Irene would blush when *he* talked.

Yoshio coughed, stretched slowly, and leaned back in his chair.

-Tomorrow we see Mr. Shintani, he said. It's all arranged.

Irene glanced at him, alarmed.

- Do you think that's a good idea? He's been on Niihau long enough to be one of them, not one of us.

-There is no them or us, said Yoshio abruptly. Anyway, Old Shintani is well respected by Mr. Robinson for his beekeeping. Howard will not want to defy him.

-But why involve someone else? asked Irene.

-Shintani understood every word the pilot told him that day. So he's already involved. And I'm sure he understands the peculiar situation of being Japanese at this time—clearly he hasn't told anybody, not even his wife, that there's a war on. And Howard is much more likely to take him seriously—he's an elder and he's been on the island for so long.

He looked at Irene with what he was sure was his most confident face. He wanted to see in her eyes what he had seen the evening before, when he'd agreed to make a plan with the pilot. But it wasn't there. Outside, the heated air settled into evening. A horse brayed. The lights on Mount Paniau were again being shone. He wondered what it would be like to see the silver flash of a propeller in front of him, hear the roar of an engine ready to do his bidding. To the stars, he thought.

At seven o'clock on Friday morning, Yoshio and Nishikaichi met with Old Shintani in his apiary. Outside in the shade, the new guards—large Hanaiki Niau and Ben's nephew Joe Kanahele—were bored. Joe decided to go fishing. Hanaiki shrugged and closed his eyes.

Inside the apiary Shintani spoke in rapid Japanese.

-Nothing I can do. Don't know where the papers are, or how to get them. Now leave me alone to do my work, eh?

He kneaded his large-knuckled hands and turned away. His cheeks sagged, his chin was square, his graying hair was cut short by an inexpert hand, possibly his own. His mouth turned downward of its own accord, as if by gravity; his neck was thin. His skin was burned into a deep brown and he had deep lines in his forehead. He held himself slightly forward, as if pushing against a wind, and from the side, with his jutting neck, he looked like a small, angry goose.

-Go ask Howard, urged Yoshio, putting a large hand on the old man's shoulders. Look, what will we tell the Japanese navy when they land? That you refused to help your country?

-Niihau is my country.

Yoshio blinked. He was at a loss for a moment.

- It is for the good of the whole island that we do this. Niihauans don't understand war, or Japan. They're waiting for Robinson to come. But Kauai's been taken.

-Taken? Shintani jerked his head from one man to the other, his skin graying, his mouth, thought Nishikaichi, working like a fish's.

Yoshio nodded.

-And there's little time to save our families, Mr. Shintani. The Niihauans too. You must cooperate with Airman Nishikaichi.

Nishikaichi suddenly stepped forward.

-The emperor demands it of you, Shintani-san.

Shintani raised his eyes. He looked at Nishikaichi full in the face.

-The young are more impudent than I remember, he said.

-Our Divine Emperor, the Son in Heaven, Nishikaichi murmured, but he could not hold the old man's stare.

-My obligations are to my family, Shintani said finally. He frowned.

-Forgive me, Shintani-san, said Nishikaichi, bowing now. It's just that—

-Big *pilikia* for everyone if we don't cooperate with the Japanese navy, Yoshio interrupted. Time you did your part.

Shintani stiffened.

-You would tell them that I did not cooperate, Mr. Harada? he said.

-It won't be up to me. What can *I* do against a group of soldiers? Yoshio cried.

-And why, Mr. Harada, don't *you* talk to Howard? Shintani stared at him, half beseeching, half furious. Leave me out of this.

Yoshio hesitated. He knew that Shintani was not a perfect choice; he had not shown any interest in being anything but far away from the pilot and the situation. He was married to a Niihauan—he was Niihauan in many ways. But at his core he was Japanese—not even an American citizen, like Yoshio and Irene—and he would see that in the end he had little choice. But Yoshio also knew that in his heart of hearts he was picking Shintani to do this one last thing for another reason: Yoshio was not sure he could himself ask for the papers without trembling just a little. As much as he believed that he was doing what was best for the island, he would not be able to lie to Howard Kaleohano. He was, finally, too weak to look into his neighbor's eyes and deceive him without a blink.

Nishikaichi looked from one man to the other, beginning to regret this course of action. The old man looked so frightened. Yoshio had become uncommonly agitated, as if he had convinced himself of something that even Nishikaichi did not know. The island itself had just yesterday seemed so beautiful, so *lyrical,* and yet now it was back to the dirty business of the war. Nishikaichi felt suddenly tired, as if he had just spent hours flying his plane through the dark, staring at both the dimly lit instruments and the black funnel of night in front of him. Flying like that, by compass, was exhausting. Your senses played tricks on you, your body lied. Your mind whispered that the plane was in a turn when the instruments plainly indicated it was not; your eyes were sure that the nose was pitched too far upward when there was only blackness and not a reference to be found. Finally you might see the tossing lights of the waiting ship, but they blended with the stars so that you were sure until the last minute that you would land somewhere on the moon, not on the deck of an aircraft carrier. It was a fight not to disorient yourself right into the water. As Shintani whipped his head back and forth, telling Yoshio something in Hawaiian, Nishikaichi fought the urge to sit down and lean against one of these bee crates and forget all of this. He wanted only to think about the fishmonger's daughter, perhaps take a swim in the warm, comforting ocean.

-Don't anger the navy, Shintani-san, Nishikaichi suddenly barked. Let's get on with this or there's no saying what will happen to you both. He stared at them as fiercely as he could. He fought the need to close his eyes and sleep. Get my papers. Meet us back at the house of Harada-san. Nishikaichi shook his fist. To punctuate his outburst he started to stalk out of the bee house, until he realized that there were guards outside. No matter how lax they were, he was still a prisoner.

-Harada-san, he said with a lowered voice, but his nostrils still flared. Let's go.

Howard was taking a lunchtime nap and Mabel was at Ella's, so Shintani had to pound vigorously on the door before it was answered. Old Shintani was not one for visits, so Howard was surprised to see him, but not so much that he didn't launch into a long explanation of the dream he'd been having before Shintani woke him up.

-The papers, interrupted Shintani. You have?

Howard blinked at him.

-Of course.

The papers were no secret; they were shown off the first night to the crowd of onlookers, and since then, to individuals like his wife, Mabel (numerous times), and Ben (twice). Nishikaichi had continued to ask for these papers, which Howard had made proudly clear were *hidden away*—which meant they were under his mattress. The pilot's insistent badgering had gradually become more and more annoying. The polite Niihauans had not said so to their guest, however, but endured them with a smile and a look of pleasant incomprehension.

What the papers showed were maps of Oahu and the approach for fighter planes through the pass. There were also rows of radio channels and some sketches of American warships. But Howard had been to Oahu only once, by steamer; his view of the island had been horizontal and three-dimensional, not the two-dimensional bird's-eye view that the Japanese pilots needed. He remembered the long, low coastline, behind which rose startlingly green mountains, and two large hotels, one pink, one white. To the far right jutted the high cliffs of Diamond Head, an old volcano that from the boat had looked like one long, rocky beard, well-groomed and flowing into the sea. There was nothing on these papers that resembled this. Instead Howard assumed that the papers detailed Japan, and told everyone so with an authority they didn't question. But now he had to face what had become evident early on, when he'd looked closer at the sketches of large warships on subsequent pages. The map was of the United States, perhaps even of Kauai or Niihau. Whatever it was, it had something ominous to do with the Hawaiian Islands.

The plane, the papers, the gun. Howard had at first refused to worry, thinking that the Old Lord would arrive soon enough to handle it. But he hadn't arrived, and now, on this fifth day after the Old Lord was due, Howard decided that a little worrying might be good. Already he knew that others were going to *heiaus* to pray to gods other than Jesus, that faith was being lost in Mr. Robinson himself.

Well, now that the beekeeper Shintani was here, maybe he'd get some more answers, thought Howard. He walked into his bedroom and pulled the sheaf from under his mattress. He returned to Shintani, who was gulping and shifting from foot to foot in the doorway. Howard waved the papers; Shintani wiped his hands on his shirt and then reached forward, in a move half hopeful, half hesitant. But Howard spread the papers out on the kitchen table without noticing that Shintani kept his open hand in front of him, his fingers wiggling.

-What do you make of this, Mr. Shintani? It's a map of something, perhaps Kauai, and here, pictures of ships. He tapped the Japanese letters. Maybe you can recognize these, tell me what they mean.

-I don't read, Mr. Kaleohano, Shintani said, but let me get them to Mr. Harada, who can.

-Tell Mr. Harada to come here, said Howard.

-No, no, give them now, Shintani stuttered, and began to rake the papers into a pile.

-Whoa, old man, Howard said, grabbing Shintani's arm.

-Big *pilikia* if you don't give them to me, Shintani cried. For the good of Niihau! And Jesus Christ! he added for good measure, as if this final appeal would make the most sense to a man like Howard.

Howard pushed him away roughly. Weeping, Shintani grabbed for his sleeves.

-You must! The papers!

-No! yelled Howard, turning his back to gather the maps and sketches. A keening sound came from Shintani, and the sound of something falling onto the ground, the chair, Howard thought without turning.

-The Japanese navy will kill us all, Shintani moaned as he backed out of the house. Howard swept wildly at the pages and didn't look back around until they had all been stuffed roughly into his pockets for safety. When he was done, he turned to see the chair on the floor, Shintani gone. For a moment Howard stayed still, letting his heart relax its frantic beating. All the unease, the finger-light but unremitting anxiety he'd felt all week now thrummed in his ears and made his hands shake. *The Japanese navy will kill us all?* Things were starting to look frighteningly clear, and the war that he had managed to put in the back of his mind pushed forward again. Things were wrong, he couldn't avoid it anymore. And it would do no good to wait any longer for Robinson. The Niihauans would have to take this into their own hands now.

24

Yoshio laid the double-barreled shotgun on the table and stared at it grimly. It had a thin gossamer of dust on it and an unnatural heft, but perhaps that was only because he had not handled a weapon in so long. The gun had been his idea, but the sight of it made him reconsider. Years ago, under orders from Aylmer Robinson's father, all the wild goats—offspring of those first goats brought by Captain Cook—had been slaughtered with this gun. Otherwise guns were prohibited on Niihau; this one had been pushed to the back of a shed, almost forgotten.

He glanced at Nishikaichi, then back at the gun.

-Well, he said. Here it is. He nodded at the butt, as if it was invisible without his direction.

-Does it shoot? Nishikaichi frowned.

-It doesn't need to shoot, said Yoshio. It's just for scaring, right? To get Howard to cough up your papers.

The pilot picked the weapon up and blew at the hammer. He put it on his shoulder and squinted down the barrels. He wanted to fire a test shot but knew that this was out of the question.

-We can't be sure it works, he said.

-But that doesn't matter, insisted Yoshio. No shooting, remember?

The pilot averted his eyes from the gun and stared at Yoshio.

He flickered them back and swung the barrels sideways, taking aim at someplace near the wall. Then, with a sudden movement, the shotgun was off his shoulder and broken open, the cartridges exposed in their chambers.

-Right, Nishikaichi said offhandedly. At least it's loaded.

He would have to hope that it worked.

-If it's loaded perhaps I should carry it. Yoshio shifted and held out one hand. I don't want you getting too aggressive.

-You want to carry a gun? Nishikaichi smiled. Okay, then.

He put a hand on Yoshio's shoulder amiably.

Yoshio frowned. He looked at the gun and back at the pilot.

-All right, all right. I don't like guns, okay? You take it, but no shooting.

Nishikaichi nodded. Yoshio watched as he laid the gun back on the table and walked to the window, staring out with a grim set to his mouth. Yoshio knew that, from under downcast lids, Irene also watched the pilot. With surprise he realized that he truly no longer minded. It would just take Irene a little while to see that her husband was a different man than a week ago; he was stronger, more decisive, a man of action, like the soldier she stared at. Idly he wondered what the pilot was thinking about. Perhaps he imagined his beloved emperor, or the orders he was finally about to carry out, and how soon he would be free. Perhaps he had a girl at home whom he was pledged to marry. Perhaps he thought of what life would be like here in the United States, under Japanese control. Would he stay? Would he settle here, in Hawaii?

Nishikaichi thought of surfing.

He wanted to fly across the water just one more time. But the gun was on the table. Mrs. Harada stood near the radio, her triangular face flushed and somber, the child at her feet. Harada-san was looking at him with a worried expression tinged with surprise, as if he had just stepped off the shallow sand into a deep part of the ocean and could not remember at the last moment whether he could swim. Looking at their faces, he suddenly saw his parents. They sat on the floor, saying not a word. The sun dappled their knees, and once or twice his mother looked up at his father, and perhaps she smiled. Is this how they would look after they got the news that their son had died for their country?

Nishikaichi turned slowly. He felt suddenly that Irene and Yoshio were waiting for him to say something important, something that a brave commander would say to his troops before a battle. But he was not a commander, and he never would be. He was a soldier, born to carry out his duty by giving the only thing he really had to give, which was his life. The speech given to him and his fellow pilots on the aircraft carrier *Hiryu* had been all about that: how they were sure to die, and how honorable that would be, how the waves that would cover the bones of their corpses would always be lifted and formed by winds from their beloved Japan. It had been a stirring speech, and buoyed by it Nishikaichi had felt elated to be in the air in his Zero, with little chance of surviving the Pearl Harbor attack.

Nishikaichi cleared his throat.

-May the wind, he began. The wind on the waves . . .

Irene looked at him, puzzled. Yoshio straightened his shoulders, his eyes bright, his face still. Nishikaichi frowned. The words did not have the spirited ring he had heard on the carrier. They seemed flat and meaningless.

-We will remember that the grass, Nishikaichi started again, realizing that if they were to die, it would probably be on Niihau's hard red soil and not in the ocean. That grass that will grow from the nutrient of our corpses . . .

Irene's eyes widened and Yoshio paled. Nishikaichi did not seem to notice.

-That grass will sway, always in a wind. It will be nourished by our honor and humility. It will sway always—he raised his voice now, straining for a grand finale—in a wind that blows from Japan!

Then he lifted both arms awkwardly in what he hoped was triumph and inspiration, but Irene gave a small cry and turned away. Yoshio pulled his hand abruptly from where it rested on the table and the shotgun.

-This isn't about death, Airman Nishikaichi, Yoshio whispered. That's exactly what we want to avoid. Isn't that the point of all this, to avoid bloodshed?

Nishikaichi blinked. An honorable death was his own wish, but an Americanized Japanese couple would never understand this. He looked from the man to the woman in front of him, and then to their little girl on the floor. He should not be too harsh about their weakness—hadn't he avoided death for the love of the fishmonger's daughter?

-Harada-san, he said, bowing slightly. It's a metaphor. An ancient Japanese metaphor. Nothing to worry about.

He felt heavy suddenly, weighed down by the inevitability of the coming hours. He would die by his own hand, once the plane and papers were taken care of. But he would make sure that Yoshio was safe and sound. That would be his final *giri*, his obligation to the older, more timid man.

-We go now, Nishikaichi said, smiling slowly. Afterward, when our mission is complete, and the island is safe . . .

He shrugged.

-Then we will surf.

At four-thirty that Friday afternoon, Yoshio tried to dismiss Hanaiki Niau, but the man just smiled and said Howard had told him to stay, it was no trouble. Yoshio retreated to the house and became agitated, until Irene suggested a second way out. Later, he asked Hanaiki to escort Nishikaichi to the outhouse with him. Hanaiki obliged, but halfway down the path, Yoshio cocked his head toward the honey shed.

-We stop for a moment? Yoshio asked Hanaiki, who nodded amiably.

The three men traipsed to the shed.

When they stepped inside, Hanaiki did not notice that the pilot had blocked the doorway they'd entered, or that he had pulled the shotgun from behind a door, just where Irene said she had put it the hour before. Hanaiki allowed himself to be marched to the back of the honey shed, but not without turning back once or twice to look at Mr. Harada, just to ascertain that the whole thing wasn't a joke.

-You mean this? Hanaiki asked.

-Just do as we say, Mr. Niau, and everything will be fine, Yoshio said. He too kept glancing at the weapon in Nishikaichi's hands, held up to one of his eyes and trained steadily at the Hawaiian's spine as if Hanaiki was not three hundred broad pounds, but a small target to be sighted carefully.

Yoshio indicated that Hanaiki should sit, which he did, slowly, his eyes on Nishikaichi and the gun.

-Tie him, said Nishikaichi.

-No, he's fine, said Yoshio, and then to Hanaiki, with apology in his voice. Stay here, don't move, he said. All for the best.

-You feeling okay? To Hanaiki, the situation was so absurd that he felt more curiosity and surprise than fear. He didn't like the way the Japanese youth was working his jaw from side to side and standing in the doorway with a shotgun at the ready. But Yoshio had always been a man whose most obvious trait was his blinking amiability. How he had found himself allied with a soldier and a gun was beyond Hanaiki's immediate comprehension.

-Don't make trouble, said Yoshio, and everybody will be fine. The soldier needs his papers, and when the Japanese come everyone will be protected.

-Japanese?

-There's war, said Yoshio as he turned to go. He hesitated, as if he wanted to put a hand on the big man's shoulder. That's why Mr. Robinson doesn't come. Everything has been taken by the Japanese.

Hanaiki's large mouth hung open. Yoshio was at the doorway.

-They'll treat us well, if we help the pilot.

And then the two men were gone, leaving Hanaiki stunned and blinking over the word *war.*

Yoshio walked quickly down the path, Nishikaichi behind him. They would head for Puuwai and Howard's house there. Yoshio had wanted to take two of Robinson's Arabians—the thought both thrilling and scaring him—but the pilot did not know how to ride a horse, a fact that stunned Yoshio. I fly, the pilot had said. What use are horses? And Yoshio had agreed. They would walk then, leaving the cart for Irene and Taeko to use if necessary. When Yoshio passed the kitchen window on the way to the dirt path that led to Puuwai, he looked sideways, hoping to see Irene watching him with what he imagined was awe and approval. But there was no movement behind the window, no telltale silhouette. There was just the reflection of his distorted face glancing momentarily at the glass. He walked on, ignoring his own disappointment. He turned only once, ostensibly to make sure the pilot was behind him, but really to catch one last glimpse of his house. And then he saw a brief flicker behind the front window. A shimmer of a pale shoulder, a flash of a *holoku*. Then all was still again.

A cart trundled slowly along the road—what good luck.

-Hide the gun, ordered Yoshio, who then waved at what he

made out to be Hanaiki Niau's wife, Hannah, on her way to the store perhaps, or to see her husband, who was now—unbeknownst to her—locked away. Her three younger children sat on the seat to one side of her. On the horse that pulled the cart sat her older daughter, Louisa, and behind her, one hand on the horse's rump, sat Lily. Hannah was half turned to the child next to her, so she did not see Yoshio or the pilot. Only when he yelled extra loud and began to run did she pull up on the reins. The cart came to a stop.

-Mr. Harada, Hannah began, pulling her youngest boy onto her lap as if to make room.

-Please, said Yoshio as politely as he could. Will you take us to the village? Irene is sick and—

-How terrible, clucked Hannah. Will she be all right?

-I think so. But . . .

Yoshio hesitated. How would he convince her to head away from the house immediately?

-Now! cried Nishikaichi suddenly in Japanese. He brandished the shotgun from behind his back. Even Yoshio was shocked, and took a surprised step back, as if the pilot threatened him as well. Hannah let out a cry. The pilot shook the weapon at her, and kept speaking angrily. Quickly, Hannah herded her kids to the ground and dropped her own large frame nimbly off the cart; she did not need to understand the words to know what he wanted. Yoshio, recovering, grabbed the bridle with one hand and Lily's ankle with the other. It was meant to be a soothing gesture but she jerked away with a whimper.

-It's okay, he tried again. Just the cart and it'll be fine.

-Mr. Harada! cried Hannah fiercely. She pushed her three younger children behind her legs and began batting her hands in the air at him.

His heart went into a fusillade of nervous leaps; he wanted to take the time to explain the whole plan to them—how the Japanese navy would be kind to the islanders after this, that this was scary but not terribly dangerous—they weren't really going to *shoot* anybody. But Nishikaichi had jumped onto the cart and stood with his feet planted and his face a blank mask, and Yoshio had a moment of pure, cold fear that this was not as he had planned.

-What's wrong with you? he cried to Nishikaichi. We treat these people with respect.

-Get in, Nishikaichi replied, staring at Hannah in case she decided to rush the cart.

-The children—

-Now, said Nishikaichi, waving with impatience.

Yoshio gestured wildly at Lily and Louisa, who seemed frozen with fear.

-Down, *keikis*, he yelled. Get off the horse!

They dropped to the ground and ran to Hannah, who had begun to yell a mixture of Hawaiian invectives and prayer.

-We'll get your horse back, Yoshio cried. He reached for Hannah's arm to reassure her, but she recoiled with fear and something that—to his astonishment—looked like disdain. Stung, he pulled himself onto the cart and seized the reins. He yelled *Ya, ya* at the horse, and with a heave they were off toward the plane.

-Are you mad? cried Yoshio. He urged on the excited horse, and then found the balance to turn and glare at Nishikaichi. You promised—

-I have only one promise, Harada-san. The pilot gripped the wooden sides and shouted over the crackle of the steel shanks, the roar of the wheels. And that is my obligation to the emperor. There is no more time to be patient.

-But—

-Enough!

Nishikaichi forced himself to frown at the passing countryside, ignoring his building need to cough out the dust in his lungs kicked up by their flight. He knew that there was something else that fueled his sudden anger, but it was not something he could discuss with Yoshio.

The little girl who had helped him surf.

He hadn't expected to see her. He'd overreacted, steeling himself against any sudden onslaught of regret or feeling. Anger had been the only way he could hold on to his martial spirit, but he had scared her. He was hit with a clearer idea of why so many of his brother soldiers had gone so crazy in China. They were fighting beauty and love because otherwise they would be weakened by it. Hatred and violence were the perfect armor. Still, he had not liked the fear on the little girl's face. It made him feel ashamed.

He coughed. The dust was too much. He wiped his eyes. He could see the spire of the place of worship, and by the way the horse was pulling, they were near the outskirts of the village. He set his jaw. He was a soldier above all else now. Soon, this would all be over anyway.

They veered right, to Howard's house. Yoshio jumped from the cart and threw the reins over the Kaleohanos' rock wall. Neither of the men spoke, just stared out at the field.

His plane was not as Nishikaichi had remembered it. Even broken it had been formidable that first day on Niihau, but now it looked like what it was: a shattered machine that would never rise again. He couldn't believe it had once been such a mighty thing, his Zero, the best fighting plane ever made.

He began to walk toward it with purpose. The shotgun dangled at his side. Quickly he spotted Little Preacher in the shade of the *kiawe* tree, and he raised the weapon to his eye. Then he continued his walk, closing the distance between himself and the young guard. Little Preacher must've been asleep, because he made no indication that he saw the approaching pilot.

-Mother Mary, cried the young man as he rose to his feet. Nishikaichi began to bark orders that Little Preacher did not understand, so he continued to stammer, and then to pray. Yoshio had arrived by now, and began to smile and banter witlessly.

-It's okay, *keiki*, Yoshio said, even though it clearly was not. Just go to the plane and help us with the guns.

-I know nothing of guns! cried Little Preacher.

Nishikaichi prodded him hard with the barrel.

-I'm a young man of God, Mr. Harada, he pleaded. Soon of the cloth.

Nishikaichi walked to the plane. He climbed up onto the left wing and leaned into the cockpit. There were buttons and knobs missing. And what people had not taken, Mother Nature had claimed for herself—the leather seat was cracked and dry, a thick sheath of dust clogged the stick, the instrument panel was spattered with bird droppings. He picked up the radio headphones, which had fallen between the seat and the door and so had been miraculously missed by greedy hands, shook them out, and put them on. Then he began to fiddle with the knobs, more out of habit than any firm belief that he would connect with a nearby Japanese squadron. But the connections had been severed by the crash, or the battery had worn itself out, and there was only silence.

Yoshio kept his eye on Little Preacher, whose own eyes were closed as he prayed. The only other time Yoshio had been this uneasy had been on his wedding night, when he had approached Irene once they were alone and seen such fear in her eyes he had almost turned around to see if perhaps there was an intruder in the room. But no, it had been he, and the prospect of doing what husbands and wives do, which she knew nothing about except that it would hurt. He only knew a little. He had wanted to feel powerful and in control in direct proportion to her fear, but he hadn't; he'd felt uncertain and fumbling. Now he gritted his teeth and scowled at Little Preacher.

He didn't notice Nishikaichi next to him until the man spoke.

-Papers, he said simply, and then pointed to Howard's house.

They marched away from the plane, Nishikaichi still pointing the gun at Little Preacher's back.

At the front door of the Kaleohanos', Yoshio called out for Howard. A small boy appeared.

-Where's your father? Yoshio asked. The young boy, no older than eight, looked at Yoshio and then at the gun-holding pilot behind him. He pointed down the road, to the Kelly house.

Yoshio shrugged and looked at Nishikaichi.

-Okay, scowled Nishikaichi, then the machine guns. We'll dismantle them.

In fact, Howard was not at the Kellys', as his son well knew, but in the outhouse. He'd been there a long time, concentrating on his business and letting his mind wander now and then to Shintani and his petrified exit from his house only a few hours earlier. He hadn't heard the cart pull up. But he'd heard a commotion coming from the plane and, after peeking through the slats of the wall, had seen the two men in his pasture with a gun pointed at the young guard. They had walked past him and were out of sight momentarily and then had returned to the plane. A loud banging was now coming from their direction; he guessed they were trying to fix the thing and fly away.

Little Preacher strained at the bolts that held the machine gun down. He blew away dust and squinted through sweat and the beginning of tears to find the right screws. Just then Yoshio let out a cry. A figure had dashed from the outhouse, hoisting his pants (in his nervousness, Howard had forgotten to knot his much-needed rope belt), and was now fleeing toward the house. Nishikaichi whirled from his place on the wing and the whole plane shuddered. Little Preacher cried out; Nishikaichi yelled something incomprehensible, bringing the gun back to his shoulder and aiming. As he yelled he shook the tip for emphasis, as if he would shoot at any moment if not obeyed. Howard kept running. Nishikaichi screamed at him, but Howard disappeared into the house. Nishikaichi jumped from the wing, but by the time he'd begun to run, the front door of Howard's house banged open and Howard ran out dragging his boy by the hand. Nishikaichi slowed to a walk as Howard disappeared down the road. He turned around, back to the plane.

Yoshio had fallen to his knees when Nishikaichi first raised the gun. He'd let out an anguished cry as Nishikaichi yelled; already he could see Howard falling to the ground, hit. He'd thought he would faint, his stomach had bucked and churned. By the time Nishikaichi had stopped shouting and walked back to the wing, Yoshio's hands were on his ears and he huddled in the dirt.

-Get up, Harada-san, Nishikaichi snarled. I didn't shoot a single round.

Yoshio pushed himself to his feet.

-This was to be peaceful, he stammered. The gun, would you have—

-Harada-san, pull yourself together! This is war, what did you think it would be like?

-No, no, no, cried Yoshio, his hands clamped together and shaking at the air. Not like this. Not ever.

With his boy in his arms, Howard quickly became fatigued. There had been no time to get the papers; he had scooped up his son and fled down the main road toward the church, yelling as he went.

Ella was the first to appear and then other villagers quickly gathered round. Ranch hands just in from the pastures flicked at their hats and grinned uncertainly as Howard spoke

-I was shot at, he cried, setting his son on the ground and catching his breath.

-By who, what?

-The pilot! Mr. Harada and the pilot are trying to—

-Mr. Harada is one of the gentlest men around, said Ella. Shame on you! Telling another tall tale. A lie in the eyes of God, Mr. Kaleohano.

-But they had a gun! Mother of Jesus . . .

-Mr. Harada wouldn't hurt a fly.

-If you told me it was Mrs. Harada, well, someone added. The villagers laughed again.

-I swear it, on the steeple of the church, on every Bible inside, they—

Suddenly there were shouts from another direction. Hanaiki Niau stumbled into the square, and leaned against the church to catch his breath. It had taken everything he had to tear a hole in the old shed wall. His fingers were cut and bleeding. Straw stuck from his hair. He ran a hand through it, as if suddenly self-conscious of his condition, and cried,

-Mr. Harada's gone crazy!

Nishikaichi stormed through Howard's house, tipping over the few chairs, sending the one pot to the ground with a sweep of his hand. In the cupboards he pulled all the cans to the floor—condensed milk, green peas, creamed corn, string beans—they made a loud popping sound as they hit and then rolled away. He stood for a few minutes in front of a lopsided wooden cross, hastily constructed and then nailed to the wall. He lifted it from its place and dropped it to the floor. Hands on his hips, he glanced once more around the room, but everything had already been upturned, moved aside, or flung. He slammed his fist on the kitchen table in frustration, and the shotgun, which lay on it, jumped, as if alive. Where had the man hidden the papers? Nishikaichi went again to the cupboards, this time reaching to the far back and climbing on a chair to fully inspect the upper shelves.

Yoshio was in the other room, and he tried to ignore the almost hysterical commotion nearby. As he knelt to feel on the floor under the mattress, he hit his head against the corner of the bed. The sharp pain made him close his eyes and exhale sharply, and when he opened them he groped without much determination. He flapped his hands against the bed slats but, his head throbbing, decided quickly there was nothing to be found there. Who would be stupid enough to hide something in so obvious a place? He got up and walked out, not knowing that if he had spent just a few more moments his fingertips might have discerned a tumorous knob that indicated the squashed, rolled-up sheaf of papers, pushed between the bottom of the mattress and the bed slats, where Howard, after unfurling them hours before, had restuffed them.

Yoshio stepped back into the kitchen, placing his feet carefully between strewn objects. He was glad that they had decided to let Little Preacher go. The pilot was getting so angry, he was afraid that someone would be shot soon.

Nishikaichi turned around and held out his military pistol, taken by Howard upon their first encounter and pushed lazily onto the top shelf of the cupboards, where a child couldn't reach.

-Now you take the shotgun, he said.

Yoshio stepped back. He shook his head violently.

-No, no, he said. This is—I'm not—I can't.

-You're a soldier now, Harada-san. Take the shotgun.

Yoshio put his hands to his eyes. This was terribly wrong. He tried to think of Irene's face, the look she might have to see him like this. As a soldier, like Nishikaichi said. He dropped his arms at his sides, then stepped forward.

-Give it to me, he said, clenching his jaw tightly.

All the Niihauans were alerted and began to gather in the safest place they knew, their church. They barred the door, the shutters to the windows were slammed shut. Hurriedly they filled the pews, until only the biggest men stayed in back, keeping watch. It was dark, but a few candles were found and lit; they flickered weakly and threw frightening shadows. It wasn't Sunday, and the preacher from Kauai only came every so often, but they sang hymns as they usually did and Howard stood up to read from the Bible. The pages fell open to Revelation, so that he was soon intoning about the end of the world, and the Niihauans began to pale and bite their lower lips. Howard, who could hardly see the type in the fading light and who kept staring nervously at the door, skipped to the end and finished the reading rapidly. There was a moment of heavy silence as he stared from the lectern down at his neighbors. He could not see all their faces, but the church was full and he could feel their fear and his own.

-The stranger has guns and is taking more from his plane. We can pray all we want, but will that defend us against bullets? I don't think so.

There was an audible gasp from the pews.

-Okay, you think that's blasphemy. All I'm saying is that the Japanese may land any second, if what Mr. Harada told Mr. Niau is to be believed. But Mr. Robinson isn't coming, and I don't know if God is either. Now we have been betrayed by our own neighbor, Mr. Harada. At first I thought he was being forced, but I'm not so sure anymore. It's my opinion, humble as it may be, that we have no choice but to head for the caves where our ancestors went in times of trouble and hide there.

He turned to the drooping figure of Jesus, on the wall behind him, whose unnaturally incandescent white skin, mistaken sometimes for grace, could still be seen in the graying light. Then he pushed away from the lectern and hurried down the aisle.

The villagers scrambled to their feet, unused to seeing Howard so scared and flustered. They scattered, all 130 of them, into the low scrub and dry ground behind Puuwai and beyond. Some grabbed horses, some fled on foot. Howard instructed Mabel to stay close to Hannah. Then he found an unclaimed mare and vaulted onto her back.

-Signal! he cried to Hanaiki Niau. Go to the mountain! Then he galloped back to his house.

25

Ella leaned one shoulder against the outside church wall and watched her neighbors fade up the dirt road. Only her husband stood by the church door, holding it open until the last of the villagers had scurried past and then shutting it carefully and standing motionless, as if undecided about what to do next.

-Come on, he finally said. We'll get the horses and head to the caves at Kawaihoa.

-I need to talk to Mrs. Harada. Find out what's really going on. Ella picked up her lantern and sighed. Ben walked quickly to catch up with her.

-We know what's going on! And it's not good! The only thing to do now is hide and wait for Mr. Robinson.

-Mr. Robinson's not coming. There's a war out there, you heard Mr. Niau. And it's about to arrive on our island! No one can help us now but God and ourselves. No more waiting for Mr. Robinson. You run like a child to the caves if you want, but I need to talk to Mrs. Harada.

-But the woman's on their side. She must be!

-She bought *Christmas ornaments,* Ella said, as if this would explain everything. She drew up her shoulders and lifted her chin. Her hands clutched her broad hips. She glared at Ben. I invited her to string leis with us.

Ben blinked, puzzled. He shook his head and put his palms to the heavens.

-Okay, Mama, he said.

Ella rode sidesaddle behind Ben, who kept his horse at a slow canter. Just outside Puuwai they heard the heavy sound of hammering, which Ella guessed meant that the guns were being unhitched, just as Howard had said. Her temper rose again, but she forced herself to think only of speaking to Mrs. Harada, and what they would do then. It would be all right, she thought. Mrs. Harada would tell her that Mr. Harada was just playing along, waiting for the right time to alert his neighbors to overpower the young pilot.

As they rode up the final hill, Ella saw that the house was completely dark. Ben knocked on the door anyway, and there was a movement at the side window. Ella called for Irene, who finally opened the door. Her small face glowed white against the black of the house inside.

-Your husband! Ella cried.

-What about him? gasped Irene.

-He's crazy as a boar. The foreigner too, yelling, waving his guns. It isn't true, he's not helping the pilot, right?

Irene's hands flew to her mouth.

-He's been shot? she cried.

-No, Ella said with disgust, but someone will be. It's the plane, isn't it? It's made him crazy. The foreigner will kill us all. Come with us, tell him to stop, tell him to—

Ella moved forward, but Ben grabbed her shoulders to keep her from charging into the house. Irene's hands still covered the lower half of her face. She stepped back, startled, as the old woman advanced furiously.

-Please! she cried. Leave! You don't understand anything.

-There's a war on, we know that. And the pilot wants papers he had when he landed and he's willing to kill for them. You must talk to your—

-I cannot do anything. Irene's voice rose to a shriek. She slammed the door and stumbled back into her kitchen. She would fetch Taeko and they would hide in an outer shed. They would lock the door from the inside and the villagers would leave her alone. They would want to hurt her perhaps, but they wouldn't destroy Robinson property to do it.

Ella walked back to the horse as if in a trance. Ben put one arm around her shoulder but she shrugged it off.

-She's no better than a flying cockroach! She wants to kill us all. Ella shook her head in disbelief. We just went shell hunting yesterday morning . . . the most beautiful shells . . .

-Hush, Ella, said Ben. We'll get to the caves, talk about it then.

Howard stepped into his decimated kitchen. He kicked aside a few cans of string beans and bent to replace the pot that tilted against the wall. He strained to listen for sounds of breathing, but soon decided he was alone in the mess. A search of the cupboard showed they'd found the pistol—he shook his head at his foolishness. He hurried to his bedroom. He stepped over the few clothes they owned and past the tipped-over side table. He reached under Mabel's bed. It was a miracle, a God-given miracle, but the papers were still there and intact. He stuffed them into his waist belt.

He rode like he'd never ridden before, head close to his horse's fluttering mane, heels flapping against her flanks to urge her on. It was dark now and there were no oil lanterns or *imus* to guide him; everyone had fled. But he had lived here long enough to know his way around by the faint bluish light of a thinning moon. He counted the houses as he rode by—dark, hulking shadows he mentally ticked off on his fingers, until he came to his mother-in-law's.

She too had gone, but he knew of an old floorboard she had asked him to fix, which he pulled up now, scraping the skin off the tips of his fingers in the effort. At her doorway he rested, hands on his knees, breathing heavily from fear and exertion. In the quiet night, he could hear the distant sound of a hammer against the plane.

Mr. Harada and the pilot would successfully dismantle the guns soon. Howard felt his heart lurch. Still breathless, he mounted his mare and kicked her toward Mount Paniau.

Howard found men already there. Hanaiki Niau, with a cut on his knee and a few scraps of straw still in his hair, straightened as Howard rode up.

-The lamps aren't enough, he cried. We're going with a signal fire.

-You sure? said Howard, dismounting quickly. Dangerous, with everything dry like this. He looped the reins of his horse on a nearby rock.

-Then they'll know something's really wrong, Hanaiki insisted.

-We light the fire, and then *pau,* no more relying on others to help, said Howard fiercely. We're alone, we do what we need to do ourselves, like our ancestors would've done.

Hanaiki snorted.

-Okay, brother, what do you have in mind? Shoot them with slingshots? Throw pebbles? They've got guns, these crazy Japanese.

-We paddle to Kauai, Howard said.

-You're crazy now. Hanaiki shook his head with disgust. You and Mr. Harada both.

-Just like our ancestors, urged Howard. It's only sixteen miles.

-There're headwinds.

-And a moon we can guide by.

-Currents.

-We'll get Captain to guide us. He's a good fisherman; he knows these waters like his horse.

For a while no one said anything more. They worked fast to clear a safe space for the fire and soon someone rode downslope to collect kindling and firewood. Howard rolled his shoulders once or twice to loosen them and then stared out to sea, toward Kauai.

-They're all dead? asked Hanaiki, following his gaze. This war the Japanese told us about, it's killed everyone out there?

Howard said nothing.

-Mr. Robinson doesn't come, that can't be good, Hanaiki said quietly. I can only think the worst.

-We'll take our chances with the lifeboat, said Howard. It's built for heavy seas.

-Crazy again. It's a sheep trough with oars, said Hanaiki.

This was true. And it was old, used mostly to ferry goods ashore and, back when ships found Niihau a place of interest, to rescue seamen from a luckless boat. It was built for short trips and stability, not a channel crossing.

-God helps those who help themselves, Howard said.

When Howard rode back down the mountain, he looked back only once. He wanted to see the bonfire as Kauai might see it, a celestial rising from the ocean, a volcanic eruption. He kept his horse to a trot and glanced only quickly, but in that brief moment his mouth dropped and his scalp tingled. The flames leaped high. Black smoke began to cover the stars. Even from this distance he heard the angry crackle of wood giving way. Sparks ricocheted like glowing bees. He didn't want to look too long, afraid it might hypnotize him or beckon him back to the peak, which now seemed imbued with the fire's power, a sacred, untouchable place of spirits and gods. He imagined his neighbors staring at their tremendous bonfire with mournful eyes, their large hands in their pockets, not speaking much. O God, keep the wind down, he prayed. O Ancestors, keep the air calm. Had they taken on too much? And now he was proposing to row across the ocean.

Howard kicked his horse to go faster down the scree.

Yoshio called repeatedly for Howard, but the air was silent. Except for the occasional stamp of a horse he could not see, the whole village of Puuwai was deserted. It was eerie, and for Yoshio, disappointing. Finally, he'd hoped to explain to his neighbors why he and the pilot were doing this. That there was a war on and a Japanese squadron was on the way. They were taking a long time (Pearl Harbor had been bombed five days ago, he calculated), but perhaps that was the way war was. He would assure his neighbors that the pilot would keep them safe as long as they cooperated. But there was no one to speak to. No doubt, Mrs. Niau had told the whole village that Mr. Harada had stolen her cart. It hadn't been that way of course—they'd only borrowed it to make things go more smoothly. But he remembered that look she'd given him, of disdain and fury. Now they had fled from him, ignorant, as usual.

They had walked around the church twice before Yoshio raised the lantern and turned to Nishikaichi. It threw fearsome shadows under the pilot's face.

-I wish it hadn't turned out this way, said Yoshio. The people running from us.

The pilot only shrugged. He looked toward the church. The white walls glowed bluish in the moonlight.

-Open the door.

-We leave the weapons outside, said Yoshio.

Nishikaichi looked at him without understanding.

-It's a house of God, said Yoshio.

-Not our god, Harada-san.

Yoshio had been inside the church only a few times—once to fix a pew and another to deliver a new batch of Hawaiian-language Bibles that had arrived with the store supplies. He hadn't thought much of it then—it was like any of the rural churches on Kauai, crowded with pews, dusty, the eaves full of yammering birds. But tonight long, black shadows thrown by the lantern light swayed on the walls. The outline of that wooden Jesus sprawled like a large bat in front of him. Tonight the church was speaking to him, warning him, and he was scared. He wanted to run down the aisle and push his way outside. But Nishikaichi walked behind him and peered at every pew. He hissed at Yoshio to direct his lantern here, there. Yoshio concentrated on slowing his breath and stilling his shaking hands. He ignored the bang of the pilot's gun against the benches.

Then they heard it. The unmistakable whimper of a human voice. When Yoshio swung the lantern, he saw a kneeling figure in the front pew.

Nishikiachi leaped onto a wooden seat and pointed the gun at the person, who wept raucously now.

-He'll shoot, cried Yoshio. The figure sobbed louder.

-Little Preacher? said Yoshio. Again?

The boy blinked rapidly as the lantern light hit him. His hands jerked to his face. Well, it made sense he'd be here, pleading with his god. His faith had not wavered.

-Get up, Yoshio said as gently as he could. Little Preacher did not move.

-I mean it, said Yoshio. I can't account for the pilot and what he'll do with his gun.

-Yellow heathen, gulped Little Preacher. Japanese devil.

Yoshio reared back as if he had just been hit.

-What did you say?

-Japanese devil! Little Preacher sobbed.

There was a silence as Yoshio seemed to be deciding something. Little Preacher, startled by his own vehemence, sobbed louder. Yoshio blinked. Despite the noise he heard something low and harsh in his ear. *Yellow sissy,* came a whisper from somewhere inside him. *Put your hands together and beg.*

-Get up! Yoshio was suddenly yelling. One of his arms was flapping, swiping the side of his own face as if something had bitten him. Little Preacher, shocked, terrified, covered his head. I'm in charge here! Yoshio screamed. Move or I'll send you to your white god!

They marched him through the village, Yoshio pushing a shotgun in his back with quick, forceful jabs.

-Please, come . . . come back . . . , Little Preacher began shakily.

-Louder, say it louder, grunted Yoshio.

The young Niihauan began to call and shout and yell for his neighbors. The pilot wanted to get as many prisoners as possible, in order to pressure Howard into giving the papers back. Yoshio pushed the barrel hard into Little Preacher's back, feeling the vertebral resistance and pushing harder. His hands were white hot. His eyes felt as if they had expanded in their sockets. This was a new feeling for him. He had felt angry before, but now he was angry and powerful.

-Louder, he hissed again. Or I'll make you beg. You hear me? You'll beg on your hands and knees.

Moments later there was an answering call from behind one of the houses.

Kaahakila Kalimahuluhulu, a young cowboy known as Kalima for short, ran onto the road toward them.

-Okay? Little Preacher, you okay? Kalima said breathlessly.

They tied Kalima's hands, though they kept Little Preacher's free, which in later years would plague him. Had he not been enough of a man? Had they realized that he was not a threat to them, that he did not have the guts to do anything unexpected, that he was not wily and strong like Kalima, but a weak-willed, tearful boy capable only of empty prayers and acquiescence? When he became a minister a few years later, many of his sermons were about how the meek would inherit the earth, though he wasn't so sure. Later in life he began to shun the New Testament, reading and preaching the Old Testament only, so that his parishioners always left his sermons slightly unhinged by his long descriptions of plagues and bloody animal sacrifices.

But he didn't think of any of this now. He was too busy repeating the Twenty-third Psalm as he lifted a machine gun from the plane and staggered under its weight.

Nishikaichi, without a word, watched Little Preacher struggle. Yoshio, encouraged, started to say something disparaging about the young Hawaiian. But the pilot was uninterested in Little Preacher; he was staring instead at his plane.

-It's perfect, he murmured. Yoshio frowned. What did the pilot say?

-The plane, Nishikaichi repeated. It's perfect.

Even as he said it, he knew it was not entirely true, at least not mechanically. The Zero was the best fighter plane in the skies. It flew higher and faster than anything else. But there was one fault. Nishikaichi knew it, all her pilots did: the Zero rolled too slowly when it turned to the right. The left turn was balletic, a welcome snap, a gut-wrenching twist. But the right: it was as if an unseen current pushed back on the wing. A novice airman did not notice, but the seasoned pilots felt it under their palms, in the pits of their stomachs, against their right shoulders. Too slow. They tried to adjust; each had a technique that they shared in training: dive first, less rudder, more rudder, dive late. But there was no real answer, just hopeful tactics and, for some, small superstitions—candles were lit over the rudder pedals, fruit laid on the right wing. After a while none of the veteran flyers talked about it much. But, Nishikaichi knew, if the American enemy found out this small weakness, the great strengths of the plane would be useless. It was the silent Achilles' heel.

Little Preacher fell to the ground suddenly. The clatter of the gun startled both men. Kalima shouted anxiously to his friend, who got to his feet clumsily and wiped his face.

-To the cart with that gun! Yoshio turned from the pilot and his odd, intent focus on the plane. He became menacing once again, poking Little Preacher with the nose of the shotgun and shouting. The two walked away, leaving Kalima cross-legged on the ground, his face collapsed in a scowl, his arms tied tightly behind him. Nishikaichi stayed too, and picked up the earphones one more time and fiddled with the radio knobs as if somehow, by a miracle, it would be working now, when he needed it to, as if the whole fact that his mighty plane was crushed and crumbled and disappearing into the earth was simply a trick of the light and that somehow, in the darkness, it had repaired itself.

Little Preacher returned, looking shaken and exhausted. Yoshio was behind him, a strange shine to his face. His eyes were greedy and wide, his mouth sagged down at the edges.

-You okay? said Nishikaichi.

-I'm going to send Kalima to tell Irene we won't be back tonight.

-He won't go, said Nishikaichi. He'll just run and hide.

-These Niihauans do what they're told, hissed Yoshio. He poked the shotgun into Kalima's chest.

-Run to my house, tell Irene we'll be back in the morning. He grabbed the ranch hand under one armpit and hauled him to his feet. Pushing his face close he whispered,

-You don't and I shoot your young neighbor here, and anyone else I find. Then he shoved him in the direction of Robinson's ranch.

Kalima set off, shuffling, lopsided, the ropes on his wrists burning. When he looked back and the plane and the men were out of sight, he cut into the scrub. He headed to the beach and its caves, where the Niihauan villagers hid and prayed.

26

On Friday evening Robinson fell asleep in a kitchen chair while reading a book on botany. His nose lay on *Camellia sinsensis,* but his thumb was fifty pages forward, on *Flora monacensis.* He woke to a banging on the door. Thinking it was the army officer with news at last, he sprang from the chair and threw the door open. Foreman Shanagan stood panting on the doorstep.

-They've lit a signal fire, he stammered. Lester's boy told me he heard it in town and I went'a see for myself and sure enough, it's blazing. Something's wrong if they've abandoned the kerosene lamps and gone for a fire. Let's take the boat out now, Mr. Robinson. Navy be damned!

Robinson grabbed his hat and coat. He whistled for a stable hand to saddle up his favorite horse.

-We can't take a boat, warned Robinson. They'll shell us from the air.

-But . . .

Robinson shook his head and put out a hand to calm his ranch manager.

-Stay here. I'm going to the base.

The MP at the gate shone a flashlight first at his horse's face and then at Robinson's own. Back to the horse. Another mainland *haole*, thought Robinson, about to make a crack about cowboys and Indians. For the past two days, they had come in droves, stuffed into the cargo planes that arrived hourly. The planes were large-bellied beasts with huge wingspans that heaved and groaned on landing, as if defying gravity was, in the end, too tiring. Once the men were disgorged, their pale skin and unstreaked hair marking them as mainlanders, the machines squatted on the tarmac in long, dark rows, like crows waiting for carrion. Then they lifted off again, bound for the next load.

The MP didn't make a crack, just waved him in. He recognized Mr. Robinson from his other futile trips to the base.

Just after midnight, on Niihau, six men did what their Old Lord could not. They pushed a boat into the water. Anyone nearby might have thought it was just the quiet antics of night animals—the snuffle of a swimming monk seal, the splash from a school of passing fish. The men knew how to be quiet, having hunted for years with only a knife and a nose faced into the breeze.

There was but one set of oars and Howard volunteered to go first. He rowed quickly for a few minutes, from the excitement and adrenaline and a real fear that perhaps they would be fired upon. The others watched Niihau slowly recede, a low-slung shadow on a light gray ocean. The bonfire was no longer lit, and the waning moon meant the stars were brilliant. Quickly the initial adrenaline it had taken to run to the beach, gather the oars and a jug of water, and drag the boat along the sand disappeared. The men turned to one another in bewilderment.

-We sure about this? Captain said. He would be the navigator to Kauai.

-My wife's pregnant, another said. I shouldn't leave.

Someone coughed.

-The Old Lord will be angry.

-Yes, agreed someone else. Better if we wait for Mr. Robinson to come to us.

Howard dropped the oars so that they slapped suddenly against the water.

-No choice, he hissed indignantly. No one's coming to help, we're on our own. What's to fear, our *kupuna* have done this for centuries. Even our grandmothers helped to row. You talk like this, their spirits cry in shame!

-That was in an outrigger canoe. Not some *haole* contraption, mumbled Captain.

Someone laughed. Howard did then too. He slapped Captain's knee.

-You guide us there safely, we take turns rowing. Easy as herding cattle. You'll see.

Captain navigated by the stars. He used *Akau* in the Large Bear, and then as it rose, the Cat's Cradle. Once a pod of whales swam by, exhaling loudly. Early on, when the men were still relatively fresh, Howard told stories, and invariably they were exaggerated, and he felt especially glad when one or more of the men scoffed and told him it wasn't true. In the dark and the wind, a small argument would break out and they would forget their aches and their blisters and their fear. And he prayed. He prayed that they were doing the right thing, he prayed for safe passage, but mostly he prayed that the water would stop splashing over the gunnel, soaking them all. He was wet and cold. Cold! he thought. When was the last time a Niihauan complained of cold? Despite his growing misery, or perhaps because of it, his senses sharpened; the tilled-soil smell of Kekuhina's sweat was distinct in the wind, he heard the tiny scratch of a misaligned oarlock. At one point while it was his turn to pull on the oars, he thought of horses, and then, for no reason, the thick taste of condensed milk. His hands burned from blisters. Now and then the air suddenly smelled of peppermint and he thought he saw a shark swimming just to one side, a broken, refracted shadow that slipped in and out of the dipping oars. All the men had long fallen silent, and only the occasional guttural windup of saliva aimed carefully overboard broke the wind's moan and the rustle of the water.

Back on the beaches of Niihau, villagers pulled Kalima into a cave and untied his hands.

-They're gathering enough ammunition to kill each one of us, gasped Kalima.

-They've got Little Preacher? someone cried.

-Lord have mercy! Little Preacher's mother began to sob.

The villagers spoke at once, until Kalima finally raised his hand and said, Enough!

Ella sat in the shadows to one side of the cave and listened to Kalima's story with a growing horror. Her right leg was beginning to go numb. She closed her eyes to try to sleep but saw only the plane, rising like a wounded animal, with Mrs. Harada on its back.

-We can sneak back and steal the guns, said Kalima. Who's with me? Ben?

Ben didn't answer. He sat on his haunches at the cave opening. His arms were wrapped around his knees, his head was erect, and he stared outward to the sea.

-Ben? They have guns, but we know the island. We could steal the cart—

-Heard you, Ben interrupted.

Kalima was silent. He ran a finger along the dirt in quick, nervous movements.

-Who would think, Mr. Harada, Ben said quietly.

-No one was more surprised than me when he stuck out that gun.

-He's being forced by the pilot.

-Believe me, he looked like he enjoyed it. Almost broke Little Preacher's spine, the gun into his back like that. He kept saying *beg, beg*, and laughing a kind of crazy laugh.

Ben sighed.

-Okay, he said, pushing himself carefully to his feet. His hips hurt, his back was stiff. His head was light with hunger and thirst. We go.

Nishikaichi stared at the coils of ammunition on the floor of the cart. He picked one up and felt its weight. Once the guns had been successfully removed from the plane, they had let Little Preacher go. He would be of little use, and his frightened prayers had only agitated Yoshio even more.

-We're going to have to nail this down somehow, he said jiggling the gun and frowning.

-You shoot that?

-Maybe.

Yoshio looked at its thin, dangerous snout, its splayed legs. The shotgun was ominous enough, the machine gun gave him the veritable shivers.

-None of the Niihauans are armed.

-So you say.

Yoshio laughed bitterly.

-If you knew Robinson, you'd believe me. You think he wants guns in the hands of children? Robinson views all the Niihauans as children.

The pilot shrugged.

-I am well aware of the *ai* that a superior feels for his inferiors. Funny, isn't it, how much your island here is like Japan.

He looked at the machine gun.

-This will help us destroy the plane. For now, let's find those papers.

Nishikaichi strode down the dirt road toward the church once more. Yoshio ran to catch up.

They both saw the light in the third house. Guns in hand, they entered, Yoshio calling loudly in warning to drop all shovels and knives, lest they be shot without remorse. There by the lamplight sat old Mrs. Huluwani, a woman Yoshio barely knew because she couldn't walk and rarely left her home. She read the Bible by lamplight. She looked at them calmly when they entered.

-Are you going to shoot her? asked Yoshio in a strangled voice as the pilot raised the shotgun. He looked wildly from the gun barrel to the old woman.

-*Ke Akua ke hiki ke pepehi,* said Mrs. Huluwani evenly. Only God can kill. She looked back down at her Bible.

-What did she say? asked Nishikaichi.

-She said—she said nothing here, no papers. Yoshio licked his lips. Come on, we go.

Nishikaichi raised the gun and fired it into the ceiling. Mrs. Huluwani didn't move her eyes from the page, nor did her hand jerk quickly to her throat. It was as if she had heard nothing, and Yoshio thought, after he rose a second later from the crouching position he had flung himself into, that she was deaf, or that there was something to her devout faith in her God that allowed her an implacability he would never understand.

Nishikaichi turned on his heel and left. Yoshio bent over and waited for his heart to stop pounding.

-I'm sorry, so sorry, sorry, he murmured to the old woman as he backed out of the house.

He could see the shadow of Nishikaichi beyond the porch. He stumbled down the stairs. He would say something. This craziness had to stop. But as he approached, Nishikaichi raised his gun to the stars.

-Should I shoot down another plane, Harada-san? And he fired.

Yoshio dropped to his knees again and waved his arms.

-We'll check the Kanaheles' house, he begged. Perhaps the papers are there. Then the Niaus' house. We'll check that too. Just stay calm, Nishikaichi-san. Please.

But they found nothing. By the fourth house Nishikaichi had sunk into an expressionless trance. He said they would return to destroy the plane.

But when they got to the cart, the ammunition was gone. The machine guns were useless now. Nishikaichi howled in frustration and let himself kick the dirt in a rare display of boyish temper. Then he put his head in his hands, breathed once or twice, and when he next raised his head his expression was still and unreadable, shadowed into a strange geometry by the lantern at his feet. Yoshio felt the small hairs rise on his neck.

-We burn it all, Nishikaichi said.

27

There was something fascinating to Yoshio about the flames that now destroyed Howard's house. They were sinewy, bright, gaudy. And for a moment, watching as the roof collapsed in on itself with first an unwilling wheeze and then a great crash, Yoshio understood that any part of him that thought that he was in control of his life, that things today would progress as he decided, and not with the inevitable march of a force much bigger than he, had disappeared. He wanted to run back to Irene, to face what he had mistaken for faith. He knew now that it was a certainty in his flaws and not her belief in his strengths that she had used to get him here. Irene *knew* that he was not helping the pilot out of conviction, but because she wanted him to. He had come up with the excuses later—*best for Niihau, best for everyone*—to hide what must've been obvious to her (but not to him, not until now) at the time—that he was desperate to please his wife. To make up for past mistakes. To undo what could never be undone.

He wanted to feel angry with Irene, to curse and blame her for where he was now. He wanted to roar like Howard's house was doing, in fury and discontent, in righteous anger. But instead he felt only the thin, persistent smoke of self-loathing strangling his gut. He could not hate Irene, nor blame her. At least Irene did what she did with conviction, with relentless faith. She would save her family, even if it meant manipulating her husband. Well, that was understandable. It was he who had once again blundered.

The heat from the fire was suddenly too much, and Yoshio turned his head away. He thought of how the Niihauans worshiped Robinson, and how Nishikaichi worshiped his emperor. He worshiped Irene. In this way all their lives were tightly circumscribed—the Niihauans by the perimeter of the island, the pilot by his sense of duty, and Yoshio by the defining moment of his life, when he saw what he had become: a coward in front of the *luna*. Irene was the only one who worshiped no one, and who fought gamely all the boundaries that held her in. Her belief? In herself alone.

The pilot stared at the burning house without even raising a hand to deflect the intense heat. The flicker of shadow and light on his face gave the impression of conflicting emotions parading across his features, but in fact his expression was impassive. He had seen houses burn before, from the vantage point of his plane, and he had always watched with a boyish fascination for spectacle. He would let his mouth drop and his eyes widen. He would sometimes exhale loudly at an extraordinary burst of color. But today he had emotions he could not let out at all. This burning house was different from the others. It was right in front of him, so close he could feel its furious heat, its betrayed, anguished cries. And it had context. Here, he had been fed and cared for. He had sung Japanese songs, the people had laughed. As the porch dropped from its foundation, sending sparks in the air, he gritted his teeth. He kept staring without turning his head. Keep looking straight on, he thought. Straight on, like a soldier.

Finally the fire began to settle. Nishikaichi allowed himself to wipe the ash from his face. There, he thought. If the papers were inside, they were destroyed now. He would commence to burn every house in the village. If the papers were instead buried in this hard, red soil, he was sure someone would tell him before their house was destroyed. But first there was something more important to which he had to attend. He stepped forward and yanked a partially burned piece of wood from a smoldering pile. He lifted it above his head, the burst of oxygen bringing the flame to life. Without a word to Yoshio, he turned and headed back to his plane.

Yoshio kicked at the pile and hesitated. Howard's house was heaving a final sigh, the remnants of one wall leaning precipitously. It didn't feel right to leave it, a funeral that was not yet over. But he'd had enough of the black smoke, the sound of things giving way, the smell. He walked sideways toward the sagging, smoke-swirled house, warding off the heat, keeping his eyes on the ground for an apt torch. He found a burning balustrade and picked it up. There was no turning back now. It was time to burn the plane.

Captain stood up in the boat and pointed. Someone yelled. Howard's chin had fallen to his chest and he'd begun to snore, but he jerked awake at the noise. Instantly they saw what had caused the alarm. There was a fire on Niihau. But it wasn't on Mount Paniau. It came from Puuwai.

The sky slowly lightened. Dawn was near. It was Saturday, December 13.

The pilot balanced on the wing, his torch held high above him. He stared down at the cockpit where he had spent so many hours. They had been lonely hours, yes, but also, when he'd looked from one side to the other as he flew in formation with his squadron, hours when he had felt a part of something bigger than himself. It had given him meaning, this plane. He wanted to sit in the now crumpled seat and put his hand on the stick and close his eyes. Instead, he ran his hands along the dashboard, leaving a smear in the dust and a glimpse of the dials and numbers that had once helped him across the sky. He wanted, one more time, to feel the hum of the powerful engine, see the corona of propeller. But it was his duty to destroy his Zero, and he would do it.

-Everything okay, Nishikaichi-san? Yoshio called from below. Nishikaichi had not realized that the man had followed him, his own torch held above his head.

-Everything's fine.

-We'd better hurry. Yoshio nodded at the plane.

-Yes.

Yoshio clambered onto the wing. Nishikaichi stared at the seat.

-It's going to be hard without explosives, he said.

-Everything burns in the Niihau heat, said Yoshio, and with that he unceremoniously dipped his burning piece of wood into the cockpit. Black smoke scurried sideways. The flame jumped. But Nishikaichi swung his arm into Yoshio's and the torch skittered over the door and into the sand below.

Yoshio, wide-eyed, stepped backward.

-It's mine to destroy, said Nishikaichi. And with that he pushed his own torch into the seat as if thrusting a sword into a heart.

The leather curled and shrank before it finally began to burn. Yoshio kept his distance; Nishikaichi watched the growing flame with his mouth pressed closed and his eyes narrowed against the smoke. The fire grew higher and smokier. Suddenly a sense of relief washed over him, as if the grief he'd felt had found a hole in his foot and leaked away, and in its place was this new feeling, and the realization that finally, he would complete his mission.

28

Howard watched the sky turn pink, then yellow, then blue. He no longer shivered. They had forgotten their hats in their haste and now their lips felt dry as stone. Their hands stung from salt and raw skin.

The water had run out hours ago.

But Kauai finally seemed to be getting bigger, and the currents in their favor, or perhaps it was just that they were all so tired they had acquired the feverish optimism of men in the desert who see mirage after shimmering mirage and still are sure the next one is real. The ocean had taken on a hallucinatory quality; each shadow became a fish, a bird, a man, a god. When it was Howard's turn at the oars again, he rowed with his tongue hanging out shamelessly and his eyes squeezed shut. Only the Captain kept watch now; he spotted his herd of merino sheep just off the bow, but he was quiet about it. He didn't want to startle either his shipmates or the animals.

Someone took Howard's place at the oars and he sat with one hand into the wind, palm skyward, to soothe the pain.

Despite the lack of water, the exertion, and the blinding heat, the greatest danger—and the Niihauans did not realize this—came from the air. The United States military had orders to destroy any ship on the sea. But miraculously no one saw the bedraggled crew and their tiny craft. After rowing for eleven hours, the Waimea dock came plainly into view. On it were a crowd of people who, with guns sighted, waited tremulously for the Japanese invasion to begin.

When the boat pulled within shouting distance, two *haole* police officers waded in until knee deep and demanded in English that the rowers give their names and destination. Howard stood up in the boat and waved joyously. The man on the oars found a second wind and Howard, caught unaware by the sudden change in speed, almost fell overboard. Ignoring the drawn guns, they sped by the police officers and, when the hull hit the sand, tumbled over the gunnels, waving at the Kauaians. One police officer waded back onto shore and shouted.

-No boats on the water, he yelled angrily. Can't you read that sign? He pointed to the large board with hand-painted lettering next to the dock.

-This is Mr. Robinson's boat, said Howard. He was the only one who spoke or understood English.

-I don't care whose boat it is, the police officer snarled. There's a war on and no one's allowed on the water.

The rest of the Niihauans were walking unsteadily up the beach. Some of the civilians, having quickly realized that these were not Japanese insurgents, put down their guns and reached to grab the men's arms to keep them upright.

-But it's Mr. *Robinson's,* Howard repeated. Even with a war, which they knew about by now, no one superseded Robinson's authority. They imagined that he was king of this island too, and that Makewali was his palace and the inhabitants here as beholden to him as were the Niihauans.

Howard kept asking for Robinson while the rest of the men in the boat jabbered on excitedly in Hawaiian. The *haole* police officers didn't speak Hawaiian, but they quickly recognized that the boatload weren't enemies of the state. Boozing locals, they grimaced to themselves. Ignorant natives too drunk to reason with. They told Howard to come with them to the police station. The other men would stay at the shoreline. They would call Mr. Robinson and straighten out whatever was going on.

Howard felt better once he had a little water and a seat beneath him that didn't sway. He washed his hands carefully in a sink behind the station as he waited for Mr. Robinson to arrive. He inspected the loose flaps of skin and the blood blisters and decided that for now he could handle the pain if he remembered not to shake hands, as he was wont to do, or pick up buckets or saddles. He was ready with the apologies for Mr. Robinson: *Sorry we left without permission, sorry about the fire, sorry about leaving the cattle and sheep and bees for this long, sorry about the stranger on the island . . .*

A man entered the room with a hesitant walk. The brim of his hat was crumpled, and next to the long strides of the sergeant who accompanied him, his steps were jerky and short. At the police desk he stopped as if waiting for instructions. Howard squinted at him; something was familiar.

The man turned and called his name.

Howard blinked to clear his eyes. Perhaps this was an apparition that had followed him from the water.

His name was called again, and a hand rose.

Howard raised his own hesitantly.

The froth of a horse ridden fast in the morning heat had congealed on Mr. Robinson's knees. His face was crimped with worry. He looked older, diminished, as if the air had been sucked from the interstices of his skin and left him limp. Howard's confusion deepened; it was as if the Old Lord had sent a lesser twin to greet him.

-What's happened over there, Mr. Kaleohano? There was Robinson's familiar gait now, his feet hanging in the air an extra moment, as if more comfortable above ground than on it, his sky blue eyes flashing, a big hand reaching out to grip Howard's shoulder. When Howard had regained his composure and started on his apologies, Robinson waved them aside.

-What's happened? he repeated.

-A Japanese pilot landed. He wants to kill everyone, said Howard.

-The Japs are on Niihau? exclaimed Robinson. He repeated this in English and the hubbub in the station house stopped. Men leaned forward, openmouthed.

Howard nodded. He looked around the quiet police station and sized up the police officers. He'd always suspected that Robinson had his own contingent of law enforcers. Now that they knew the enormity of the situation, why didn't they spring immediately into action for the Old Lord?

-You round up your men here, Mr. Robinson, and we leave now for the island.

-And there's only one Jap, you say? You sure about that? Robinson paused. How can the whole island be terrorized by one pilot?

-That's the bad news, said Howard, shaking his head. It's the Haradas, Mr. Robinson. They help too.

Lieutenant Jack Mizuha heard of the battle on Niihau in the lunchroom that day. Eavesdropping over his plate of rice, he kept his face composed and hard. A Japanese pilot, they said. A nisei couple. Guns fired, houses burned. He tried to look nonchalant as he pushed his tray aside. Once in his dark, cramped office, he picked up the phone to call the district commander, Lieutenant Colonel Eugene Fitzgerald.

-I'd like to lead the attack on Niihau, he told his superior.

-Now, Jack, the lieutenant colonel replied. We've got the CO handling it.

Mizuha heard him cough away from the phone, then put his hand over the mouthpiece and speak to someone in the background in muffled tones.

-Is it true that a nisei is helping the enemy army? Mizuha asked.

-Word travels farther than our artillery around here, Fitzgerald sighed. Seems these Niihauans are engaged in hand-to-hand combat and using ancient Hawaiian war techniques to defend themselves. There're rumors about bombs dropping and Jap parachutists jumping in, but we've ascertained there's only one soldier, as far as we can tell, if those Hawaiians know what they're talking about. And yes, there's a Jap couple been working there, who're shooting right alongside the pilot.

Mizuha clamped his eyes shut. Terrible, terrible news, he thought, and he wondered what would happen to his family here on Kauai when people began to find out. It was one thing to get demoted from his command of the base because of prejudice; it would be quite another to be killed.

-This thing will blow over, Jack. You're a good army man, Jack, we all know that. It's just that sometimes we have to let the stupid people run the show for a while. This is the Stupid People Show now, right, Jack? So just sit tight, I know this rankles a bit, but be patient.

-I'm not asking for my command back. I'm asking to lead the rescue party to Niihau.

-I know what you're saying, Jack. It just won't look too good, sending you.

Mizuha then heard a small, sharp *whoosh,* which he realized was the sound of a match being struck.

-You understand, Jack, Fitzgerald continued after a pause in which Mizuha could see him stretching back, a cigar in his mouth and his feet planted wide, perhaps simultaneously reaching for the can of roasted macadamia nuts he always had on a nearby shelf.

-With all due respect, sir, replied Mizuha slowly, it might look better sending me. You'll have yourself a race riot once people find out some nisei folks are helping the enemy. It'll be anarchy here on Kauai, white coming down hard against yellow, you know as well as I do. Unless we show that we're patriots, sir, this island will explode within hours.

There was a pause and a sucking sound. Mizuha waited.

-I see your point, Jack, Fitzgerald finally said. I'll get back to you.

29

When the sun rose on Saturday, December 13, there was a haze in the air that could not be attributed to dust. The villagers wandered out of the caves morosely, exhausted by their own imaginations; they pictured all of Puuwai a pile of ashes, and the *mai ka ʻaina ʻe* shooting and killing the villagers who were not accounted for. One by one they waded into the sea to wash and wake up, the children all the way in, the men up to their belt loops to splash water under their arms and on their faces, the women only to their ankles because of their *muʻumuʻus*. They moved slowly, speaking little. Their prayer session was quick and without feeling.

No one had eaten or drunk since the previous afternoon; the younger children cried first for food and water, the older children picked at their hands and looked at the ground. The women hushed the babies and brought them into the caves for shade. The men began to gather in a circle outside to discuss the whereabouts of the nearest spring and the few implements they had with which to collect water.

When it became clear to the older women that their men, who had begun to argue quietly, were no nearer a solution, Ella marched over, her hair bursting from her head, her dress dripping sparks of water from its hem.

-We just go into the village and get food and water. We can't let the foreigners scare us like this. Come on, a few of you can come with me, we'll split up and see what we can find.

-Hush, Mama, said Ben. That's foolishness. Those men have gone crazy there. They've got guns and boiling tempers. We're risking death to go back there.

-You went and stole the ammunition. Ella narrowed her eyes. Soon the children will be crying and screaming and they'll find us here anyway. I've got a bucket full of cooked poi and a rack of salted fish at the house. Shame to let Mr. Harada and his friend eat it. Doesn't seem right, even.

-Ella, that's enough, said Ben. Let us figure this out.

Ella went on as if she hadn't heard.

-We can't go much longer without water. We either hike to a spring now or people won't have the strength in the heat of the day. Or we go back to the village for supplies. The good Lord Jesus Christ will help us in our time of need. Some of you've gone back to the old ways, is what I've heard, relying on ancient stories and spirits to get you through this hard time. Well, that's a mistake—it's only God who can help us now. I say we go back to the village and see what the Lord provides. Take some of the *wahines*. Those men might have guns, but they won't shoot a woman, I tell you.

Ella marched off. Hanaiki Niau shook his head.

-Brother Ben, your Ella is quite a handful. But she has a point. Let's send a few people back to Puuwai. It can't hurt.

-Hurt! We could get killed.

-No one's had water, it'll only get worse here.

Finally they agreed that three groups would be sent. One would consist of Kalima and his two sisters, another would be Ben and Ella, another still of the Keo twins. All were ordered to bring back whatever food and water they could carry.

* * *

Ben led, Ella followed; they walked in silence. Sometimes Ben took off his hat and swung it like a rope around his head, warding off flies. Or he held back a low-hanging branch so it wouldn't ricochet into Ella after he had passed. They ignored the dust each kicked up. They kept alert for the sound of strange footsteps.

They smelled the charred remains of Howard's house before they saw it. Ben motioned that he did not want to stop, but Ella ignored him. She walked to the edge of the clearing and crouched behind a *kiawe* tree.

Howard's house looked like the skeletal remains of a steer, the ribs of the place still barely upright, the odd plank extended at an angle into the air, as if with rigor mortis. The lava wall was intact, and chickens walked its periphery in mournful confusion, having wandered back from where they'd fled only to find that their home had altered considerably.

-Jesus in heaven, Ella whispered.

-We must move on, hissed Ben.

-How dare they, she responded.

Ben pulled on her elbow, but she shook him off.

-It's that plane, she hissed. It's—

-Hush, you're making too much noise. He grabbed her more firmly, aware that she never liked to be told what to do, that this would precipitate another argument like the one they'd had the other day, he was sure, but that they had to get out of here, and soon.

-Think of the others! Ben whispered. We need to get food and water—

-That plane— Ella would not be deterred.

-There's nothing you can do about that plane. Come on.

There was a shout behind them. Ella and Ben instinctively put their hands on their heads, as if someone had warned them of a rock slide, but both of them recognized the voice immediately. The pilot pointed a pistol at them.

They stumbled into the clearing, the pilot roughly urging them toward the plane in a language they did not understand. Yoshio, who had been dozing in a seated position among the wreckage, scrambled to his feet.

-Mr. and Mrs. Kanehele! he cried. He began to push some debris aside. Watch your feet. There's glass and sharp objects everywhere.

The pilot motioned for them to sit on the ground. Ben put out a hand to help Ella but she ignored it. She pulled her *mu'umu'u* up to her shins.

-How could you have done this? she said to Mr. Harada, and snorted her disdain for him, the pilot, the situation they were now in. Ben sat nearby, glancing between the pilot and Mr. Harada as if assessing which one was more dangerous. All around them the wreckage of the plane protruded from the dirt, as if bubbling from it. Sheared parts stained the red dirt black, now and then the rising sun caught one just right, so that it winked conspiratorially. Ella looked around for a clear place to sit, and noted that the pieces weren't as shiny as the one that Mrs. Kaleohano had shown off at the Haradas' store, nor did they hold the magic Ella had seen that day. They looked like what they were, scrap metal of no real use to anyone anymore.

-What does he want of us, Mr. Harada? Ella said indignantly, lowering herself cross-legged onto the ground. Not to mention the sad fact that you've helped him on his mission of destruction. How could you do this?

-It's for the best, Yoshio stammered. He began to pace in front of her. Listen, if we help him, he'll make sure we're all okay when his commanders arrive. I did this for all of you—

But even as he said this, he knew this was no longer true. He had done it for Irene, and for his own sense of self. But for the Niihauans? Maybe there was something to salvage, so that it would work out for them. When the Japanese arrived, he would do something then. And as he thought this, he saw himself raising a hand and staring defiantly into the barrel of an Imperial Navy gun. He could feel his chest filling with determination, his shoulders squaring. Spare the villagers, he would say, and his voice would shake the ground. But then he was back in the red dirt, by the plane, facing Ella. His shoulders were slumped, his breathing short in his chest. No, he had not helped the pilot for the Niihauans. If he had done it for them, he would have told them from the beginning, brought them the truth about Pearl Harbor.

-Trust me, he finally said, lamely.

Ella snorted, and then squinted up at him.

-Howard's house is gone, she said.

-Yes, Yoshio answered. He's been foolish, refusing to hand over the papers, now he's disappeared.

-He taught you to ride, Mr. Harada, Ella said, shaking her head. Isn't that right? He put you on the big white Arabian and showed you how to be a Niihauan. And this is how you repay him?

Yoshio's hands flew together and clasped tightly.

-You can't understand what's going on out there, he cried. Out there in the *world.* There's more to life than just Niihau, Mrs. Kanahele. Things bigger than Mr. Robinson's paradise are happening.

-Bigger than loyalty? Kinship? Neighborly goodwill? I think not, Mr. Harada.

-Hush, Ella, Ben broke in. No use talking sense to them, they won't hear. Mr. Harada, I don't understand what you're up to but that man's got a gun and he seems intent on using it soon enough. Help us now, before it's too late.

The pilot must have begun to understand that the Kanaheles were trying to persuade Yoshio of something treacherous because he began to bark out commands.

-He wants to know where Howard is, Yoshio said quietly. He wants you, Ben, to go find him.

Ben knew Howard was gone, but he said,

-Fine, we'll go.

-No, not Mrs. Kanahele. Just you. He wants to keep your wife here to make sure you come back.

Ben shook his head vehemently. I'm not leaving her here, he said. No.

-The pilot's angrier than I've seen him. You'd better go.

-Go, silly, Ella interrupted grouchily. No need to be the gallant husband. God will look after His own. You're glad to be rid of me anyway. Go, and find Howard.

She kept her eyes fixed on Yoshio as she spoke, as if to strike him down with her gaze. She knew as Ben did that Howard was long gone, perhaps dead himself.

The pilot waved his gun and shouted again. Yoshio looked at him nervously and then back at the old couple on the ground in front of him.

-You must go now, Mr. Kanahele. Please. I'll make sure your wife is all right.

Ben got to his feet slowly. Ella knew that his hips hurt, that he was thirsty and hungry and very tired. Her heart ballooned a little then, and when he was out of sight, she felt unexpectedly forlorn.

Yoshio stared at the place in the thicket where Ben had disappeared. He felt nauseated and it wasn't just that he had not slept all night, or that he had barely eaten since yesterday. He had reached the point that children do after they spread their arms and twirl themselves around, the sudden unmistakable transition from giddy but balanced orientation to a sudden vertiginous confusion, a momentary regret at the silly, nausea-inducing game, and a collapse onto the grass. He did not collapse, but instead let himself fill with the realization that things were now decidedly out of his hands. He was spinning, spinning, spinning, and everything was a frightening blur around him.

He taught you how to ride. Ella's words echoed in Yoshio's mind. The horse's name was High-Stepping Son, but the islanders and even Robinson himself called him Haole for his bright white coat. He was a seven-year-old Arabian and stood eighteen hands high, as nimble as a pony and as bad tempered as a sick old man—sometimes it took three ranch hands to saddle him. Though there were six Arabians corralled next to the ranch house, the Old Lord only ever mounted Haole.

Men were picked to ride him if Robinson was away too long, because after a few weeks without a saddle, it was claimed, Haole reverted to his wilder self, suddenly remembering that he was strong enough to endure blinding Sahara sandstorms and deep, shifting dunes, command a herd of willing mares, and kill any stallion who came near. He would not be coaxed by water or food, and when he was finally caught, it was as if he had never been tamed. These men would keep a close eye on the white horse before they saddled him up. If he drew his lips back and flattened his ears and nipped at the air, they would draw straws to see who the unlucky loser would be who'd have to ride him first. Yoshio had watched this process often enough, on his way to the honey shed, or back from the apiary. But he'd never thought that one day it would be him in there, wheedling with a shaky voice for the big stallion to calm down.

Howard had put Yoshio on smaller, gentler horses first, and it was not long before Yoshio could easily stay in the saddle. But the day Howard told him it was time to ride Haole, he had protested. Howard had just laid a hand on his shoulder and pronounced solemnly that he had faith in him. *You're good with horses*, he'd said. *You can do this.*

Howard had helped steady the animal, and when Yoshio had finally pulled himself onto the saddle, his mixture of terror and elation had made him feel punishingly alive. Afterward Howard told him that *haole* meant white person, yes, but it really meant "without breath," because whites seemed so disconnected from some essential spirit. So don't be scared of a horse without breath, my friend, he'd said sagely.

Without breath, Yoshio thought. Well, I'm fast losing mine. He suddenly realized that he had been exacerbating his nausea by inhaling too fast; the tips of his fingers were tingling and his lips were going numb.

Nishikaichi now dozed on his feet, jerking awake only when his balance faltered. Yoshio swept the ground of debris with one foot and carefully sat down. He did not dare to look at Ella and into her defiant stare.

-I'm feeling very bad tempered about all this, Mr. Harada, she said once, but when he did not respond, she said nothing else.

30

The map hung on the left side of the room. Most days Lieutenant Jack Mizuha stopped to admire it on his way to lunch, stepping into the briefing room after a quick glance over his shoulder to see that no one was around. He liked the festive colors of each country, and the way the world, thus flattened and miniaturized, looked manageable (France, the benign size of a fingertip; Turkey, as wide as a hat badge; China, the width of a hand). It was in all ways a perfect map, except for an almost imperceptible smudge mark on the small yellow square of Indiana, as if that state had been tapped too often with an index finger, or moistened by an inadvertent breath. Mizuha was an educated man, but he'd never been beyond the Hawaiian Islands; he didn't know many people who had. The world was a place he pieced together by reading the local newspaper, borrowing books from the Waimea Public Library, looking at this map. And of the wide kaleidoscope of countries and towns, he wasn't sure why he wanted to visit Indiana most of all. Except that he had once heard that it was called the Heart Land; this sounded vital and beautiful to him.

Today, as he walked into the briefing room, the map was different, and Mizuha turned his head away from it quickly. A red marker pen disrupted the bright colors. Hong Kong, the Philippines, and Thailand were all circled, dates scrawled nearby with no regard for the countries that they obscured. Places that Mizuha had never bothered to inspect, which had only a week ago been small specks in the blue paper sea (Wake Island, Guam, Midway Island), were now haloed in red. Japanese military aggression now bloodied the primary colors and precise lines of Mizuha's world.

Lieutenant Colonel Fitzgerald talked to a tall Caucasian man with bushy eyebrows and a sloped posture. The man said nothing, only pulled on his hat now and then as if shading himself from a nonexistent sun. He wore old denim pants and the toes of his boots were scuffed into pink nubs. Ice blue eyes blinked at the ground as the lieutenant colonel talked. He didn't look like the richest man around. Nor did he have the bearing of someone who inspired obedience and fear. Mizuha remembered the rumors about Mr. Aylmer Robinson and his island. About him being a dictator and enslaving the native Hawaiians there. Far-fetched, he thought now.

Fitzgerald spoke for a few more moments and then looked up as if he had just noticed Mizuha. He swept his arm toward him.

- Officer Jack Mizuha will be leading the mission.

Robinson turned and looked at Mizuha for a beat. Mizuha was used to this—there was nisei hysteria all over the island—but he would give the man only a few seconds before he spoke up himself. It would be impertinent, but so what? It was rude the way the white men treated him. Mizuha clenched his jaw. Robinson continued to say nothing.

One, one thousand, two, two thousand.

Robinson coughed.

Three, three thousand . . .

He rubbed one hand against his hip.

Five, five thousand.

Robinson thrust his hand forward. He nodded.

-Pleased to meet you, he said.

The handshake was quick and firm.

-Anything you need to know about the island, we get squared away during crossing.

-That's fine, said Mizuha. He eyed the man closely.

-And I don't want any guns brought to the island, continued Robinson. No bloodshed. They're a peaceful people. They don't understand aggression.

-We'll do what we can. But this is war, said Mizuha slowly. As a—

-I'm sure that our men will be as conservative as possible, Mr. Robinson, interrupted Fitzgerald. Guns are only a last resort for all of us.

-No bloodshed, Robinson repeated. Officer Mizuha seems like a competent man. I'm confident this will go well. He tugged his hat again, lowered his eyes, and began to walk to the door.

-Mr. Robinson, sir, Mizuha called after him. Robinson turned and, with both of his untrimmed eyebrows raised, waited.

-This Japanese couple on your island. The Haradas. It isn't Yoshio Harada, from Waimea? Drove a Shell Oil truck some ways back.

-That would be him, said Robinson slowly. He's my caretaker. And a beekeeper. A good one. That's why I asked him to my island. Guess I misjudged the man.

Mizuha's heart sank. If someone like Yoshio Harada could do this, what else could happen? He shook his head.

-Well respected here on Kauai, if I remember him right. Only met him a few times, but—well, it seems impossible.

Robinson didn't respond at first. Mizuha watched his face harden and close.

-The Niihauans don't lie, he said sharply. At first I thought, well, to quote the Bible, "he knows not what he does." But in the end the reasons don't matter. As a military man, Officer Mizuha, you understand this. We must only get to Niihau and solve this situation before it turns more dire.

-Agreed, sir, said Mizuha. He watched Robinson touch his hat and walk out with a peculiar loping gait, each foot in the air a tad longer than needed, unhurried, but purposeful. He did not know if he liked the man, but he understood now how he could run an island efficiently or even, as some said, a kingdom.

31

Ella watched the two men carefully. Both were tired. This made the pilot ornery. He would doze off, she noticed, and then wake suddenly, whereupon he gripped his gun and looked around with a fierce expression, masking his confusion with anger. Mr. Harada, on the other hand, laid his shotgun across his lap and stared at it, as if he couldn't quite believe that something this heavy, this shiny, was on his thighs. His square face sagged oblong with fatigue. His hair, cut short, was blurred with dust. Old sweat had left large circles under the armpits of his shirt, which was untucked.

It was getting hot, and Ella hoped that soon they would move away from the plane and into a house, or even under the nearby *kiawe* trees. Her *mu'umu'u*, reddened by dust, now began to darken with her own sweat. For now the plane provided some shade, but it was more like a spreading stain, and this Ella did not like. And if that wasn't spooky enough, a grayish dust rose from it, as if the plane itself breathed. Ella soon realized that the cockpit was smoldering. They were, for some reason, destroying the plane.

Well, good, she thought. Perhaps that will put an end to its grasp on the island. She could name the vices that had shown up in the islanders with its appearance: greed, envy, wrath, pride, and even sloth. She couldn't account for lust and gluttony, but she wouldn't be surprised. Destroy it, she thought. I'll help if you ask.

But they didn't ask. Mr. Harada wouldn't even look at her. Even the few times she spoke, he did not respond.

There was a call from the scrub, and Ben appeared. His hands were spread to his sides to show that he was not a threat, and there was no sign of Howard. The pilot began to speak rapidly. Yoshio scrambled to his feet, his shotgun at the ready.

-Where's Howard? he called.

Ben did not answer but shook his head repeatedly as he approached. He stopped when he was abreast of Ella, and reached down to touch her head. She expected herself to be annoyed by this gesture (and he did too, so he was tentative and hesitant), but instead she thought she could hear her heart beating up into her skull and his own thundering in his fingertips. She remembered suddenly when he had been a young and earnest lover. It was absurd to think such a thing at this inopportune moment—and certainly unchristian—but there it was, the restirring of an old love, as if the plane itself offered this last thing as recompense.

-Howard is gone, Mr. Harada. He left the island to get help.

Ella recognized Ben's tone. It was the one he used to calm an old chicken that had clambered haplessly onto the lava wall, just before he throttled it for dinner.

-What do you mean, left the island?

-He took a boat with a few other of the men. They've gone for help.

-Help? Yoshio laughed bitterly. The Japanese are on Kauai. You heard me, didn't you, Pearl Harbor has been bombed, the Japanese destroyed everything.

-I'm telling you. He's not here anymore.

Nishikaichi's palms slapped the handle of his gun. Then he barked at Yoshio for a translation. Yoshio shook himself suddenly and pulled one hand across his face.

-Look harder, he hissed at Ben.

-Tell him what I said. Your pilot. Tell him.

-He's going to kill the whole village for those papers, said Yoshio mournfully.

-There's still time to help us, Mr. Harada. Together we can clean up this mess you've made. It's not too late.

- He'll kill me too, to show he means business. He's at the end of his rope.

-Fat lot of good your whining will do now, snapped Ella.

-Mama, warned Ben.

Ella spat in the grass and turned away.

Nishikaichi looked up at the blue sky. He had never shot someone at close range, but if he kept his mind on the Son of Heaven, he could do it. But he must stay clear of any thoughts of the fishmonger's daughter, push her entirely out of his mind, from his whole being. He would not think of the small native child either, and the way her hand had lodged in his and pulled him toward the sea.

-Give me the shotgun, he said. He stuck his pistol in his boot.

He imagined instead his parents, and how proud they were that he was a pilot in the Imperial Navy. Would they be proud of what he was about to do? He saw them at the table, eating. Ribbons of light fell from openings along the roof. His father would be bent over his noodles, so that the small bald spot one couldn't see otherwise would show, the chopsticks clicking lightly. His mother would wait to eat until she knew his father had everything he needed, but she would be at the table too. She had a way of sitting with her head canted to one side. Her hands would form a perfect almond on her lap. A half smile would be frozen on her lips, as if in the middle of listening to a long, expansive tale, but his father would be silent. Were they happy? He did not know. It was not a question he had ever asked himself. They did their duty: kept house and a family, offered their son to their country. That had always been enough.

The pilot looked at the two villagers. It was time to start what he had wanted to avoid. He would shoot them quickly, it would be painless. It would be the most Japanese of deaths, he thought, a sacrifice they would make for their villagers, to stop more violence. Once the rest of this island knew he meant business, they would return his missing papers. They would return the ammunition, so he could fully destroy the Zero, and then himself. These two would not understand the importance of their deaths now, but once they met in the place beyond this world, he would explain. He would shoot the man first, because women were always less of a threat. The old wife would crumble easily, he thought, once her husband was gone.

-Give me the shotgun, he said to Yoshio quietly.

Yoshio glanced at Ben, and back at the pilot. He did not protest, but his face paled. He held the gun out awkwardly, and his hands shook. The man was not good with guns, thought Nishikaichi. But that was fine, very fine, because he would do the dirty work now.

The pilot stepped forward, his arms outstretched for the gun, his mind already racing ahead to the moment the trigger would be pulled, the deafening noise, the cry of the woman as her husband fell without a word.

Something was in motion, coming toward him.

He thought for a moment that one of his comrades rushed forward with open arms to greet him. Where have you all been? he wanted to ask. I've been waiting. But it was an unearthly sound, a roar like the surf, and he knew that this could not be, and he saw the old island man clearly now, rushing, rushing, a short, wide wave about to crash upon him.

Nishikaichi calculated instinctively; he dropped the shotgun, because it was not yet firmly in his grasp, and reached for the pistol in his boot. It slipped free instantly and he fired.

Three shots.

The old man faltered at each one. Stumbled. Kept coming.

Nishikaichi was hit with all the momentum Ben had. The two men fell to the ground and the pistol skittered away.

Nishikaichi knew he would overpower this old man. His hands could feel the blood where he'd been hit. But the Hawaiian surprised him with his strength. Nishikaichi grunted and swore, but the Hawaiian continued to grapple long after he should have passed out. Nishikaichi finally pinned the old man under him. He sat up on the man's hips, and saw that his flight suit was patterned with Hawaiian blood. He stared at the old man's black eyes, glazing over now. He would make this quick, and painless. He pressed his thumbs into the old man's throat.

There was the screaming nearby, high and insistent. A bird, Nishikaichi thought, just as the metal pipe hit him across his temple. There was a great light, and a scream again.

The fishmonger's daughter held out her hand. You've done your duty, she said. But I haven't, Nishikaichi protested, and looked down at the Hawaiian man's dark eyes. They were still open, and they had grown larger, so that he dove, graceful, unhurried, into them, and began to swim. Silly bird, he thought, as it called out again, this time low and deep and somewhere inside him.

Ella had struggled to her feet as Ben charged. Her *mu'umu'u* wrapped around her calves like seaweed, and she caught the hem under her hand and slipped once. But she was used to scrambling quickly. Hadn't she pounced on chickens unwilling to have their necks wrung? Hadn't she grabbed the errant child that scurried too close to the *imu*? She got to the pilot's arm just as he fired his gun.

Ben was hit; she saw it as if in slow motion. The first bullet entered his shoulder and spun him sideways slightly. Amazingly, he regained his balance and kept coming. The next bullet hit his groin, and then as he lunged onto the pilot a final bullet blew open his hip. The blood was vigorous and messy, not like the dainty drops on the church's lovely Jesus. Then as Ben hit the pilot, Ella was thrown off balance, onto the ground. She hit hard, her arm landing on a short metal pipe she supposed belonged to the plane.

-Help him! she screamed at Mr. Harada, who had sunk to his knees and gaped at something on his shirt. Ella pushed herself to her feet and picked up the pipe. Yoshio did not move or look her way. There was blood like a dark scar on his sleeve. He may have been crying, she was not sure.

Ella raised the pipe above her head, letting out a piercing scream. From the corner of her eye she saw a small flame burst briefly from the nearby cockpit, then die. She thought of Pele, the goddess who had made her home here long ago and then, like many others, had left for other islands. There she spewed her emotions in great lava flows. Pele, goddess of fire. Now here she was, come back to destroy the plane that was desecrating her beloved Niihau.

The two men struggled on the ground, though whether these were simply Ben's agonized death throes she could not be sure. How could someone survive bullets at such close range? Her scream had not ended yet, it seemed to jettison from her like *kiulokuloku,* those gale winds from the Pacific that push over everything in their path. The pilot sat up now, her Ben underneath him. That was all it took. She swung the pipe hard and the pilot fell forward without a cry. He fell right on Ben's face, then rolled sideways. She began to pray out loud. To the rhythm of the Twenty-third Psalm, Ella pounded the pilot's head until he was still.

32

Yoshio stared at the dead pilot and the old woman who stood over him. Her expression was blank, her face flecked with blood. Her mouth was opening and closing, but he couldn't hear what she said. It occurred to him that Nishikaichi would not have wanted to die like this, at the hands of a woman. An old woman, at that. It would be, in his mind, dishonorable.

Everything was over.

He put the butt of the shotgun on the ground and leaned his belly into the barrel. It was a long reach, but he was a big man and he thought, How nice it is to be tall, to have long arms to reach with. He had never before appreciated it enough.

The sun burned on his neck as he flexed it downward. Something in this posture, its acquiescence, the way the heat pushed on him like a hand, triggered again, for the last time, that terrible day in California. It came in pictures, as it always did. First, the lopsided grins of the three white men. The smell of bad whiskey. The way the long alleyway that had, a few moments earlier, seemed like a good shortcut narrowed into a black void behind them. The first few punches thrown like leisurely pitches from a baseball mound in a warm-up game. The laughing curses spat his way. *Put your hands together and beg,* they'd finally said. And he hadn't at first but widened his fingers and spread his arms back, as if the farther apart they were the more chance he had. The cement grated against his cheek and he saw one man, tired of punching and kicking perhaps, go down on one knee and lean toward him. The man reached for one of Yoshio's wrists and whispered, *C'mon, a yellow sissy like you knows how to beg.* With his other hand he grabbed the back of his belt. *Didya hear me? I said beg.* He lifted him up, and propped him on his knees, and then delivered a hard punch to his stomach. Yoshio's breath had whooshed from him, and as he struggled to regain it, he thought, This is what it's like to die. *Beg,* the man commanded again, landing another blow, and the breath that had begun to return was whisked away one more time. Yoshio tried to speak, to tell them to stop, he'd had enough, but no words came out. *Maybe he's just stupid,* another man said. But he wasn't stupid. He put his hands together and begged. He begged and begged and begged, his fingers clasped so tightly that he wondered if they would ever let go. *Beg, you yellow sissy.* And he had.

There's something about begging that diminishes you, once and for all. The other insults that America hurled at him daily for being a nisei were nicks and cuts; this was a large, gaping wound. It wasn't just that they had made him say, *I'm a yellow sissy,* over and over, though that had hurt too. It was that he'd had to put his hands together on command and put them up beseechingly, so that they no longer could defend his stomach or his head or anything else. He had to trust that his assailants wouldn't hit him, and that if they did, he would be partly to blame, because there he was, arms raised in supplication, in utter and total defenselessness. Begging like that, he was as helpless as a child. He really was what they said he was, a *yellow sissy.* Something in him was lost that day, speeding out with his breath, never to return. Whatever was left in its place was merely the frame and joists of a person, not the essential spirit. All that remained was someone who could not tell a *luna* that his first child was in danger, who could not be at his wife's side when she needed him most.

He had never told anybody, and sometimes he thought that he himself would forget it, especially here, on Niihau. It was certainly as close as he ever came to it. All he'd ever wanted was to prove to Irene, and to himself, that he was still a man. And finally, a week ago, he'd had his chance in the unlikely form of a Zero whose gas tank had been hit. It was as if it had appeared bearing everything he had lost. It had brought a man with pride, with a mission, and with a sense of self. The Zero had said, *Here, I've kept all this for you since that day. The pilot, he is who you were. Now, come. Follow him and you will have it back*. That's all Yoshio had wanted, really. To regain what was once his. And now even that had gone awry, as if everything he touched was cursed. Finally, he must do the only thing left for him.

-Taeko, he murmured. Forgive me.

The first blast threw him to the ground. He lay looking at the sky, which still had its purple glow and the faint wisp of a cloud. It's going to rain, he thought. That's good.

He reached for the gun again and staggered to his feet. The shot had only grazed him, and he was determined to do at least this one thing right. He felt the sharp tip of the muzzle under his rib cage and pressed harder so as to lodge it there. The pain felt comforting. In the ensuing explosion, as he pulled the trigger, he saw Irene. Her eyes shone and her arms were wide.

-Come, she said to him, pulling a chair forward. Your hair needs cutting.

-Aren't I handsome enough for you yet? he whispered.

Her mouth broke open in long rays of light. She stepped forward and embraced him fiercely.

-Of course you are, she said. You always have been.

33

When Aylmer Robinson finally pulled up to Kii, with a boatload of armed men, there was no one waiting at the dock. He shaded his eyes and frowned, and then told Mizuha that they would have to walk the fifteen miles to town.

At first the soldiers walked as squadrons do: alert to every sound, guns at the ready. But soon the island took hold; their weapons sagged in their hands, sweat streamed down their backs, their gazes dropped to the ground in front of them. The land was endlessly dry, and compared with Kauai, flat. The heat was merciless. Their boots went quickly from spit-polished black to a dusty brown, their canteens emptied fast. The Niihauan men finally pushed ahead and waited at each rise impatiently, their chins pushed forward, their hands clenched in fists. Even Mr. Robinson didn't want to rest, and when Lieutenant Mizuha insisted that they do, he kept his head tilted toward Puuwai, as if listening for any sound that would tell him what was going on there. Finally, the village came into view.

Howard did not look long at the burned remains of his house, though Lieutenant Mizuha sent a few men to size up the ruined plane before they continued deeper into the village. They returned bright eyed with excitement at such a close encounter with an enemy object but reported that there was no one there. Mizuha looked around uneasily. The chickens scratched on the lava walls, the horses grazed peacefully. An *imu* smoked in a front yard, clothes hung on drying lines. But not a villager was in sight.

-Where is everyone? he said. Something's wrong.

Robinson held up his hand and cocked his head. The soldiers stopped shuffling and slapping the butts of their guns to listen.

-You hear? he said.

They turned their heads, tried to hold their breath. But all they heard was the wind and the scuffle of their hearts.

-Listen, listen, insisted Robinson. They're singing.

They heard it now, over the breeze and the pounding of their blood.

-They're in church, Robinson said. That's what it is. It's Sunday, of course, the day of our Lord.

At the church Robinson told the soldiers to wait while he entered and spoke to the Niihauans, but they pushed past him with their guns drawn. The whole congregation stopped singing. They turned with closed faces. They watched the disheveled squadron as they crab-walked down the aisle, each soldier's head dipped into his rifle sights, each mouth tight and nervous.

-It's over, Mr. Robinson, Ella Kanahele said from the back pew. She did not bother to rise. We took care of it.

Ka Haku Makua walked toward her.

-But Ben, she added, he needs a doctor.

After many weeks someone remembered about the bees. Howard knew only a little about beekeeping, but he rode to the Main House anyway. It was silent—Mr. Robinson had gone back to Kauai to help in the war effort and there had been no mention of who was to take care of his home now that the Haradas were gone—Yoshio dead, and Mrs. Harada and her child shipped to the mainland and a prison there. Howard stared at the Main House for a while, assessing its size and the maintenance it might need. Then he led his mare to Irene Harada's store—now closed and boarded up—left her to graze, and walked to the apiary.

Things had changed on Niihau. Every afternoon a low echo would rumble through the scrub. The villagers would turn their heads toward the only road out of town, once little more than a footpath for a sturdy cart, now widened and tamped down into what could pass for a street. A jeep would appear, dark green against the red soil, puffing smoke and dust. Soldiers hung on to the seats as if for dear life. When the jeep pulled to a stop on the bluff, their helmets would rocket sideways on their sweaty heads, their guns would tilt askew from their shoulders. For a while the soldiers would scan the horizon. Then the machine would rev up, sending clouds of red dust into the air. Slowly the jeep would turn, then speed back to Kii, and to the new makeshift army base there.

The jeeps had fascinated the Niihauans at first, as had the electricity poles, the large refrigerators, the gun installations, and everything else that had suddenly been foisted on Niihau within weeks of the Japanese pilot's death. Fraternization between the outsiders and the Niihauans had been strictly forbidden by Mr. Robinson, but something had changed now and even the children visited the small army base on the sly. Lily went, and saw that light could be turned on as if by magic, cool air blown by whirring fans, drinks pulled completely cold from large white containers. What else is out there? she wondered. What other mysteries of the world? Already, Niihau seemed smaller than it had just a season ago. When she was older, in just a few more years, she would go and see things for herself. She told her parents and they scoffed, but worry glinted in their eyes. She was not the only child speaking this way, and even the adults looked up from the beaches now, their hands shading their brows, and stared out to the horizon.

The men also visited the base, bringing back tales of cheap beer smuggled in under the mailbag. Of soldiers who smoked and took the Lord's name in vain. Who complained of the dust and flies so aggressive that they called them "dirty Japs" while slapping them angrily. Who didn't go to church and some who didn't even believe in God, not anymore at least, not since Pearl Harbor. The men came back smelling of cigarette smoke themselves, and sometimes of beer.

For a while the downed Japanese plane had been a distraction for the bored recruits, but it turned out to be of little interest. A Zero in far better shape had already been examined by government experts; this one yielded no new information. The Niihauans found this hard to believe. How could something that had changed their lives so much be considered unimportant? Even the papers that Howard had handed over to their officer—the ones that helped cause so much trouble—had been of no military interest. Just a bunch of drawings of Pearl Harbor, which now lay in ruins anyway.

All that, the Niihauans thought, for nothing.

They got news of the war from the soldiers, and this was passed from house to house. *Not good*, they were sometimes told. *Good*, other times. Places that were hard to pronounce were named and then mangled by each Niihauan family in turn, so that in the end the cities and towns where bloody battles were being fought on far-off islands they would never visit all sounded the same. The Niihauans didn't like hearing about the war, but they considered it their war now. After all, a bloody battle had been fought here, on this red, rocky soil. It was only right that they be kept informed.

* * *

Howard hesitated at the apiary's periphery, as anyone unused to bees was apt to do. The workers would be in a cluster now, keeping the queen and their hive warm until the spring, so that there would be little activity outside, and no chance of being stung. Part of him didn't care what happened to these bees because they were Mr. Harada's pride and joy. Still, he could brush away windblown leaves and scrub, which he did, and walk between the hives looking for signs of unrest or hapless invaders—ants, beetles, rodents. Everything seemed calm until he reached the last hive.

These bees had broken from their winter huddle. Some clung to the slats at the entrance, some were listless on the floor of the apiary, as if they'd walked from the edge of the hive and had no energy left to beat their wings. Alarmed, Howard squatted and peered as close as he dared. There was no other explanation: the queen had died. Every bee in that hive knew it, had known it, within hours of it happening, the information passed by scent from one bee leg to another in a kind of mournful waltz. He imagined their desperate sighs, their slowing wings, their gathering confusion, and perhaps even grief.

At any other time, Howard would've asked beekeeper Shintani for advice, but the old man had been taken away with Mrs. Harada and her child, and the islanders had been puzzled, because his part in the whole tragedy seemed small, insignificant. *He's Japanese*, Mr. Robinson had said simply. Now Howard frowned, and backed away. They would need another queen immediately. Usually Mr. Robinson sent one in by boat; she was de-boxed and unwrapped and placed carefully in the faltering hive. But Howard also knew that bees could make their own queen. It took time and it wasn't reliable—but then, what was? He stared at the white wooden box, the sad, slow bees. A leader could emerge from deep inside that hive, he thought, one of their own. He walked back to his horse and mounted. He glanced once more at the Main House, and even as one part of him was wondering whether he should use the radio at the army base to get word to the Old Lord about the unproductive hive and its dead queen, the other part knew that in the end he would not say anything at all.

Ella stopped to watch the jeep disappear over the bluff that afternoon. She was on her way to sort shells at Hannah's house, where the Kaleohanos were temporarily staying until their own house was rebuilt. She did not start walking again until all the red dust the machine had kicked up had disappeared into the hard blue sky behind it. She liked that quiet moment of watching it rise and blend into the sunlight. She liked everything quiet these days. Ben had returned from the hospital on Kauai, but it would be a while before he walked without crutches or rode a horse. Ella would not admit it, but she liked him there, something solid and sure, parked near the window and peering disconsolately at the dry fields beyond Puuwai, where his beloved cattle wandered without him. When they talked they didn't fight, now that the plane had been picked over by the soldiers and what remained seemed little more than a huge trash pile, not really a plane anymore, and certainly not a powerful spirit. She thought about other things instead: about Ben, for one, and about whether she would go to heaven, now that she had killed a man. The official account was that Ben had done in the Japanese pilot, because it wasn't seemly that a Christian woman could bash in a human head, even that of an enemy. Mr. Robinson insisted on this version of the story; he had always fretted openly about the sensationalist press and said that he did not want to read more of their indictments of his "mystery island." These journalists will write the same old hoo-ha they always do, Mr. Robinson complained. He was tired of hearing that the Niihauans were brainwashed, subjects in a feudal kingdom, not free to make their own decisions. Now he'd be reading that there were Jap sympathizers in every small wooden house, and that Niihauan women killed men as handily as they gutted fish. So the official version held Ben as the man who had dealt the fatal blow, and there were rumors of a medal for both him and Howard, for their valiant efforts in what was now called the Battle of Niihau.

Ella did not stop at Hannah's house but continued walking. She knew she would turn around soon, but for the moment she liked the bedrock feel of the land under her feet, the way its red-dust surface rose and wrapped around her, then misted away into the air. *Inuwai* began to blow, bringing the smell of the sea to her nose. Soon, it would be spring. The bees would start feeding their queen, the *papipi* would briefly flower. She stopped at the bluff that overlooked the beach and gazed westward, where no other island was in sight. She was suddenly sure that no matter what humans tried to do, Niihau would always float here, cradled by water, rooted somehow to the earth. Changes had come to Niihau, yes, but even these would not last. They would transform into something else again. Only the island itself was constant, immovable.

Perhaps it would rain soon, she thought, and turned back toward the village.

Author's Note

Though many of the events in this book really happened, this remains a work of fiction. This means, among other things, that while all of the major characters are named after real people who experienced this strange, tragic week on Niihau, I have added dialogue, attributes, and motivations of my own imaginings. The island of Niihau does exist, and it is owned by a family named Robinson. A Japanese Zero did crash on Niihau after the attack on Pearl Harbor; the pilot did survive; the island was isolated and largely uninterested in the machinations of the outside world; the island's Hawaiian residents were unsure why a foreign military plane was so close to their island, while the three Japanese-speaking inhabitants immediately knew full well what had happened. Those are the bare-bones facts I used as a springboard for the story I wove. To fill in the gaps I did extensive research, but often historical documents contradicted one another.

My most baffling challenge was trying to uncover when the Niihauans knew that Pearl Harbor had been attacked. Specifically, how did they find out? There was no consensus in any of the materials I looked at. In this and other instances I chose the scenario I thought most likely, and also the one that best exemplified both the isolation of Niihau and the heartrending identity issues that

Japanese Americans, and indigenous Hawaiians, faced at that time. Also, in places, I added small scenes to bridge the larger, historically verified ones.

I did get confirmation on the events that ended the so-called Battle of Niihau during a wonderful, synchronicitous event in Reno, Nevada. I had never been there, nor had I often played blackjack with real money. But there I was at one in the morning, in a brightly lit casino, getting help from a table of amiable strangers. The man next to me told me he was from Hawaii, and I, who had spent a lot of time on Oahu and Kauai, asked him, "Which island?" Well, he said, I grew up in California, but my father was from a place you've probably never heard of, called Niihau. I almost dropped my chips. The odds at blackjack might be fairly good, but what are the odds that I would meet someone with connections to an island of 130 people? He told me that Ella and Ben Kanahele were direct relations. I caught my breath and asked him if the way I have portrayed the ending here is the way it actually happened. Oh, yes, he said with a smile. No doubt about it.

There were other surprises. Documents state that the events on Niihau were a major influence on the decision to intern Japanese-Americans in February 1942. So this small, alomost forgotten historical footnote has had large historical reverberations.

I asked for permission to visit Niihau and talk directly to the people there about any remembrances they had of those seven days back in 1941, and to hear any stories that might have been passed down from relatives and friends. Unfortunately, my request to the Robinson family, who still own the island, was never answered. Perhaps this is fitting, because the book is a work of fiction; in addition, their continuing reserve ensures that the "mystery island" remains a mystery, even today.

CPSIA information can be obtained
at www.ICGtesting.com
Printed in the USA
LVHW042340140622
721301LV00006B/157